PRAISE FOR KATEE ROBERT

"Robert easily pulls off the modern marriage-of-convenience trope . . . This is a compulsively readable book! It's more than just sexy times, too, though those are plentiful and hot! . . . An excellent start to a new series."

—*RT Book Reviews*, on *The Marriage Contract*

"*The Marriage Contract* by Katee Robert is dark, dirty, and dead sexy. I want a Teague O'Malley of my very own!"

—Tiffany Reisz, author of the Original Sinners series

"A definite roller coaster of intrigue, drama, pain, heartache, romance, and more. The steamy parts were super steamy, the dramatic parts delivered with a perfect amount of flair."

—*A Love Affair with Books*, on *The Marriage Contract*

"The series is a hit all around, and I'm already loving it."

—*The Book Cellar*, on *The Marriage Contract*

"If you like angsty reads, this book is right up your wheelhouse."

—*Heroes & Heartbreakers*, on *The Wedding Pact*

"I loved every second. A minus."

—*All About Romance*, on *The Wedding Pact*

"There are moments of heartbreaking betrayal, loss of life, family secrets, and expressions of love. The premise is exhilarating, and the characters are dynamic and charismatic."

—*The Reading Café*, on *The Wedding Pact*

"With *The Wedding Pact*, and its compelling protagonists of Carrigan and James, Katee Robert has cemented her standing as a must-read author. I can't wait to read more!"

THE
DEVIL'S
DAUGHTER

ALSO BY
KATEE ROBERT

The O'Malleys Series

The Marriage Contract

The Wedding Pact

An Indecent Proposal

Forbidden Promises

The Foolproof Love Series

Foolproof Love

Fool Me Once

A Fool for You

Out of Uniform Series

In Bed with Mr. Wrong

His to Keep

Falling for His Best Friend

His Lover to Protect

His to Take

THE DEVIL'S DAUGHTER

KATEE ROBERT

Montlake
Romance

Text copyright © 2017 Katee Robert/Katee Hird
All rights reserved.

Published by Montlake Romance, Seattle

www.apub.com

Amazon, the Amazon logo, and Montlake Romance are trademarks of Amazon.com, Inc., or its affiliates.

ISBN-13: 9781503940918
ISBN-10: 1503940918

Cover design by Mecob Design Ltd

Printed in the United States of America

To Bailey.
It will be years before you're allowed to read
this book, but your fascination with the weird and dark
side of the world inspires me endlessly.
Love you, Little Miss!

CHAPTER ONE

The girl ran.

She ran with everything she had in her, her thin arms pumping and her bare feet slapping the dirt. The long grass sliced at her skin, each piece a tiny razor blade. It hurt. Everything hurt. But if she was caught again, it would be so much worse.

Get to the road. Get to the road. Just get to the road.

Already her strength was flagging, her body failing her despite the desperation driving her on. She couldn't stop. She couldn't rest. She couldn't do anything but run.

The ground changed beneath her feet, and it took her three full strides before she realized it. She turned a full circle, trying to get her bearings. It was so hard to think past the blood pounding in her head and the dozen sharp pains that screamed to make themselves known now that she'd stopped moving. *Maybe I could just . . .*

No.

She had to get to Clear Springs.

The irony there wasn't lost on her, even in her current state. All she'd ever wanted was to get out of that little hellhole of a town, and here she was, putting everything she had into doing the exact opposite. She frowned, trying to see farther down the road. It shouldn't be so difficult to figure out which way to go. She'd spent years on these little two-lane roads that crisscrossed their way through this part of Montana.

If it were day . . .

If she weren't so tired . . .

If, if, if.

Just *move.* She took a deep breath and put one foot in front of the other, picking a direction at random. The words became a mantra, a promise. *Just get back to town. Just get back to town, and this will all be over.*

She wasn't sure how long she'd walked before headlights cut through the darkness, blinding her. The girl went to her knees without having any intention of doing so. She lifted a shaking hand to shield her eyes. "Please."

The driver's side door opened, and footsteps padded over the asphalt. She squinted against the light, her heart skipping a beat at the familiar profile. "No . . ." *I got away. I was so sure I got away.* Behind the figure, she could make out the faint, familiar lights of Clear Springs. *So close.* It might as well have been the moon. She had the same likelihood of reaching it.

She tried to get to her feet, but her body failed her once again, her legs giving out. She barely caught herself before she face-planted. "Please. I'll do whatever you want. Just please don't hurt me anymore."

A hand touched her head, all the more horrifying because of its gentleness. "You know I can't make that promise."

The girl had thought herself beyond tears, but that moment proved her wrong. She stared at her scraped and bloodied knuckles, a horrible knowledge settling in her chest. There would be no college, no life beyond the little town that had felt like a prison for most of her life, no future family where she could learn from the mistakes her parents had made.

Nothing.

There was nothing but the hand on her head and the pain lying in wait for her.

◆ ◆ ◆

"You have to do something."

Zach Owens had heard variations of that same demand ever since he moved back to Clear Springs and took a job as a deputy nine years ago. Now, as sheriff, he heard them a whole hell of a lot more often.

This one was different.

He sat forward and pinned both Robert and Julie Smith with a look. "You know I've been doing everything I can." For three days he'd been working his ass off to figure out where the hell their daughter had wandered off to. They didn't get missing persons a whole lot around here—if someone went missing, it was because they didn't want to be found. He still wasn't convinced Neveah Smith wasn't in that category.

"This isn't like the other times." Tears welled in Julie's eyes. "It's that Martha Collins. She's got her hooks into my girl, and she's lured her out to that damned cesspool of sin."

"Julie, language."

Zach sighed. It was just like Robert Smith to call his wife out on her language when their daughter might or might not be missing. The Smiths were good people. They made a point to get to church every Sunday and do all sorts of community outreach, even if they were a little zealous about some of that shit. Julie Smith had made it her personal mission to see the cult up on that hill brought down in flames.

But it wasn't Zach's job to tell her that Martha Collins was too smart to start snatching teenagers off the street.

"The folks up at Elysia aren't responsible for everything that goes sideways in Clear Springs." In all the time he'd been back in town, he couldn't remember a single thing they'd done that would shine the light of the law on themselves. Groups like that didn't make it far if they weren't able to keep their noses clean.

"Maybe not before. This is different."

She kept saying that. Zach knew her well enough to know she wasn't going to let this go. The woman might be sweet as pie, but she was like a terrier with a bone when she got her back up. Having her only daughter up and disappear was more than enough to do that.

The problem was that Neveah was a little troublemaker. She liked to worry her parents, and she loved getting herself into questionable situations. It would be just like her to disappear for a few days and then waltz back into town with a shit-eating grin and some boy in tow.

Robert wrapped an arm around his wife's thin shoulders and gave Zach a significant look. "I'm sure she'll show up before too long, but could you go talk to those freaks? It'll make Julie feel better."

The very last thing he wanted to do was go out to that commune and sniff around. He wouldn't find anything they didn't want him to find, which made the whole endeavor pointless. Martha and her people would smile and chat him up, and he'd walk away empty-handed. "I can do that, but you know as well as I do that they aren't likely to give me anything useful."

He showed the Smiths out, making more promises to go out to the commune that very morning. If it'd make them feel better, he'd do what he had to do.

"Trouble?"

He glanced over at Henry. The man had been working at the Clear Springs station since Zach was a teenager, but when the sheriff position opened up, old Henry wanted nothing to do with it. He liked being a senior deputy, and he wasn't interested in adding more responsibility to his plate with retirement only a few short years away.

Zach turned to face the west. He couldn't see Elysia from here, but he could pinpoint its exact location. Some days it felt like that damn cult cast a shadow long enough to encompass the entire town.

He rubbed the back of his neck. "The Smith girl might be missing."

"I'll bet she is. Probably missing right up to Augusta, or even over to Great Falls. The girl gets around."

He shot Henry a look. It didn't matter what either of them thought of Neveah Smith. What mattered was giving her parents some peace of mind until she found her way back into town. "They think Martha Collins has something to do with it."

"That Julie Smith." Henry snorted. "The Winchesters had a whole batch of bread turn up unexpectedly stale last week, and who do you think Julie thought was the cause? Martha Collins. How she thought the woman managed that is beyond me, but Julie ain't exactly a neutral party, you know?"

"I know." Hadn't he been thinking the same thing? "We still have to check it out."

"By all means." Henry grabbed the keys from the stand. "I'll drive."

That was just fine with Zach. It'd give him some time to think. He headed for the cruiser and settled into the passenger seat. As much as he didn't want to discount the Smiths' fear, he couldn't help thinking that Henry was right—Neveah Smith would turn up sooner or later, and it wouldn't have had a damn thing to do with Elysia.

The trip took a good thirty minutes, but only because the roads were hardly anything to write home about. The narrow asphalt lane was full of potholes and uneven grooves, which made going more than thirty miles an hour a health hazard. There was no road directly into Elysia from the main highway—something he suspected was intentional.

For someone to get to the commune, they had to *really* want to.

Terrain was tricky out here, and distances didn't always match up the way one expected them to. That was why the hill the main settlement of Elysia was on seemed to rise out of nowhere. He knew that, but it didn't stop some instinct inside him insisting that he needed to sit up and pay attention.

Everything about that damn cult was smoke and mirrors, but he'd be the first to admit how dangerously compelling both Martha and her people could be. He'd listened in on their talks a time or two when he was young and had a chip on his shoulder a mile wide, and the whole back-to-nature way of life appealed to him. If that's *all* this place was, he wouldn't have a problem with it.

But it wasn't.

They wanted obedience as much as they wanted anything—more, in fact—and when he couldn't get anyone to give him a straight answer about their belief system or what living on the commune entailed, he'd gone with his next best choice and enlisted in the Marines.

It had been the best decision he'd ever made.

Or that's what he comforted himself with on the nights the nightmares had him by the throat.

Henry pulled to a stop about a hundred yards from the gates of Elysia. They were framed by the eight-foot whitewashed fence that circled the main buildings, a direct contrast with the rest of the fencing that wound around the rest of the property, which was closer to something one would find on a cattle ranch. It marked the territory, but if someone was determined, it'd be easy enough to slip through. Doing so was something of a rite of passage with Clear Springs teenagers these days, and the Elysians seemed to tolerate it well enough that they only called him when one of the kids ventured too close to their homestead itself.

Today the giant gates were closed, giving him a full view of their intricate design. The damn things were thick wood, a good ten feet tall and carved with a design he couldn't quite make out at this distance. He knew what it was, though—a scene of a woman being dragged through a giant crack in the ground, a second woman on the surface reaching for her, both their expressions of fear and determination. Not exactly feel-good stuff.

He got out of the cruiser and eyed the two men standing before the gates. The older man held a rifle in his hands with an ease that said he knew how to use it, and the other one had a bright smile on his face that was as false as everything else about this place. Zach lifted a hand. "Abram. Joseph."

Joseph moved forward, his smile not so much as flickering. Abram stayed back, which was just fine with Zach. There was something just *off* about Martha's right-hand man. Just being within eyesight of him had instincts Zach thought were long dormant perking up and taking notice.

"Howdy, Sheriff. What can we do for you this afternoon?"

He'd never liked Joseph. The man was as pretty as he was false, and he had a nasty habit of whisking through Clear Springs and paying too much attention to the married women for anyone's peace of mind. As far as Zach knew, no one had crossed any lines there—and even if they had, it was hardly his jurisdiction to police cheating spouses—but it didn't sit well with him. He'd always thought the only reason Martha kept the little shit around was because he could have passed for an Abercrombie model, right down to the short blond hair and chiseled jawline. But then, that might be Zach's personal dislike for the man showing through.

He nodded at the gates. "We'd like to speak with Martha."

"Sorry, but that's not possible." Joseph's brown eyes flicked to the police cruiser behind him and then back, the only part of him he didn't bother to lie with. He might appear relaxed and easygoing, but he'd categorized everything about the situation the second Zach pulled up. "She's deep in meditation."

Meditation, his ass. He crossed his arms over his chest. "It's important."

"Not going to happen." Joseph's smile widened. "But I'm more than happy to deal with whatever brought you all the way out here. As a courtesy in the name of cooperation, of course."

Of course.

Zach exchanged a look with Henry. They were hiding something. That wasn't new, but usually Martha and her inner circle fell over themselves to let him wander around in an effort to prove that they weren't, in fact, a cult. He couldn't remember the last time the gates were closed to him. He was pretty sure they never had been.

Holy hell, what if Julie is right?

He leaned against the cruiser, putting every effort into appearing relaxed and unconcerned. "You know Neveah Smith?"

Joseph shrugged. "Sure. She's been up a few times."

He blinked. He hadn't expected the man to admit it.

And, damn it, Joseph knew it. He laughed. "There's nothing wrong with letting the kid attend a few services. If she's not supposed to be here, take that up with her and her parents. We haven't violated any rules."

They knew something. He was sure of it. There was no other reason for them to close him and Henry out. "You seen her around lately?"

"Not in a couple weeks." Joseph flashed a grin again. "Apparently we weren't exciting enough for her tastes. She was expecting crazy orgies and drugged-out parties." Joseph leaned in and held a hand to the side of his mouth. "We don't start that sort of thing until they turn eighteen."

He was fucking with Zach.

Zach knew it, but it didn't stop his blood pressure from rising. He'd rather deal with just about anyone other than Joseph, if only because the idiot liked to make a joke of everything.

This was serious. Or it would be if the girl was actually missing.

But he wasn't getting anything from the Elysians today. He pushed off the cruiser. "You call me if she comes around."

"You have no jurisdiction here."

"That's where you're wrong." As much as some of them liked to pretend otherwise, they weren't an independent state. As far as he knew,

Martha didn't even preach that sort of nonsense. But the Elysians were an insular sort, and they didn't take too kindly to what they viewed as civilians telling them how to live their lives.

Too damn bad. He didn't make a habit of meddling in their business as long as they didn't break any laws, but that didn't mean he'd look the other way if they *did.*

Zach headed for the passenger seat. "Don't cross me, Joseph. If she shows up, I expect a call."

"I'm scared. Really, I am." Joseph pointed at himself. "This is me, shaking in my boots."

There was a time when Zach used to solve his problems with his fists. He'd never thought he'd miss it until this moment. Punching in that smug bastard's face sounded brilliant—except he was an officer of the law, and sheriffs weren't allowed to go around assaulting people who made them angry. "See you around."

"Sooner than you think."

Once they were back in the cruiser, Henry backed away, but Zach kept his gaze on the two men the entire time. "They're up to something."

"Seems like it."

But what? On the grand scale of things, Elysia might irritate the hell out of him, but they hadn't set a foot outside the law since they'd bought the hundred acres out here. And if one of Martha's flock stepped out of line . . .

He shook his head. When he'd been maybe sixteen, he remembered her hauling in her own daughter to the police station to report that the kid had stolen a violin. That was the only time she'd ever been in the station, and the only time she'd asked for outside help. She'd always gone above and beyond the call of duty to present the facade that Elysia was really just a harmless commune.

For her to refuse to see him and close the gates . . .

Yeah, something was up.

The radio crackled, Chase Moudy's voice cutting through the cruiser. "Zach? Zach, where the hell are you?"

He exchanged a baffled look with Henry. *What now?* The other deputy sounded like he'd seen a ghost. Zach picked up the radio. "I'm here."

"You gotta get here, and fast. There's . . ." Chase's voice broke. "There's a dead body out on the Parkinsons' property. It's a girl, man."

Neveah.

CHAPTER TWO

Zach's stomach surged into his throat as he climbed out of the cruiser. They'd followed Chase's instructions out of town to the north. The dirt road led off Highway 434 and into the foothills of the Rocky Mountains. He spotted the only other police cruiser Clear Springs had to its name off the side of the road, Chase's long frame leaning against it. He had his head in his hands.

Considering the man had seen a thing or two when he worked homicide over in Seattle before moving here a few years ago, that didn't bode well. In the time Zach had known Chase, he'd never seen the other man riled—or as hopeless as he looked now.

The Marines hadn't been a cakewalk for Zach. He'd experienced things in the desert that he wished he could wipe out from his mind, even nine years later. This was different. Nearly a decade working in Clear Springs and the closest he'd come to a murder case was a lost hiker who'd wandered miles off course and ended up freezing to death near Sawfoot Ridge.

That was it.

This was worlds different.

"Call it in."

Henry gave him a look like he was crazy, his bushy gray eyebrows sliding up his forehead. "To who?"

That was the question, wasn't it? He took a deep breath and tried to *think*. Clear Springs was small enough that they didn't even have their own mortuary. They didn't have detectives. They didn't have a damn thing except him, Henry, and Chase. "Call the coroner over in Augusta. Keep it quiet. I don't want the Smiths to hear about this before we have a chance to confirm—"

"You think it's Neveah?" The shock in Henry's voice made him feel like a monster.

Zach opened the door. "I won't know until I get a look at the body. Make the call." He got out. It was tempting to take some time, to do something to prolong the moment when he had to walk around Chase's vehicle and look at the body of a girl who had once lived and loved and laughed. But that was not why he was here—he was here to do right by her, whoever she was.

So he braced himself and tapped Chase's shoulder. "Tell me."

Chase gave a full-body shudder, but his voice was almost calm when he said, "I got a call from old-man Parkinson about some teenagers trespassing on his property. I took my time, because you know how he is."

Zach knew. He could also hear the guilt in his deputy's voice. "You couldn't have known."

"But—" Chase shook his head, his brown eyes wide as if he were in shock. "Right. You're right. This shit is just messing with my head, you know?"

"I know." He realized he was still stalling and motioned his deputy over. "Talk to me while I take a look."

Walking around that car was hard—harder than it should have been. Seeing the flash of pale skin down in the bushes on the side of the road was harder yet. Zach walked to the body on leaden feet and crouched down. The girl was on her stomach, one arm outstretched as if she was reaching for help and the other curled underneath her. Her dark hair was a tangled mess that hid her face. And she was naked.

Chase cleared his throat. "I was going to cover her, but . . ."

"You did the right thing." As much as he wanted to grant her that respect, they needed to gather evidence before they moved her.

He examined the ground. There was one set of footprints—Chase's—that circled the body, and scuff marks where he'd obviously checked for a pulse. No other marks, except for a set of bare footprints that must belong to the girl. He frowned. Surely she didn't walk here and fall over dead?

Zach sat back on his heels and looked around. They were a good ten miles from town, but ten miles wasn't that far in the grand scheme of things. With the mountain range rising in the distance, there was no reason for her to be lost. Every local knew that if you put the range at your back and started walking, you'd run into some sort of civilization sooner rather than later. He put that in the back of his mind and returned to his examination.

Faint bruises covered her back and ran down her arms and legs, ranging in size from what could be fingerprints to large ones indicating a more serious blow. The colors varied, too—some nearly black and others faded to a sickly green-yellow. So, not all new. She certainly couldn't have gotten them all in the few days she'd been missing.

You're getting ahead of yourself.

Right.

He leaned closer, carefully putting his hand on the dirt to stabilize himself. There was a marking between her shoulder blades, a smudge of blue-black that looked like ink. A tattoo? There was another on her hip, and yet another one on the wrist of the outstretched arm. *What the hell?*

Whatever the origin of these marks, he doubted they were something she'd consented to. Time would tell, though, and he'd have to wait to hear from the coroner to know for sure.

Only one thing left to see.

He lifted the curtain of her hair, and froze.

The girl wasn't Neveah Smith.

◆　◆　◆

It's finally happening.

Eden Collins sat in her car and told herself for the thousandth time that she was a fool. She shouldn't be here. There was nothing she could offer the situation that wouldn't make everything worse. She tapped her finger on the steering wheel, staring at the entrance to the Clear Springs police station. Growing up, she'd been in there once or twice when her mother decided that some outside help was necessary to rein in her rebellious daughter.

She'd never thought she'd walk in voluntarily.

She'd never thought she'd come back to Clear Springs at all.

She sighed. There was no help for it—either she needed to turn the car around, drive back to Missoula, and catch the next flight out to Virginia, or she needed to stop trying to talk herself out of this and walk in there and offer her services.

I don't want to go back. Please don't make me.

It was the cry of a child in the dark. She'd worked very, very hard to leave that child behind, but the little-girl voice had the nasty habit of popping up at the worst times. Eden had known coming back to Clear Springs for the first time in a decade would rouse all sorts of inner demons she'd been so determined to forget. It didn't make it any easier to bear.

"This is stupid. Get out of the car. Get out of the car right now."

She threw her body into motion, half-afraid that if she didn't force herself to move, she'd sit there until someone decided to report her for being creepy. *Who am I kidding? The people in this place are just as likely to knock on the window and ask me if I need any help.*

The fall air had a little bite to it, and she closed her eyes and inhaled deeply. *Home.*

No. It's not home. It'll never be home again.

She'd made a life for herself in the FBI, and if she didn't have much in the way of roots . . . well, she'd left the possibility of roots behind when she left Clear Springs. Most days it didn't even bother her that much. She was doing good in the world, using her nontraditional childhood to give her an edge that had helped her make a name for herself over the last six years in the cult division. She was Eden Collins, FBI agent. She wasn't that scared little girl. Not anymore.

One step at a time, she made her way into the police station. She'd half expected it to be a whirl of motion, with people rushing here and there, trying to come to terms with the fact that death had touched their small town. But there was no one in the room except a man sitting behind the desk in the corner, glaring at the phone on his desk.

Zach Owens.

The golden boy of Clear Springs in every sense. His blond hair was still cropped short, harkening back to his days as a Marine, and his body was obviously well taken care of. This wasn't a man who'd let his years working in a sleepy little town turn him soft.

While Zach took her in, she conducted her own perusal. She'd never met him personally, but she knew him by reputation and pieces of information stolen via eavesdropping. He'd gone off to war a boy and come back a man with shadows in his eyes. Or maybe she was just seeing him with rose-tinted glasses, the tragic figure representing everything she'd never have. Acceptance. Loyalty. The love of the people here.

Something like jealousy curled through her stomach. It was silly and childish, and she was better than that, but it was hard not to resent someone who so obviously *fit*. Eden had done a bit of traveling since she'd turned eighteen and run as far and fast as she could from her mother, but she'd never found a place that was well and truly hers.

He caught sight of her and narrowed his eyes. "Can I help you?"

Being pinned in place by those blue eyes made her second-guess the intelligence of her plan yet again. It didn't matter. He needed her help, even if he didn't know it yet. She stepped forward. "I'm here about the body."

His shoulders dipped a quarter of an inch before rising again, the tell so slight, she wouldn't have noticed if her business didn't rely on seeing what other people missed. He frowned. "How the hell did you hear about it already? It's only been a few hours."

And here's the kicker. She pulled out her phone and brought up her e-mail. "This was sent to me yesterday afternoon." Zach cursed, and she didn't blame him. The photo showed the dead girl, her hand outstretched as if begging for help. *As if begging* Eden *for help.*

"Who sent this to you?"

"I don't know." When she tried to respond to the e-mail, it had bounced. Eden had thought it was some sort of prank, but she'd done a search through the FBI data banks on Clear Springs just in case . . . and discovered that a body perfectly matching the one in the photo was currently in the Augusta morgue.

A body that shared at least superficial similarities with Eden.

He looked at her as if seeing her for the first time. "As much as I'm grateful for the heads-up about a potential leak, who are you and why would this picture be sent to *you*?"

This was it. The moment of truth. She straightened and did her best not to appear as nervous as she felt. "I'm here because I recognize that tattoo on her back." She held out her hand, proud of herself when it didn't shake. "I'm Eden Collins, and you've got bigger problems than you realize."

CHAPTER THREE

Zach was half-sure he'd heard her wrong. Hell, he was still trying to process the fact that she'd walked in here with a picture of his crime scene. He recognized it—the damn thing had been taken by the Augusta coroner before the man took the body—which meant there was a leak somewhere along the line, and hell if that didn't make his job a whole lot harder. Now he had strangers showing up claiming to be . . .

Fuck.

The woman didn't look like someone who could help him—in those worn jeans and leather jacket—but he'd learned a long time ago that appearances could be deceiving. "Can you repeat that?"

"You have trouble—"

"I heard that. The other part."

She gave a wry smile. "The part where I said my name was Eden Collins?"

Yep, that was it. There was only one Collins he knew of, and it was one Martha Collins, cult leader. He looked Eden over again, trying to reconcile what she appeared to be saying. "You're related to—"

"She's my mother."

This was Martha Collins's long-lost daughter? The Elysians tended toward nondescript clothing and plain hairstyles—the exact opposite of the woman in front of him. Oh, there was nothing overtly flashy about her long dark hair or her clothing, but something about the way she held herself spoke of combat training. *She's dangerous.* "If you think this is funny, it's not."

She sighed. "Let's get this over with so we can move on to what actually matters. My mother and I don't get along—or we didn't when I was growing up. We haven't spoken in ten years, though she's reached out to me a few times." Something passed over her face, gone too quickly for him to identify. "That's not why I'm here. I'm here because I recognize that tattoo in the picture."

"How? It's barely more than a blot on the screen." It'd been barely more than that when he'd actually seen it in person. He was hoping the coroner could get more once they cleaned the body.

The body.

It was such a cold way to refer to a person, even if whatever had made that girl a person had fled long before Zach had ever walked on the scene. *Focus. You're not doing her any favors by dwelling on that fact. She needs you to find her killer.* Then *you can mourn the loss of life.*

If there even was a killer. He needed more information before he determined that fact. While it seemed fucking unlikely that she'd stripped naked, tattooed and beaten herself, and then hiked out to die on the side of a road, stranger things had happened. She could have been partying and wandered off.

And maybe you're just praying like hell that was what had happened.

He forced himself to focus on the woman in front of him rather than the one on the slab at the morgue. "Explain."

"I know what it is because I have one." She shrugged out of her jacket and turned around, her tank top baring her upper back to him. It took him several seconds to find the spot in the midst of the swirling ink marking her skin, but there it was—a small circle with that familiar image in the middle of it. Eden's was less blurred than the girl's he'd found, but it wasn't as clear a picture as he expected.

"What is that?"

"A bat."

Now that she mentioned it, he could see the rough outline of a bat. Or it would be if a toddler had drawn it. The lack of expertise behind that particular tattoo only stood out against the skillfully drawn art that was the rest of her ink. "Why?" He didn't realize he was going to ask until the word was out of his mouth.

She pulled her jacket back on and faced him. "It symbolizes death and rebirth in general, and Persephone in particular. Bats are sacred to her because they were thought to carry the souls of the dead in some cases."

A slow dread uncurled inside him. "You're not telling me—"

"I am. Every follower of my mother has the same tattoo. Several of them, in fact." She pointed to her hip and her wrist—the same places that had been marked on Jane Doe.

Fuck me. He'd known something was up when Martha wouldn't see him and the gates had been barred, but he never would have guessed this. *Except . . .* He eyed this stranger claiming to be Martha Collins's daughter. There was no proof, and taking her word for it on something like this was too much to ask. "Can I see some ID?"

She flashed that same wry smile she'd given him before, but she pulled out her wallet and passed a Virginia driver's license over.

He examined it, and sure as shit, her name was exactly what she'd claimed. "You'll understand if I can't just take your word for it."

"Naturally." She accepted her ID back and handed him a card. "This is my number. Eventually you're going to have questions, and I'm the only one who's going to be willing to give you answers. I'm staying at the bed-and-breakfast for a few days if you change your mind."

He read the card, half-sure he was processing the words wrong. "Eden Collins, FBI."

"Not right now. I'm on vacation." She walked away before he could say anything else, the door to the station closing softly behind her.

Zach dropped into his seat, frowning at the card. "And here I thought my day couldn't possibly get weirder."

Eden couldn't help the sense of relief that settled over her as she crossed the parking lot to her car. The sheriff—Zach—wasn't going to call her. He thought she was a nut, and rightfully so. She hadn't exactly done anything to disabuse him of that notion. But she'd done her part—she'd offered her help. It would have been so much easier to call, but her conscience wouldn't let her. He would have dismissed her out of hand, and she'd had to make him sit still long enough to *listen*. After that, if he didn't take her up on it, that was his choice. She could move on with her life with her conscience intact.

He wants justice done. She'd seen that in his eyes, in the way his attention had lingered on the photo of the body, the guilt there an almost physical thing. This was his town, and at least a part of him felt responsible for the fact that a girl had been brutally murdered here.

It set him apart from some of the local law enforcement she'd dealt with who just wanted the problem to disappear so it wouldn't further ruin their day.

She froze in the middle of reaching for her door handle, the hair on the back of her neck standing on end. "I'm not back."

"You look back."

The voice sent ice cascading down her spine. Every instinct screamed at her to run, to hide, to do anything but turn and face the monster at her back—which was why that was exactly what she did. *I've dealt with scarier people in the last six years.* But, as she turned around, she didn't quite believe it. She kept her shoulders back and her hands at her side as she surveyed the man before her. "Abram." Her mother had a habit of renaming people who became her followers, but there was something about Abram that made Eden think he could have actually been born with the fire-and-brimstone name.

The years had been good to him. She thought hard—he had to be nearly fifty by now, his hair gone silver, the lines on his face slightly more pronounced. It *should* have made him more approachable, or at least easier to dismiss. Instead, he looked even more menacing than he had the last time she'd seen him.

"Your mother requests your presence."

How many times had she heard those same words from him in that exact tone of voice? Too many to count. They never meant anything good. She doubted *that* had changed in the intervening decade. "I'm not a minor anymore, and I'm not inclined to see her." Though it sounded calm and reserved in her head, the words came out petulant, as if she was still the child who'd fled.

"All the same." He didn't so much as move, but he seemed closer, invading her space and making it hard to control the fear pulsing higher with each heartbeat.

She glanced at the police station, but if Zach saw Abram confronting her, he wasn't rushing to her defense. And why would he? As far as he was concerned, she was a crazy person who was related to an even crazier person. This was just family business.

Except it wasn't.

She knew how this played out. She could get in her car and drive away—Abram would probably even let her—but sometime soon, she'd turn around and he'd be there, and he wouldn't be so accommodating in that future interaction. So she could do this on her terms or on her mother's.

That's a lie. Nothing was on Eden's terms—not when it came to Elysia. There was only Martha and her indomitable will.

Bend or be broken.

Those were the only true options.

I am a damn FBI agent. I can handle this. The sooner I figure out if Martha is at the bottom of this, the sooner I can get the hell out of this town and back to my life.

She slipped her keys back into her purse. "I'm not going to Elysia."

Abram stepped back and motioned to the coffee shop across the street. It wasn't a Starbucks—nothing in Clear Springs was brand-name—and it looked all but deserted at this hour of the afternoon. *Too close to school being out for the stay-at-home moms and teens.* Apparently her mother didn't want much of an audience. A first.

The walk across the street seemed to take forever, and yet nowhere near long enough. This was the very thing she'd spent so much time and effort trying to avoid, and she'd willingly walked back into a confrontation she wasn't sure she was ready for. Worse, it was all for nothing.

Inside, the coffee shop looked like a thousand other coffee shops across the United States. Dim, intimate lighting, close seating, and a counter that ran the length of the back wall. There was one other customer inside, but he was packing his laptop into a backpack as fast as he could. *Good to know Martha still inspires that reaction.*

With nothing else to focus on, she finally looked at her mother. The years had treated her just as well as they had Abram. She might have a few extra pounds around her waist, but it made her appear happier—more like the benevolent matriarch she claimed to be.

As she always did when faced with the woman who'd brought her into the world, she went down a mental checklist of features they shared. It wasn't long—Eden was lean where her mother was bulky, several inches taller than Martha, and she had a violinist's hands, much to her mother's chagrin. All of which came from the father she'd never met.

From Martha, she got medium-brown hair, though she'd lightened hers, and Martha's was more gray than brown these days. They shared the same mouth, wide and full, the kind of mouth meant for spilling lies.

And then there were the eyes.

The rest of it she could escape. Eden didn't smile the way her mother constantly seemed to be doing while she was growing up, the spider in the middle of a web of her making. She'd changed her hair deliberately, distancing herself from the girl she used to be.

But when she held still long enough to stare in the mirror, it was her mother's eyes staring back. Whiskey-colored eyes, the tone too deep to be termed a mere brown.

Martha turned a sunny smile on Eden, and it was almost enough to have her heading for the door—only Abram's presence at her back kept her moving forward.

If forced to choose between Martha and Abram, there was only one way to go. At least she was reasonably sure she'd walk away from a confrontation with her mother. With Abram, there were no guarantees.

"Martha."

Her mother's eyes lit up, and she half pushed to her feet. "Eden. I admit, when Abram told me you were back in town, I could hardly believe it."

"I'm not back."

Her smile dimmed, and Eden called herself an idiot ten times over for wanting to do something to bring it back. *Manipulation, that's all it is.* Martha motioned to the cups in front of her. "I got your favorite."

There was nothing else to do but take the empty seat and get this over with. She took a sip—sweet with lots of cream—and didn't bother to tell Martha she'd switched over to drinking her coffee black a few years back. It would serve no purpose, and her entire goal was to get out of here with the least conversation possible.

"It's been a long time."

She shifted, not sure how to take the searching look her mother was giving her, as if she was trying to memorize Eden's features—or, possibly, was comparing them to the ones she'd had ten years ago. What was there to say? *I hated the life you created and forced me into, so I left. You won't change, and neither will I. This will never be what you want it to be.* She couldn't force the words past her closed throat, so she took another drink of coffee.

Martha hesitated and then mirrored the motion. "A lot is different from when you were last home."

Not nearly enough, she'd wager. But if her mother was offering information, she'd be a fool not to get everything she could from Martha. "Oh?"

"Our community has grown. It's flourishing." She gave a small self-deprecating smile. "But, then, you didn't come back to talk about Elysia. How have you been?"

Over the years, she'd received phone calls from Abram, demanding information at odd times in that quiet, terrifying way of his. He'd never asked more than a few questions, and she'd never offered more than was strictly necessary for those forced check-ins—whatever it took to get him off her back. She didn't want to now, either. "I'm still working for the government." Safe enough to admit, since her mother already knew about it.

Sure enough, Martha's lips thinned. "The FBI."

"Using the skills I learned from you." She knew better, but she couldn't help the dig.

"I'm sure I have no idea what you're talking about."

Of course she didn't. Because Elysia most certainly *wasn't* a cult. Right. She didn't roll her eyes, but it was a near thing. "You might like to pretend otherwise, but I know for a fact that Elysia has been on the FBI watch lists for years, so you're not fooling everyone."

"Eden Magdalene, you might be a woman grown, but that doesn't mean you can take that tone of voice with me."

Or speak too many truths, apparently. Eden stared at her coffee cup, suddenly exhausted. "I don't suppose you know anything about a photograph showing up in my e-mail yesterday?" It had all the hall-marks of one taken for an official police investigation, but that didn't explain how it had found *her*. She'd had a friend in the tech depart-ment try to trace it, but it had been routed through several IP addresses before disappearing into the Internet ether. Call her paranoid, but her first instinct was to suspect her mother had had something to do with it. *How* was the question, though.

Martha cocked her head to the side, frowning. "I'm not sure what you're speaking of."

Of course she wasn't, though Eden was at a loss to decide if that was truth or because she didn't want to admit to somehow being the leak in a murder investigation. She sighed. "What am I doing here, Martha? You know very well we couldn't sit in the same room without going for each other's throats when I was eighteen, and it would seem nothing's changed since then."

"I want what I've always wanted, baby. I want you to come home."

There's no home for me to come to, not now. Not ever. No matter how much I wish that wasn't true. She cleared her throat. "I—" *Think. Think fast.* A hard no would just have Martha digging in her heels, and she wasn't sure yet if Zach would change his mind. "I'll think about it." The lie rolled off her tongue with the ease of long practice. She wasn't going back. She'd set herself on fire before she willingly walked through the gates of Elysia and put herself under her mother's control again. The only reason she was here was to make sure no other girls turned up dead.

"It would mean so much." Martha's smile brightened, and a trai-torous part of Eden brightened in response. It was how it always was with her mother. She rarely had to take the stern role when she could manipulate much more effectively with a soft word and a particular look. And when that wouldn't work? Well, she wasn't above getting her hands dirty, either.

Did you do it? Did you see that girl killed?

Eden couldn't ask. The sheriff had already refused her help, and she'd have to be a special kind of stupid to go investigating on her own. There was nothing she could do without the power of the law on her side. If she tried . . .

Well, if she tried, there were plenty of unmarked graves in Elysia. What was one more?

CHAPTER FOUR

Zach had only had cause to sit in on an autopsy a few times in the past. Never a pleasant experience by any means, it was so much worse seeing this young woman, who was little more than a kid, her dark hair spreading across the cold metal table, her skin waxy-looking and pale in a way that no living creature could mimic. Wrong. So fucking wrong.

He cleared his throat, wishing he could clear out the smell of the room as easily. Hospitals were never his favorite places, but here in the damp basement, the underlying stench of death couldn't quite be scrubbed out, no matter how much antiseptic was used.

The medical examiner adjusted his tools and took a deep breath. "We don't see a lot of murder in these parts."

"I know." Augusta was quite a bit bigger than Clear Springs, but their crime ran toward theft and domestic abuse—not cold-blooded murder. "But that's no excuse for the damn leak. We've got to do this one by the book, William. That means keeping the information on lockdown until we have a suspect in cuffs."

"I don't know how it happened, Zach." He cleared his throat. "But there won't be further issues. Of that I can assure you."

It was the best he was going to get. He nodded at the girl. "Let's get started." Twelve hours since the body had been found, and he needed to know who she was—and if she had any connection to the fact that Neveah Smith still hadn't turned up. *No way around it. We're going to have to put together a search party.* The chances of Neveah having wandered off and gotten lost were slim to none, but with this girl on the slab in front of him, he had to admit that it was just as likely they were looking for another body.

Fuck.

William nodded, his snow-white hair poking haphazardly out from his head. He looked a lot like the professor from *Back to the Future*, though Zach would never say as much. William Reynolds might be quirky to the extreme, but he was good at his job. His job had just never entailed something quite like this before.

And someone in his office sent a picture to the daughter of a woman who could very well be a suspect. Just fucking perfect.

He began the autopsy, muttering under his breath. "You don't need to be here for the entirety of it, Zach. I'll go through the preliminary stuff and send you the rest of the report by the end of the day."

He wasn't sure if William was offering it as a favor to Zach or because he worked better alone, but he wasn't going to complain. The sound the sternum made when the coroner cracked it was enough to cause Zach nightmares even with all the shit he'd seen. He crossed his arms over his chest. "Okay."

William went through it methodically, combing out the girl's hair and depositing the detritus from the brush into little baggies. "Looks like mostly weeds that are local to the area, but I'll go through it more closely when I'm done."

It lined up with how they'd found her. "Can you tell cause of death?"

The coroner raised his white eyebrows. "I'm getting there." He touched her neck gently with a gloved finger. "See these bruises?"

Zach leaned closer. "Those weren't there when we found her this morning." Though he might not have noticed, considering the rest of the bruises covering her body. "These were, though."

"The others are older. The range in color means they weren't all done at once—some of these are days old, if not closer to a week or more."

So unless she was held somewhere for more than a week, chances were those bruises had been caused by someone other than the killer. *Don't make assumptions until you have all the facts. This could have been an abusive boyfriend who took things too far.* That didn't explain the tattoos, though. Zach eyed her throat. "I don't suppose we could get prints off her skin?"

"We can try, but it's unlikely we'll pull anything." William rested his hand against her neck. "Mediumish grip—I know that's not specific—so could be either a small man or a large woman."

"Personal to kill her like that. Killer would have to get right up close and watch the light fade out of her eyes." His chest tightened at the thought, memories hovering at the outer edges of his mind. It had been a long time since he'd been in combat, long enough that he'd mostly emerged on the other side of it, but that didn't mean there weren't bad nights. He had a feeling tonight would number among them.

"Takes some considerable strength, too. Easier to do it from behind with your arm or a rope or something." William motioned to his fore-arm and then moved back over the body. "These tattoos are new, all four of them."

"Four?"

"Between the shoulder blades, sternum, right wrist, and left hip." William nodded at the table behind him. "I took pictures beforehand so you could take them with you when you go."

"Thanks." The tattoos made him think of Eden Collins showing up in his station this afternoon. She'd known about them—she *shared* a few of them—which seemed to support her theory that they were somehow connected with Elysia. Though she was keeping things from him if she'd only told him about three of them . . . or she didn't actually know the fourth existed.

She could have done it.

He made a mental note to call the FBI and double-check that she was actually one of them. Easy enough to make up a card that said whatever she damn well pleased. He hadn't asked to see her badge—something he regretted now.

"There's nothing beneath her nails, no new injuries with the exception of cause of death." William hesitated. "She had sexual intercourse recently. I'm running a tox screen, but I have to ship it over to Great Falls, so God knows how long it'll take to get back. They're backed up just like every other lab in the country. I can try to push, but this isn't going to ring any bells for them."

Zach hated that. She should be more important to everyone. There should be outrage that her young life had been cut so short. But there were thousands upon thousands of deaths and murders on any given day across the country. There was no reason *this* one would make people sit up and take notice.

Unless there ends up being more.

No, he couldn't think like that. He had to work the case he had, not the one he feared. As of now, there was nothing connecting Neveah Smith's being missing with the body in front of him.

He just hoped like hell it stayed that way.

"What do you mean my flight's been canceled?"

"I'm sorry, ma'am. There seems to be some weather causing problems in Chicago, which is your connecting city."

Eden should have known better than to connect through Chicago, but it was the only flight she could book last-minute. Silly her, she'd only caught a one-way from Quantico. Over the years, it'd become something of a superstition—the only time things went sideways seemed to be when she had concrete plans in place for travel back home. She hadn't even thought about it when she'd flown out to Montana.

Now it seemed she was going to pay for it.

She squeezed the bridge of her nose. "Can you fly me through a different connecting city?"

"I'm sorry, ma'am. With all the travel being diverted, there simply isn't another flight until two days from now."

Two days.

She'd told Zach she'd be in town for a few days, but after the run-in with Martha, the thought of spending a minute more than necessary in Clear Springs had her threatening to break out in hives. She'd come straight back to her room at the B&B and locked the door, but that hadn't stopped her from glancing out the window repeatedly, half expecting to see Abram standing on the curb on the other side of the street.

It wouldn't be the first time.

Should have booked a room over in Augusta instead.

Ultimately both her pride and common sense had gotten the best of her. If she stayed outside Clear Springs, it was as good as waving a sign saying she was uncomfortable here—that Elysia and Martha still had power over her. There'd been the added consideration of being close on the off chance Zach actually took her up on her offer.

None of it mattered now. She was here, she was spooked, and the sheriff didn't want her help. All she wanted was to go back to Virginia.

Eden shuddered. "Look again. Please."

The customer-service agent sighed. "Ma'am, I understand your frustration. Believe me, I do. But there's simply nothing else I can do."

She knew that. It didn't make it easier to swallow. Eden cleared her throat. "Then book me the flight two days from now—and not through Chicago if at all possible, please."

The man sounded relieved. "Yes, of course. Would you like me to e-mail you the updated itinerary?"

"That would be great." She waited for him to confirm he'd done that and hung up. Eden dropped her phone onto the bed and cursed. The temptation to get in her rental car and start driving was strong, but it wasn't logical. She'd get back to Quantico faster by sitting here and waiting for her flight in two days than by driving—and be less likely to get herself killed because she fell asleep behind the wheel.

She moved to the window again and flicked the curtains back, just enough to see out. Darkness had fallen while she was on the phone. She hadn't even been in Clear Springs twenty-four hours and it still felt like a lifetime. *What was I thinking, coming back here?*

That was the problem—she hadn't been. She hadn't stopped to think from the moment she'd seen that photo. Britton probably thought she'd lost her damn mind.

Eden ran her fingers through her hair. Britton ran a tight ship back at Quantico. He'd taken over for the last director right around the time she'd joined the BAU, the Behavioral Analysis Unit, though sometimes she felt like he'd been there for time unknown. He had that ageless quality that made it impossible to put a number on him—he could be anywhere from thirty-five to fifty.

He had to think she was crazy. She'd rushed into his office this morning and asked for a week of personal time for a family emergency. He hadn't commented on the fact that in six years, she'd never once made an effort to see her mother, let alone demanded emergency vacation for it. He hadn't pointed out that she and Vic were about to be sent out on a new case. He'd just approved her time off and told her to do what was necessary.

"A couple more days isn't going to kill me." Maybe if she said it enough times, she might actually start to believe it.

Eden shivered, the hair on the back of her neck standing on end. While she'd been staring out into space, the few people on the street below had disappeared, as if fleeing the coming darkness. It was a fanciful thought—the truth was most people in this area had homes and children that required dinner on the table at a reasonable hour—but she couldn't shake it.

A flicker of movement against the corner of the building across from her window caught her eye, and she frowned, leaning close to the glass. Seconds ticked by, leading into a minute, but nothing else moved. "Weird." She closed the curtains and flicked on the television, turning it to a mindless comedy. It wouldn't help. No matter what she did, she could feel her mother's presence looming over her, waiting for her to miss a step so she could sweep her back into the Elysian fold.

I'm not going back. I promised myself that when I left, and nothing has happened to change that.

CHAPTER FIVE

Zach's day started off with the identity of his dead girl and went downhill from there. Elouise Perkins. He'd thought he knew everyone in town, but the Perkins family kept to themselves. They lived in a little trailer just outside town on ten acres that nobody wanted despite their trying to parcel it off for years. He'd had a few run-ins with Michael Perkins over the years since he'd been back in town. The man liked his booze, and when he got rolling, he liked to pick fights.

Zach climbed out of his cruiser and walked to the trailer door. Informing the family of their only daughter's death was a new one for him, too, and he wasn't looking forward to it. Hell, he wasn't liking his job all that much right now. He *liked* the slow small-town life. The calls he usually went on were for petty little things like noise complaints and property-line disputes. Michael Perkins getting into a bar fight was the worst he had to deal with, and that was just fine by him.

It took nearly ten years, but death followed me home.

Zach knew it wasn't that simple, knew that this murder had nothing to do with his time away, but a small, superstitious part of him couldn't help wondering. As much time and distance as he'd put between himself and what had happened in the desert, if he closed his eyes, he could be back there in an instant, a coating of dust on the back of his tongue, his hearing half-gone from the deafening sound of gunfire, his vision narrowed down to bright splashes of red against the background of browns.

I'm not there. One thing has nothing to do with the other.

The door opened before he got there, Ruby Perkins staring at him with lifeless eyes. They'd been in the same year at school before she'd dropped out because she was pregnant. *Pregnant with Elouise.* The thought made him sick to his stomach. "Ruby."

"You're here about my girl." Her voice was just as empty as her dark eyes. "She's dead, ain't she?"

That stopped him cold. "What makes you think that?"

"Heard that you found a dead girl yesterday, and here you are with *that* look on your face, so that means the dead girl is *my* girl."

"You heard about the body being found?" Damn it, even without the coroner office's leak, keeping information under wraps in Clear Springs was downright impossible.

"Everyone has." She stepped back, opening the door farther for him. "You might as well come in. You want something to drink?"

"No." The word came out sharper than he intended, but nothing about this encounter was going like he'd thought. "Why didn't you come to the station if she was missing?"

A rustling in the back of the trailer made him turn as Michael Perkins walked into the main living space. It had been a few weeks since he'd been in the back of Zach's police car, and he looked even worse than he had then. His belly hung over his jeans, escaping the white tank top that was a few sizes too small, and his hair stuck out oddly, not hiding the fact that it was thinning rapidly. His face had the vaguely red and bloated look of a regular drinker, and Zach had to fight against coughing at the strong stench of whiskey coming off him. *It's always whiskey.*

He took a careful breath. "Michael. I've come about Elouise."

Michael flopped onto the couch and held out his hand. Ruby scuttled over and handed him a freshly opened beer, her head ducked and her shoulders hunched. It made Zach sick to his stomach. He knew those signs. He'd seen them often enough during his time in the force. They didn't have much in the way of domestic abuse in Clear Springs—not since a few families moved out—but it was known to happen from time to time.

Apparently it happened here.

He thought of the rainbow of bruises on Elouise's body and went cold. "When's the last time you saw your daughter?"

"A few days. Maybe a week." Michael waved that off. "What I want to know is how you're going to make this right?"

If anything, he got colder. "We're pursuing all avenues—"

"Not that." Another casual wave, though there was nothing casual about the way his bloodshot blue eyes watched Zach. "People are talking, talking about how she was found, how everyone saw all there is to see of our girl. It's not okay."

"I'm not arguing that."

"Then you need to make it right. Can you really put a price on the kind of pain Ruby and I have experienced because your people didn't stop those dipshit kids?"

Zach stared. Surely he was hearing the other man wrong? "You want me to *pay* you?"

"Emotional trauma. It's worth a pretty penny."

It was everything he could do to hold himself perfectly still and keep his voice calm. "I'm sorry for your loss—both of yours. We'll find out who gossiped about the state Elouise was found in, and they'll answer for what they did. Once the medical examiner up in Augusta is finished, we'll release Elouise's body to you for burial."

Michael sneered. "Guess we're going to be expected to pay for that, too. What a crock of shit."

"Get the fuck over it." The words were out before he could think better of it, but he wasn't in the mood to play nice, not when this idiot was shitting all over the memory of his daughter. He clenched his jaw. "What can you tell me about the last time you saw her?"

"Dunno."

He wanted to hit Michael so bad he could practically taste it. Zach had never liked the man, but now he was finding that he actually loathed him. Needing to distract himself, he turned to Ruby. "What about you?"

Her shoulders hunched a little more, like she was trying to close up on herself. "She was leaving." She disappeared down the hall, reappearing a few seconds later with a small stack of papers in her hands. "She got into college without telling us." She passed them over, and sure enough, there were half a dozen acceptance letters from state schools. One had even offered her a full ride. He kept reading, the ice in his chest spreading at the mention of a wonderful letter of recommendation from none other than Martha Collins.

Fuck.

He motioned to the letters. "Can I take these?"

"Go for it." Michael spoke from his spot on the couch. "Now get the fuck out if you're not going to be helpful."

Zach ignored him, taking a moment to meet Ruby's gaze. "I'm going to find out who hurt your daughter. Justice will be done."

For a second, something like life sparked in her dark eyes, but it was gone almost as fast as it came. Instead of answering, she went to the fridge, opened another beer, and delivered it to Michael as he was swigging the last of his first one. They both ignored Zach, so he saw himself out.

He started up his cruiser and just stared out the windshield. The visit had opened up too many possibilities. If Michael knocked his daughter around, chances were that her trying to leave Clear Springs behind for good had pushed him over the edge and he'd killed her. Most homicides were perpetrated by the people closest to the murder victim—he knew enough to know that, and there was the whole thought process that said the simplest answer was most likely the true answer. The simplest answer was that Michael Perkins was an abusive son of a bitch, and he'd finally snapped.

But there were the new tattoos to consider.

And the fact that Martha Collins had known the girl well enough to write her a recommendation letter.

There was no help for it. He was going to have to go back out to Elysia and give talking to Martha another shot. He cursed and threw the car into gear. The trip took twenty minutes, and he was greeted by the same closed gates as last time. At least it wasn't Joseph leaning against the fence with the shotgun held casually in his hands—it was Lee.

She has to know something's up. Even if she closes the gates on a regular basis, she wouldn't leave one of her favorite three out here at all times if she wasn't serious about keeping everyone away.

He had to wonder if it was the murder that caused this change of behavior—or if it was the return of her daughter.

Zach shook his head. "This is going to be a goddamn nightmare." He climbed out of the cruiser and waved. "Lee."

"Howdy, Sheriff."

Of Martha's three core men, Lee was the least aggravating to Zach. He seemed to be exactly what he was—an attractive black guy in his late twenties who always had a ready smile and rolled with the punches. Zach wasn't dumb enough to think he was exactly what he appeared to be, but it made it easier to talk with him. He nodded at the gates. "More meditation?"

"You know how it goes." Lee's smile was white against his dark skin, as if inviting Zach in on the joke. "Martha gets her mind set on something, and that's how it is. Three days of nonexposure to the outside world is exactly what our people need." His smile disappeared. "She's not wrong this time, either. World's a terrible place."

"You know something about that?"

Lee shrugged. "I know enough. We might not have television here, but it's impossible not to hear what's going on out there. War, murder, rape, corruption on every level. It's better in Elysia. Simpler. Martha takes care of us, and we take care of her right back." The edge to the words stung.

Zach raised his eyebrows. "I have no problem with Martha and her flock—never have. But I do have some questions for her regarding an ongoing investigation, and I'd really appreciate it if she'd oblige to talk to me—sooner rather than later." He didn't much like groveling to get an interview with the woman, but he'd do that and worse to get some answers where Elouise Perkins was concerned.

"Investigation? That sounds awful official for some kids just trespassing again."

If Lee knew about the murder, he was a better actor than people gave him credit for. But then, he was also one of the more public faces of Elysia, the pinnacle of what a person could accomplish by joining up and signing over everything they had in search of a simpler life. That meant Zach couldn't trust him as far as he could throw him. Even if Lee didn't know a damn thing, he'd cover for Martha, no questions asked.

He wanted to drop the information to see if he got a response, but if Martha didn't know about the murder yet, he wasn't going to give her a chance to practice her reactions. So Zach just nodded at the closed gates. "Tell her that I want to see her when you're open again."

"She already knows."

Because I was here yesterday. Not because she's some kind of prophet.

He tipped his hat. "See you around, Lee."

"You, too, Sheriff Owens." At least coming from him, it didn't sound like the threat it had from Joseph. That just meant Lee was the more dangerous of the two, because no one would expect a blow coming from his direction.

Did you extend that same charm and easy smile to Elouise Perkins? Coming from the life she had, she was ripe pickings for the likes of Lee and the Elysians. They prided themselves on scooping up lost sheep and offering them a safe home, something Elouise desperately needed.

But then, for all intents and purposes, it looked like Elouise had planned on attending college. He'd have to have that verified. He called Chase as he headed back to town.

"Sheriff?"

"I need you to call Montana State and see if they have any record of Elouise Perkins signing up for classes, going through registration, anything that would set up a timeline for when she was last seen." If they could confirm she'd been down there, he might have to send someone to talk to anyone who might have seen her. The last week of August was registration week, and it was a nightmare with so many people coming and going, though, so it was going to be something like searching for a needle in a haystack.

"What about her parents?"

Thinking about them was enough to have him tightening his grip on the steering wheel. "They haven't seen her in at least a couple days, if not a week, which means we can't rely on them to pinpoint the day she was taken. We need to know *exactly* who saw her last."

"Roger that. It's pretty early, so I should be able to get ahold of someone in their registrar's office."

"I'm headed back to the station now. See you in a few." He hung up; the sheer number of unanswered questions he had staggered him. As much as he wanted to pin all the blame on Michael Perkins—and he would pursue that avenue without fail—it was starting to look more and more like someone up at Elysia was involved.

And it was equally likely they'd keep stonewalling him until kingdom come. He might not have started any problems with Martha, but that didn't mean she was going to bend over backward to be helpful.

If she or one of her people was involved, she'd do everything in her considerable power to keep it from him.

Zach cursed. Really, there was only one avenue open to him, as much as he didn't like it. He pulled the cruiser over to the side of the road and dug out Eden Collins's card. It took twenty minutes to get ahold of someone over at Quantico to confirm she actually was an FBI agent, and then another ten to get in contact with the director of her branch of the BAU, Britton Washburne.

"Washburne." The deep tones of the voice that came on the phone soothed him almost instantly—and Zach had no doubt the man on the other end used that as a tool at his disposal when it suited him.

"Zach Owens here. I'm sheriff of Clear Springs, Montana, and I have one of your agents here in town."

"Eden Collins."

He didn't have to ask how the man knew whom he was talking about. Not much got past the FBI when it came to their own people, he imagined. "She says she's here unofficially."

"She's on her own time, yes."

Which wasn't the same thing at all. Zach narrowed his eyes. "Just how much do you know about where Eden comes from?"

"I know enough. I'm sure you're not calling and wasting my time to gossip about family connections she left in the past nearly a decade ago."

He tapped his fingers on the steering wheel, hating that he felt like a kid tattling to the principal. "You trust her?"

"You *are* wasting my time, Sheriff." Washburne sighed. "I trust her with my life—several times over. She's been above reproach from the time she went through the academy. Is there a reason for your call? Or are you on a fishing expedition?"

He was beginning to feel like the latter. "Thank you for your time."

"Have a good rest of your day." Washburne hung up.

He didn't think that was likely. In fact, his day was going to hell in a handbasket faster than he could say, *Fuck this.* Zach dialed the number on the card Eden had given him.

"Hello?"

There was no point in beating around the bush. "Are you still in town?"

She hesitated. "For the time being."

"I've reconsidered your offer. Can you meet me in Augusta in an hour? There's a little coffee shop just outside town on 435."

"I know it." Another hesitation. "I'll see you there."

She didn't sound happy about it, but he couldn't really blame her. There wasn't a single thing about their current situation that inspired happiness . . . and he was about to go and shit all over her day.

CHAPTER SIX

Eden arrived early and took a table in the back corner where she could see the entirety of the coffee shop from her seat. *Why do people always meet in coffee shops? This is a conversation better suited to a bar—or at least somewhere that serves alcohol.* Zach Owens was going to ask her for help. There was no other reason he'd be calling her. Something had happened that had pushed him over the edge if he was truly considering her as a resource.

She wanted to get up, to climb into her rental car and start driving. The desire had only been building since last night, getting harder to resist with each minute that passed. If her flight hadn't been canceled, she'd be gone, away from here and her mother and Elysia and Zach Owens.

Speak of the devil.

He walked into the coffee shop, paused, and started forward when his gaze lit on her. His faded jeans showcased a truly impressive set of thighs, and a Carhartt jacket that just screamed low-key man. It was worn and a little dirty—the clothing of a man who spent his life out in the world. It all added up to the same thing she'd found the last time they talked. Zach Owens was most likely a good man who worked hard, enjoyed living in his little town, and, what was more, he *fit* here.

And now he was in trouble and here she was, the perpetual outsider, offering help he desperately needed.

The irony wasn't lost on her. Eden pulled her coffee closer when he sat down and then mentally cursed herself for doing so. She was telegraphing how much she didn't want to be there for anyone to see—if they paid attention to that sort of thing—and she knew better. She was *trained* better.

The sheriff leaned forward, propping his elbows on the table. "Does your offer still stand?"

No. She bit back the word, studying his face. He looked like he'd been through the wringer in the last eighteen hours. *Probably didn't get much sleep.* It shouldn't have made him more attractive, but the tiredness evident added a layer to his handsomeness, deepening it. "What happened?"

"Can you get into Elysia? They've been stonewalling me since before I even knew this girl was dead."

That wasn't a good sign. Her mother never did anything without purpose, and normally she shut the gates only when there were visitors and she was showcasing how much better "back to nature" living was. It was easier to control whom the potential new members came into contact with that way, and get the indoctrination started. The established members were allowed to come and go as they pleased, venturing down into Clear Springs when the need arose. Most of them stuck close to the compound despite that freedom, which was just the way Martha liked it.

She sipped her coffee. "Are you sure they aren't entertaining?"

"No." His blue eyes were steady on hers. "They don't usually bring new folk through town, but I still tend to hear about it when there are strangers in the area. There aren't. And even if there were, I can't remember the last time those gates were closed."

Eden could. When Martha was first getting started in Elysia, immediately after the big gates had been built, they'd always been closed. The cult was a lot more stable now than it had been when she was in grade school and Martha was more secure in her power, so there was less need to resort to keeping people contained. Her mother had always preferred the softer method of control. "That doesn't mean anything." *Why am I arguing this? The whole reason I came out here was because I was convinced someone in Elysia had something to do with that girl's murder.*

Now that she was faced with actually having to put her money where her mouth was, fear made it hard to breathe. She hadn't realized just how much she'd trusted that she'd be turned away until it was no longer happening.

He pushed his coffee to the side. "Can you get into Elysia?"

"Yes." *Probably.* Martha kept asking her home, so it would be strange if she suddenly recanted her invitation the only time Eden actually accepted it. Her mother wasn't stupid enough to think it was for real, but she'd be unable to pass up the chance to play doting Demeter. The only thing Martha loved more than power was a show with her in the center.

It made Eden's stomach churn to even think about. "But that doesn't mean they'll tell me anything." *God, I don't want to do this.* She took a careful breath. "I'm going to need more information, though. If I don't know what I'm looking for, I'm not going in. It's too much risk for too long of a shot."

He hesitated like he was considering her. It struck Eden that she made an excellent suspect. She had a connection to Elysia, and the killings hadn't started until right around the time she'd shown up. It would have been child's play to slip into town a few days prior and pick off the victim—at least in theory.

And obviously the possibility has occurred to Sheriff Owens.

She straightened. "Either you trust me or you don't, but I'm the one taking all the risk by being here unofficially. I'm not going in without enough information to figure out what I'm looking for." She already had a pretty good idea—it was her job to hunt human predators, after all—but she didn't know squat about the victim, and that was a vital missing piece. Every profile started with the victim and worked its way back to the killer. "The girl. What's her story?"

After one last hesitation, Zach leaned back. "She's a local teenager. From what I can gather, there's an abusive situation at home, and she was planning on leaving Clear Springs in the rearview in favor of college. We're trying to pin down a timeline right now, but we know your mother had at least some contact with her, because Martha wrote a letter of recommendation to Montana State."

Eden set her coffee down, her stomach turning. She'd suspected there was a connection with the cult—hell, she'd been sure of it—but getting outside confirmation made it so much more real. "She's spent time at the commune."

"That would be my guess."

Martha was more than capable of playing a long game. She'd probably offered a sanctuary for the poor girl, extended a helping hand to give her a leg up into college—and to give her an excuse to keep in contact. Cults recruited across all ages and demographics, but Martha was fond of playing mother hen to disillusioned youth. Kids who were out in the world with their training wheels off, often suffering from situational depression because reality wasn't as shiny as what they'd expected. She offered them what appeared to be the life they'd always dreamed of—one filled with happiness and simplicity.

It was a lie, but a good portion of them never figured it out.

"I'm going to need to know when the girl went missing." Now it was her turn to hesitate. Putting herself out there in assistance was one thing—barging completely into the investigation was another. A thin line, but one she needed not to cross. If Britton found out she was dipping her toes into this mess, he'd yank her out of Montana so fast her head would spin. *Not to mention my meddling could completely compromise the investigation if it comes to light that someone from the cult is the unsub.* "I might need to see the body, too."

"Impossible." Zach leaned forward again and lowered his voice. "I don't trust you. I think your showing up is too damn convenient by half, even if you check out. But putting that aside, if you're right and this links back to Martha and her flock, I can't have your prints anywhere on the investigation. You're too close to it, and any defense attorney worth their salt would use that as leverage to allow their client to walk."

He'd checked her out. She forced her shoulders to relax. Of course he'd checked her out. She would have done the same thing. It didn't change much, other than the fact she was going to have to call Britton and do damage control. She might be here on her own, but that didn't mean her actions couldn't cause potential negative consequences for the BAU.

And he was right. If he'd officially requested help from the BAU, they never would have sent her. "Then why are you agreeing to this?"

"Because I don't have another goddamn option." His blue eyes showed frustration for a moment before he got it back under wraps. The man had a hell of a poker face.

The man had a hell of a face in general.

She hated the blush that rose at the thought. She wasn't here to check out the local flavor, no matter how attractive that flavor was. But it had been a long time, and she was only human. She cleared her throat and did her damnedest to focus on what really mattered, rather than her hormones trying to get the best of her. "It's possible that the cult has nothing to do with this."

"How likely do you think that is?"

That they weren't involved? She wanted to say she was certain no one in Elysia was, if only because it would give her an out she desperately wanted, but she couldn't lie to him. "The tattoos aren't something they advertise, and it isn't something a charity case of Martha's would have—or even know about. If this girl was leaving, she wasn't a full-fledged member—not yet, at least—so Martha never would have tattooed her. Not officially. There are approximately two hundred active members of Elysia at the compound, and another hundred scattered strategically in small groups in nearby cities, all of whom have knowledge of the tattoos. Though the fact she was found here seems to indicate it was one of the local group responsible. Take out children and minors and you have about one hundred and fifty suspects." Too many, but still a smaller pool than they would have otherwise. It gave them a place to start investigating, which was worth its weight in gold.

He raised his eyebrows. "For someone who hasn't been back in town since she was a teenager, you have a whole hell of a lot of knowledge about your mother's operations."

"My mother is the head of a cult." The words came out flat because she was fighting so hard to keep her turmoil of emotions repressed. "A cult that I grew up around, though her manipulations never quite stuck." *Mostly.* "A good portion of cults never do more than steal people's life savings and get some free labor, all of which lines the inner circle's pockets. But a small percentage turn violent and/or suicidal. I might not have been back here, but I'd never forgive myself if I knew things were shifting that way and didn't try to stop it." The Elysians had all the markings of a cult that would turn, though she couldn't tell him that without getting into exactly what practices they believed in.

Something she did her very best *never* to think about.

"Like now."

"Like now." She caught herself rubbing her sternum where the key tattoo had been forced on her. It didn't take much to slip back into that night when she was seventeen. She hadn't wanted the ink any more than she'd wanted the others, but she'd flat out told her mother no that time.

So Martha had ordered Abram to hold her down and had done it while Eden screamed and cried and begged her to stop.

She shook herself, fighting off the memory. "I'll go out there in the morning."

Something like compassion flickered over Zach's face. "They really did a number on you, didn't they?"

"It's nothing I can't handle." She just hoped it was true.

He grabbed a napkin and pulled a pen out of his jacket to scrawl on it. "You get into trouble—you even *think* you might be over your head—you call me. You hear?"

She accepted the napkin and tucked it into her pocket, deciding not to comment on the fact she already had his number in her phone since he'd called her to set up this meeting. It didn't matter. What mattered was that he was offering her a life raft. "I thought you didn't trust me."

"I don't." He shrugged. "But I can't have you getting yourself among the victim list if someone out there *is* responsible. So be careful."

"Got it." She stood. "I'll call you when I know something."

"Wrong. I'll take you out for dinner tomorrow night and we'll compare notes." When her mouth dropped open, he smiled. "We've both got to eat."

She didn't trust his one-eighty any more than she trusted anything in this town. Zach showed every evidence of being a smart man, which meant he fully intended to keep her close, though whether that was to protect her or keep an eye on her was anyone's guess. Both, most likely. Eden just nodded. "See you then." She dropped her cup into the trash and headed out into the brisk evening. The temperatures dropped with the sun around this time of year, and it would be bitterly cold before too long.

No one jumped out to accost her, and she made it to her rental car and locked the doors. *Old habits die hard.* There had been a case a few years back where a killer would wait for single women to get behind the wheel and turn on the engine, and then he'd jump in the passenger seat with a gun and tell them to drive. He'd killed five women before Eden and her partner caught up to him. She shuddered.

As tempting as it was to leave things until morning, there was always the chance she'd been wrong about her welcome. *Wouldn't that just be ironic? I make this big claim that I can always walk through the gates of Elysia and then I'm turned away.* She brought up her mother's contact in her phone and pressed "Call" before she could talk herself out of it.

Two rings and Martha picked up. "You never changed your number."

Her stomach lurched, the coffee threatening to rebel. "It seemed like failing if I did."

"And you've never failed at anything, have you, baby?"

She wasn't about to touch that with a ten-foot pole. "I've changed my mind. I'm staying in town for a little bit. I'm not of the mind that reconciling with you is even possible, but I'm willing to give it a shot." *Lies, lies, and more lies.*

"This wouldn't have anything to do with that girl who was found yesterday morning, would it?"

She wasn't surprised Martha already knew about it. She made it her business to know everything that went on within her realm of influence—especially if it was something that could be used to benefit her—and this girl's murder fit the bill. Eden turned onto the highway. "Does it matter?"

Silence for a beat, and then another. When Martha spoke again, her voice was warm enough to bring a smile to Eden's face—if she didn't know any better. "Not if it means my baby girl is coming home."

"I'm not coming home. I'm staying in Clear Springs—not in Elysia."

"For now." Martha kept going before she could correct her. "And you know you don't have to ask, baby. You'll always have a home in Elysia, and the gates will never be barred to you."

She gripped the steering wheel, fear and anger creating a toxic mess inside her. Her mother had always known exactly what buttons to push to edge her into whatever reaction Martha desired. No matter how superficially welcoming she was, she couldn't help sticking Eden a little, while she was at it.

She wanted to scream that Elysia had never been home—would never *be* home—but that reaction would just allow Martha to pat her on the head, secure in the fact that she knew her daughter well enough to provoke the desired response.

It didn't matter if she was right. Eden refused to give her the satisfaction. "I'll see you tomorrow."

"And what a tomorrow it will be with my baby coming home. I'll see you in the morning after communion." She hung up.

Of course she didn't question that Eden would still know Elysia's schedule, even after all this time. The most screwed-up thing about it was that she *did*.

She tossed her phone onto the passenger seat. "Into hell I go."

CHAPTER SEVEN

"Neveah Smith has been missing for three days now. We've confirmed that she's not in any of her usual haunts, and her phone has been turned off." That fact alone signaled trouble. Every single time Zach had seen her during the last two years, she'd had the thing attached to her hand, so he couldn't think of a good reason she'd turn it off completely.

He looked at the faces around the room and did his damnedest to project confidence he didn't feel. "Her parents have talked to her friends, but we're covering that ground again. I'm not prepared to bring in Randolph from Augusta, but if we don't get some sort of lead by the end of the day, that'll be the next step."

Chase rubbed a hand over his face. From the bags under his eyes, he didn't look like he'd had much sleep since finding Elouise's body. "I'm still following up with the colleges. You want me off that?"

"No." There just wasn't enough manpower to cover both a missing person and a murder, and the murder had to take precedence. Zach just hoped with everything he had that that's *all* this was. They weren't equipped to deal with this level of shit. But he had a sick feeling in his gut that the trouble in Clear Springs wasn't going to end with a single murder. "Henry and I'll get it started. I have a few of our volunteers coming in, too." They were mostly retired folk who put in time at the station on the rare occasions when schedules just didn't line up because of sickness or vacation.

He ran his hand through his hair. "Chase, you call me the second you get some answers from the registration people. I'm pursuing some unconventional paths, but we can't afford to let this thing with Neveah sit, either." He shook his head. "We're in over our heads, guys. So just do the best you can until I can get more hands on deck."

Henry pushed to his feet and stretched. "You already put the call out to Augusta?"

"Her picture has circulated over there, and I've passed it on to the stations in Great Falls. They have quite a bit bigger population, so I don't know if it will pop even if she's been there, but they've promised to get it out there and see if anything comes of it." He felt like he was going through the motions for no reason, but they had to pursue every avenue until they found the girl.

Or found her body.

"Henry, who was that kid she was running around with? The one with the priors?"

"Aaron Johnson." Henry crossed his arms over his chest and glowered. "He's a little punk."

Zach wasn't about to argue that. The kid had a mouth on him and the morals of an alley cat. "The Smiths say she was done with him, but—"

Henry snorted. "Parents would be the last to know."

"Exactly. Track the kid down and see if you can get him to tell you when the last time he saw her was."

Henry nodded. He might be more gentle giant than anything else, but he could put a good front on it when it suited him. Idiot kids with sticky fingers brought out that side of him. He'd have Aaron Johnson pissing his pants with one stone-cold look. "I'll check the school first, but that little punk has more truancies than the rest of the junior class combined. It might take some time to hunt him down."

For a small town, there were plenty of places for kids to get into trouble if they were so inclined. Zach had gotten into his fair share when he was in school, too, though he'd never resorted to the shit that would actually get him arrested.

Probably because his father had been the sheriff.

He nodded at Henry. "Best get to it, then."

"I'll call when I have some answers."

"Good." He watched the older man shrug on his jacket and head out the door. It was only then that he turned to Chase. "Go home. Take a few hours."

"What?"

"You're not doing anyone any favors if you're running yourself into the ground. Those college offices don't get up and running before nine, so get out of here for a while and catch some shut-eye." It was an order, so he didn't bother to phrase it as a question.

Chase didn't move, his eyes stark in his pale face. "I can't get her face out of my head, Zach. Up here, I know there's nothing I could have done." He pointed to his head. "But that doesn't take the guilt away. This is our town. *Ours.* Nothing like that is supposed to happen in our town."

Zach couldn't argue that. Part of the reason he'd chosen to come back to Clear Springs in the first place was because of the fact that things like brutal murders didn't happen here. He'd seen enough violence in the desert to last him a lifetime. There was nothing more fucked-up than having men he'd trained with and gone on mission after mission with gunned down in front of him. Or worse, blown up past the point of recognition. Violence like that wasn't supposed to happen in his hometown. It was supposed to be safe.

But someone had gone and taken away that safety—and it was his job to figure out who had done it.

"We'll find the person responsible." It didn't matter if they were in over their head, because letting something like this happen to another girl in his town wasn't an option. He very carefully didn't think about the fact that they hadn't found the slightest evidence of where the hell Neveah had gotten to. Zach took a deep breath. "But you won't be finding a damn thing if you fall asleep behind the wheel or while you're on hold. Take a few hours, Chase."

It was entirely possible that, wherever Neveah was, those few hours wouldn't make a single bit of difference in her fate.

He didn't say that. He barely let himself *think* it.

Zach had learned the hard way that it was vital to focus on the positive and keep going. If they stopped long enough to think about all the shit beyond their control, they'd lose their damn minds, and he'd find his deputies curled up in a corner, rocking, with a wild look in their eyes.

He'd been the one in the corner a time or two in his twenties. He had no interest in returning.

One step at a time.

Chase hesitated and then finally gave a jerky nod. "Three hours. No more."

"Take four and make sure you get something to eat while you're at it." He didn't know if his deputy would actually sleep, but maybe getting him out of the police station for a bit would be enough to ground him again.

"If you're sure . . ."

"Go. Don't make me say it again." Once he was sure Chase would obey his order, he headed for his cruiser. The high school kids would just be hitting homeroom right around now, which meant it was a good time to yank Neveah's friends out of class and see if any of them were going to change their story about what had happened over the weekend without their parents looking over their shoulders. Technically, he wasn't allowed to interview underage suspects without a parent present, but the principal would stand in, and since none of these kids were actually suspects, he was willing to bend the rules. All that mattered was finding the missing girl. He could give two fucks about underage drinking or any of the things that would tie parents up in knots. Once he made that explicitly clear, he hoped it'd get *someone* talking. At this point, all they knew was that Neveah had been at school on Friday, but no one claimed to have seen her since the last bell rang.

Someone was lying. Zach just had to figure out *who*.

CHAPTER EIGHT

The gates of Elysia rose up like something out of Eden's nightmares. She knew the scene by heart, every little detail tattooed on her brain over the years. Her mother had the same image painted in vibrant color in the chapel. It was a work of art, but that didn't change the fact that Eden despised it. She knew what Martha had always wanted—mother and daughter running Elysia.

It was never a dream Eden shared.

But then, she didn't have her mother's total lack of moral code.

She pulled through the gates and parked her car in front of the main building. It was part chapel, part gathering place, part cafeteria. The members were here several times a day for various activities—or that was how it used to be. They cycled through so half were working and half were worshipping . . . and all were under the watchful eye of Martha and her inner circle.

Back when Eden had been a kid, Abram alone had been that inner circle. He'd been Martha's first follower—or that was the story her mother told. She wasn't sure if it was reality or fiction. Elysia had come into being before Eden's living memory, so she was fuzzy on the truth. If her mother was to be believed—and she couldn't trust a damn thing out of Martha's mouth—the idea for a simpler place had come to her when she was pregnant. She'd traveled until she found just the right spot and began to preach. From there, followers had flocked to the one true way.

Bullshit.

She'd seen the records. Martha had inherited the land Elysia stood on from a distant uncle back when she was all of eighteen. She hadn't done anything with it, but it seemed like one day she'd just appeared with a group in tow and set up camp. The commune had grown from there.

Through the years, some things had changed, but she doubted very much that Abram's place at her mother's side had. She just didn't know. As much as she'd presented herself as an expert in all things Elysia to Zach, it wasn't the truth. She had numbers, yes, but numbers were easy to get ahold of. Years ago, Martha had petitioned to have her "religion" recognized as a nonprofit, and won. Eden still wasn't sure how she'd managed that, because the IRS had spent years fighting the Church of Scientology before buckling to the pressure. Either way, as a result, she had to report her numbers to maintain her status—and get her much-needed tax breaks.

In this world, nothing can be said to be certain, except death and taxes.

Old Ben Franklin doesn't know the half of it. Eden relaxed her grip. She wasn't turning around and driving out of here like the hounds of hell were on her heels. She was going to let go of the steering wheel and get out of her car and face the demons from her past. Once she'd gathered enough information, she'd drive back to Clear Springs and compare notes with Zach. Simple.

But she couldn't quite make her fingers unclench from the faded plastic.

A knock on her window startled her damn near out of her skin. She managed to keep her shriek inside, but only barely. She turned to find a man grinning at her from the other side of the window. *Blond hair, brown eyes, attractive in the conventional way.* She categorized his features before her memories caught up with her mind. She knew this man. Eden frowned. "Joseph?"

"So you do remember me." He laughed. "You going to get out of the car or sit there all day?"

She got out of the car.

Eden couldn't stop staring at him. They'd both grown up in Elysia, though he'd been four years older, an age gap that meant they were never quite in the same stage at the same time. She hadn't liked him then, had found him too loud, too pushy, but when there were only so many children in the commune, they'd been forced into close interactions countless times over the years.

He'd still been in that awkward postadolescence stage when she'd left, all gangly limbs and bobbing Adam's apple. He was a whole lot prettier now, having grown into his height and jawline, his blond hair cut and combed in an artful way that looked professional. *He's pretty enough to be a model now. I bet that suits my mother's purposes nicely.*

At least until a person met his eyes. Her mother could lie with her eyes—Eden had seen it time after time, and even now, she wasn't sure she could tell the difference. Joseph wasn't that skilled. His eyes gave him away as rotten to the core.

His grin turned downright flirtatious. "Damn, Eden, but you sure did grow up nice. Guess some things really do get better with age."

She raised her eyebrows and gave him a single sweep, refusing to let him know how much his come-on revolted her. Joseph had been a bully when they were children, and bullies were like sharks—the scent of blood in the water would drive them into a frenzy. *Show no weakness.* The mantra of her life. "And some things don't."

He turned a mottled red and forced out a laugh. "You always were a bitch."

And he'd always had a temper, now that she was thinking about it. *Enough of a temper to murder someone in cold blood?* Back then, she wouldn't have thought so, but people changed—and often not for the better. She cocked her head to the side, letting the insult slide off her. "You spend much time with that girl who was killed a few days ago?"

His lips pressed into a hard line, his attractiveness fading with the ugly look on his face. "I told Martha you weren't back for her, but hell if she was willing to listen. You go and break your mama's heart, and I'm going to break you."

Well, that escalated quickly. Strangely enough, his threats grounded her. She wasn't a helpless teenager anymore, no matter how coming back here made her feel. Years of training and experience had made her deadly in her own right, even if she put that to use in the name of law and order.

But all the training and experience in the world weren't enough to deal with her mother.

She lifted her chin. "Speak of the devil. Where is she?" She'd expected Martha to meet her with bells on. Her mother always liked a good show. It seemed like she was missing an opportunity to proclaim that her prodigal daughter was home at last.

Eden looked around. The commune had expanded a bit in the last ten years. Before, there had been only the main building and a scattering of houses behind it. Now there were two more buildings flanking the chapel, creating a U-shaped courtyard of sorts. Since morning prayers had ended well over an hour ago and lunch wasn't for another hour, it was strange that the only person out and about seemed to be Joseph.

Maybe she's actually listening to what I say for once and respecting it.

As soon as the thought crossed her mind, she gave herself an inner shake. Martha didn't respect anyone's needs but Martha's. If it appeared she was being sensitive to Eden, it was because she was buttering her up for something. The woman did nothing without reason, and Eden highly doubted her mother was about to start now.

Joseph opened his mouth as if he was about to say something else insulting, but caught himself at the last moment. He crossed his arms over his chest and looked down his nose at her. "She was called away.

She said to make yourself at home in the chapel and she'll be with you shortly."

So Martha wasn't being sensitive. Something more important came up.

Eden followed Joseph into the building, doing her best to smother the complicated tangle of emotions inside her. Part of her was relieved that she was right, but it was doing battle with the strange disappointment stemming from the same reason. She had no business being disappointed. Hell, she had no business expecting *anything* from her mother.

Especially answers.

She pushed it all aside and focused on her surroundings. The decorations leaned toward the light and airy—white walls, simple wooden pews that were expertly crafted, white prayer cushions for when kneeling was called for. The only thing extravagant about the room was the mural behind the podium, painted in vivid color.

The fear on Persephone's face had always resonated with Eden. Here was a girl who also wasn't in control of her own fate, who was being thrust back and forth between two powerful forces. Eden had always privately held that there was relief lingering in her eyes. Hades might have dragged her into the underworld, but the silver lining was that he'd effectively removed her from her mother's influence. And what kind of person—goddess or otherwise—put her own grief before the well-being of the entire world? Persephone had dodged a bullet, and it was only because she'd failed to eat enough pomegranate seeds that she was forced back aboveground once more.

But only for six months. And when they were through, Eden imagined she welcomed the shadows of the underworld and Hades' uncomplicated attentions. He didn't expect her to be subservient. He wanted her to rule at his side.

There had been more nights than she cared to remember where she lay in bed and prayed for her own Hades to come and save her. To take her away from the world she'd been trapped in—away from the woman who ruled her with an iron fist and a sweet smile.

In the end, Eden had been her own savior.

She just had to remember that—remember that she'd walked back into her own personal hell of her own free will. She could leave whenever she wanted to. "Not much has changed."

Joseph watched her with muddy brown eyes. The sheer hate there made her flinch before she caught herself. She started to reach to touch the butt of her gun before she remembered that she wasn't on duty and she wasn't carrying it.

He gave her another slow visual rake. "You want to know something?"

The only thing she wanted was to get the hell away from him. "No, thanks."

He continued as if she hadn't spoken. "If you'd stayed, she would have given you to me. She told me so."

If that wasn't just another indication that her leaving was the right thing to do, she didn't know what was. "Guess I dodged a bullet." *In so many ways.*

His grin didn't reach his eyes. "There's still time." Had her mother resorted to giving her followers drugs? Because there was nothing short of insanity that would have him being *that* confident he'd ever have a chance with Eden.

Drugs . . . or an unrelenting belief that every word that came out of Martha's mouth was the gospel.

If her mother said Eden would come back into the fold, he believed her. Of course he did. Martha was convincing in the extreme. If she wasn't, she wouldn't have gotten this far—or have a decades-long history of bending people to her will.

You have to at least try *to be convincing. Coming in here with verbal fists swinging isn't going to open any doors.* "If you say so."

Joseph turned and strode out of the chapel, leaving her staring at his back. It took her a few minutes to get moving once the door closed behind him, but she blamed that on culture shock caused by coming to Elysia after so long away. Eden wandered around the chapel, but nothing had really changed. The pews were of better quality—and probably more expensive—but everything else was exactly the same.

It took a grand total of ten minutes for her to become unbearably bored. She'd never been good at sitting on her hands when there was work to be done, and with nervous energy thrumming just under her skin, that was doubly true.

She peeked out the door, but the foyer was just as empty as the chapel. Apparently Joseph was confident she'd do as she was told. She snorted. Obviously he didn't remember her as well as he seemed to think.

The hallway directly across from the chapel led back to what used to be the classrooms, but it was eerily silent, so she figured that must have changed. Curious, she headed that way on silent feet. The first room used to be designated for grade school–age children, but now it held several adult-size desks with new computers and corded phones. There was no one around, but the scrawled writing on the giant whiteboard indicated this was the working command center.

Around eight years ago, Martha had taken her weaving business countrywide. Alpaca products were trendy, and their popularity seemed to be growing as time went on. While the majority of Elysia's property was designated for growing plant-based things, they had fields upon fields that had been converted for the alpacas. Eden had seen the tax records of their earnings—or what they claimed were their earnings. She wasn't stupid enough to think they'd reported every penny brought in, nonprofit or no.

Business was good. That was for damn sure.

But she wasn't here for their tax records. If that girl had been killed by someone in Elysia, she very much doubted it had to do with money.

Ruling out that motive completely would be foolish, but for now she would focus her attention in other directions.

As she moved farther down the hall, a soft humming sounded from the next room. Eden hesitated, but then figured the worst that could happen was someone would report that she'd wandered off—something she wasn't exactly trying to hide at the moment—and poked her head into the room.

A woman scrubbed at the wooden floor with a hand brush that meant the job would take hours. A mop would have made more sense, but Eden had intimate knowledge of this particular punishment. Fingers rubbed raw from the chemicals in the soap, shoulders and back seizing up because of the hours spent hunched over.

She wanted to shake the woman, to tell her that nothing she'd done could have been deserving of this punishment, to yell that this was abuse and anyone who claimed otherwise was a goddamn liar.

She didn't do any of that. She just stood there until the woman sensed someone watching and looked up.

Recognition rolled over Eden, and she gasped before she could stop herself. *"Beth?"*

"Eden!" Beth dropped the brush and lunged to her feet, only to stop short. "Sorry. I know it's been a long time."

But Eden was already moving, pulling her into a hug. Beth had always been petite, but she felt downright frail now. Breakable. That didn't detract from the strength of her hug, though. She kept hold of Eden's shoulders when they stepped back. "Martha said you were home, but I was almost afraid to hope."

"I'm not home." She hated the way the other woman's face fell, but she thought a lie would have been more damaging. "But I will be visiting a bit for now."

Beth's smile returned, practically lighting up the room. She had an ethereal beauty, with her pale skin and white-blonde hair that Eden had thought she would outgrow. Instead, age had only sharpened it, giving her the look of some otherworldly being who'd wandered into the room. "I've missed you so much."

"I've missed you, too." To her surprise, it was true. If she'd had one friend growing up, it was Beth, though Eden had never made the mistake of assuming their friendship would take precedence over Elysia.

Her gaze fell to Beth's left hand, and she froze. "You're married?"

"What? Oh, yes." She beamed. "Almost ten years now. Jon and I are very happy." Her gaze fell. "We haven't been able to conceive yet, though."

Eden wasn't going to poke at *that*. She was too focused on the idea of Beth marrying Jon. His mother had brought him into Elysia when he was ten, but when she left six months later, she'd left him behind. He'd always been quiet and restrained to the point of being antisocial, something she identified with thoroughly at the time—still did, if she was honest. She vividly remembered meeting his gaze over the heads of the bowed Elysian subjects during one particularly brutal sermon and seeing him roll his eyes.

It blew her mind that he'd stayed, let alone that he'd stayed and married Beth, whom he'd never shown the least bit of interest in. *At my mother's command, no less.*

She did some quick math. "But that means you were married—"

"On my eighteenth birthday." Beth's smile never wavered, her face giving no indication that she was anything but elated by that turn of events. "It was a very beautiful ceremony."

She gritted her teeth, trying to decide if she should pursue it, but ultimately Eden couldn't help herself. "I didn't realize you and Jon were dating." They hadn't been—she was sure of it. Beth wasn't capable of lying, let alone to her best friend. If she'd been seeing Jon, Eden would have known about it. Hell, she would have sworn up and down that Jon would take the first bus out of Clear Springs on his eighteenth birthday.

Apparently she'd been wrong on both counts.

"We weren't." Beth shrugged. "Martha had a dream."

She blinked, trying to process *that*. "A dream." *That's new.* Or apparently not new, since it had happened ten years ago.

"Yes. It was, well, it was after you left. She was very upset and it opened a channel inside her that was closed previously."

I'll just bet it did. Prophetic dreams. Eden looked around, wondering what else had changed since she'd been gone. It struck her once again that she couldn't take anything for granted. Just because she'd grown up on this land and under the influence of her mother didn't mean a damn thing anymore.

Good thing I've learned a trick or two since then. I'm going to need every edge I can get.

It brought her right back to the reason she was here in the first place. She affected an easy smile. "Well, then, I'm happy for you. I take it things are going well?"

"Oh, yes!" Joy suffused her face. "I've reached Adept, and this winter Martha is personally going to be training me to allow myself to be a conduit for Demeter in dreams."

Adept meant Beth was near the top of the hierarchy, one step below Abram and the rest of the inner circle. Eden searched her gaze for any kind of cold ambition, but there was nothing but childlike happiness. *A true believer.* It made her skin itch just thinking about it.

But she wasn't here to convince her mother's flock of the error of their ways. She was here about the dead girl. "Beth, do you guys get a lot of teenagers from Clear Springs out here?"

"There you are!"

Beth went even paler and fell to her knees. "I wasn't shirking my duty, Martha. I promise." She grabbed the brush and went back to scrubbing with vigor, keeping her head ducked so her hair hid her face.

Eden clenched her hands but managed to keep the anger off her face as she turned to her mother. "It was my fault. I saw she was working and distracted her anyway."

"You always did have the tendency to play fast and loose with the rules." Martha motioned her forward. "Now, let's leave poor Beth to her cleaning and have that talk I know you're dying to have."

Interesting choice of words. It was deliberate. She had no illusions about that fact. Eden was convinced she'd have a better chance of getting information out of Beth, but that wasn't an option at this juncture. She made a mental note to corner her former friend at the first available opportunity, then followed her mother deeper into the building.

CHAPTER NINE

"Tea?"

"I'm good." Eden took a seat across from her mother, the years flashing away as if they'd never passed. Suddenly she was sixteen again and about to receive yet another lecture on how she wasn't living up to the Collins standards that Martha's followers expected. She gritted her teeth. *I've got to stop doing that. I'm not a child anymore, and she doesn't have power over me.*

It didn't feel like that, though. It felt like her whole life had been working to one moment, to when she sat down across from Martha. Not as mother and daughter, but as adversaries. She studied her face, tracing over the new lines and eyes that practically shone with kindness. Martha had let some gray bleed into her hair, but she was still attractive. She looked like the kind of woman who'd gather lost souls to her and hold them until they were whole again.

Which was exactly why she was so dangerous.

She was like one of those deep-sea fish with the dangling light, drawing its prey in closer and closer until it was too late to escape. By the time anyone realized the danger, they were so far under her spell, they never saw the light of day again.

Martha turned on a freestanding electric kettle and sat back. "You have questions. I won't pretend to have all the answers, but I will do my best."

The worst part was that she sounded earnest. So much so that Eden would have believed it was the truth if she hadn't seen this particular act—word for word—before. She drummed her fingers on the arm of the chair. There was nothing for it. If she accused her mother of lying right out of the gate, Martha would shut down, and any information she was willing to impart would go up in smoke. There was no guarantee she'd tell the truth, but she was playing along for now, which meant Eden had to do the same.

She'd trained for this. There had been many interviews over the years since she joined the BAU, suspects and witnesses ranging from hostile to borderline comatose. A conversation with her mother shouldn't even rank in the top ten most difficult.

And yet here they were. She considered Martha, debating her next words. She could ask after Elysia, after Abram, but her mother would most likely call her on trying to butter her up. Better to go directly for the meaty subject—the real reason she was here. "The girl who was found dead—Elouise Perkins."

Her mother pressed her hands to her mouth. "Oh, that poor, poor girl. I had heard that there was a death, but I had no idea it was her." There was nothing but surprise on her face, but Martha had learned to lie in every way that counted before Eden was born. Everything from the identity of Eden's father to the details of Martha's childhood was fabricated. She knew, because it was the first thing she'd researched when she got access to the FBI's databases.

No history of her mother attending school in the state of Georgia, let alone the prestigious all-girls school she'd apparently made up as well. No history of Eden being born in Saint Joseph's Hospital, despite what her birth certificate said.

The deeper she'd dug, the more like a lucid dream her entire childhood had felt.

She took a careful breath and pulled herself back to the present—back to what really mattered. "You knew her."

She didn't frame it as a question, but her mother answered it anyway. "I had seen her around town from time to time, and it was brought to my attention that her relationship with her father was . . . problematic."

Problematic. What a careful way to phrase it. Eden frowned. "He hurt her?" If there was the slightest chance there were other suspects beyond Elysia, why the hell had Zach sent her out here? She pressed her lips together. *You're looking for a way out, and you know it. Zach had his reasons, same as you . . . though he had better explain them tonight.*

Domestic violence doesn't explain the presence of the tattoos. Remember that, even if nothing else is true.

"He was abusive, yes. She often wore scarves despite warm weather, but that could be one of those teenage fashion statements." Martha waved that away. "I wasn't sure until one of my men witnessed Michael raising a hand to her."

There was so much pride in her tone, it didn't take much to connect the dots. "Your man stepped in. Brought her back here." *Out of the frying pan and into the fire.*

"Yes to both. We offered her a place to stay without any conditions—no, don't look at me like that, Eden. I know what you think of me, but there truly were no conditions. She was in trouble so we gave her shelter."

And made a very public display of their charity to new members. Martha never did anything without reason, and Eden highly doubted she'd started with Elouise Perkins. "You wrote her a recommendation letter."

"I wrote her several." The kettle began to whistle, and she poured the boiling water into the waiting cup. "You're sure you don't want any?"

"I'm sure." She didn't exactly think her mother would poison her, but the myth of Persephone struck a little too close to home. It might be silly to think that eating on Elysian ground would be enough to trap her here, but Eden was feeling particularly superstitious at the moment. Best case, it represented a white flag she had no interest in offering. Worst case . . . well, there was a murderer on the loose, wasn't there? The MO might not match, but she wasn't about to take any chances.

Martha stirred some honey into her mug. "Where was I? Yes, the recommendation letters. I offered her a place in Elysia, of course, but she was determined to attend college."

"Of course you did." Eden didn't even try to keep the sarcasm out of her tone. "Do you know which college she chose?"

Martha gave her wide eyes. "I'm surprised you and that lovely sheriff don't. She was planning on attending Montana State."

Since she had a feeling Zach already knew that, she let the passive-aggressive comment go, though it rankled. A lot. She'd known she was on a need-to-know basis, but her pride stung at showing up here and having her lack of information thrown in her face. "I don't suppose you know when she left?"

"Ah, let's see." Martha closed her eyes, a habit she had when trying to remember something. "I believe school started on the seventeenth. The last I saw her was . . . September second. Yes, it was the second. Abram was kind enough to give her a ride to the bus stop so she didn't have to walk."

By her count, the suspect list was just adding up. Abram was on there solely because of personal bias, because he'd been all too willing to torment her at her mother's command when she was younger. She was inclined to add Joseph to the list simply because she despised him. And her mother . . . well, Martha was the puppeteer. It was impossible to imagine that anyone in Elysia breathed wrong without her say-so. "How kind of him."

"It was, yes." Martha said it without a hint of irony.

Eden started to say that she doubted Abram had done a kind thing in his life, but she stopped herself before the words left her lips. Insulting him wouldn't get her anywhere, no matter how true it was. She cleared her throat. "Is there anything else you can tell me?"

"I don't know what you want me to say, Eden. As much as I'd like to be able to tell you I know exactly who killed her so they can be brought to justice, it simply isn't true. If you're looking for the criminal here, you're looking in the wrong place."

Either she didn't know about the tattoos or she was a really great liar . . . which Eden already knew to be true. She recrossed her legs, hating that this meeting was creating more questions than answers. But then, she'd known the only way she was going to get real information from this place was to snoop on her own. She'd bet her last paycheck that Martha had rehearsed how this little tête-à-tête would go before she'd agreed to Eden coming out here in the first place.

I need a chance to get some more alone time with Beth.

It wouldn't be today, though. Which meant she had to smile and play whatever game was necessary to be allowed back.

"Tell me what's new with you, baby." Martha took a careful drink of her tea. "It's been so long since we talked."

For good reason. She set her hands in her lap, digging her nails into her palm. "I spend a lot of time working. Traveling for work. Training for work."

"You're very good at what you do." Only her mother would make the statement sound like a bad thing.

"Yes, I have a perfectly respectable percentage of closed cases." There were certain ones that had stayed with her—and would always stay with her. Victims' families who'd have no closure. Killers who'd struck again. Leads that had gone from hot to cold to downright dead. She wasn't any better at letting go now than she had been as a kid. "It could be better."

"You really haven't changed." Martha gave a sad smile that pulled at her heartstrings despite her best efforts to shield herself against it. "Always something you could do better, something you were downright determined to do better."

"There's nothing wrong with wanting to be better."

"You never wanted better. You wanted perfect. Perfection doesn't exist, baby."

She'd always said that. It drove Eden so damn crazy, because there was nothing wrong with aiming to be *more*, to have a better life than she had. It wasn't in her nature to settle—never had been. That was what her mother had done—burrowing deep and creating a nest here for herself that she rarely left and ruled with an iron fist. Eden wasn't like Martha. She refused to be.

She pushed to her feet. "I think that's enough for today." She hadn't gotten what she wanted, but she wasn't sure how much more of this she could take.

"You'll be back."

It wasn't quite a question. In fact, it was a whole lot like a command. She fought down the instinctive need to say she was never setting foot in this place again. It didn't matter that she wasn't actually giving Martha what she wanted. Her mother knew she was here to investigate that girl's murder, and she wasn't above using a horrific situation to further her own aims. She wanted Eden back in the fold, with whatever tool she needed to make it happen. "I'll be back."

Martha's smile was beatific. "Elysia's gates are always open to you, baby. You know that. You may come and go as you please."

She ignored that through sheer force of will and concentrated on keeping her posture relaxed and her face unconcerned. *Show no weakness.* "That works for me."

Did you kill that girl, knowing I'd come back, that I'd have to come back?

And what if she did?

Many people blindly sent money to Martha because of those damn commercials she'd commissioned six years ago, and there were more who lived in the commune itself. If Martha was indicted for murder, her property would be forfeit. If she didn't cash it out to pay for an attorney, it would fall to the next of kin.

Me.

The mere thought made her sick, but she couldn't shake it. There was too much knowledge in her mother's whiskey-colored eyes, so similar to her own. Eden stared. "If you had something to do with this murder, you will pay. It doesn't matter if you're my mother or if you have all these people eating out of the palm of your hand. Justice doesn't care about either of those things."

Martha shook her head, her expression sad. "Baby, don't you know? Justice is a lie. All this world cares about is power—and I have that in spades."

Zach's phone rang exactly at five o'clock, and he was desperately glad for the distraction. "Owens."

"I'm going to call in an order to Hakeem's. In about twenty minutes, why don't you go pick it up and meet me at my room?"

It took him several seconds to connect the exhausted voice with Eden Collins. She sounded nothing like she had during their last few encounters. He double-checked the caller ID just in case. Yeah, it was most definitely her. "I thought we were meeting in Augusta."

"Martha knows what I'm here for, which means she'll be expecting me to be in contact with you, regardless of whether you think I'm a suspect or not. There's no reason to hide that we're talking. And, forgive me for being blunt, but today was fucking beyond rough, so if you want a report, coming to me is your only option."

He wanted that report. There was also the added bonus of being able to talk frankly with her without worrying about an audience or someone connected with Elysia eavesdropping. She'd probably thought of that, tired or not, because Eden didn't seem like the type of woman to let a rough day get the best of her. "I'll be there in thirty."

She hung up without saying good-bye. Zach set his phone on his desk and sighed. Today had been dead end after dead end. None of the kids at the high school claimed to know a damn thing about where Neveah had gotten to. When he'd asked about potential parties, they'd clammed up across the board, which led him to believe there *had* been a party last weekend, though he was at a loss to figure out if she'd been there. He bothered to break up bonfires only when the kids were trespassing or there was a high fire-risk warning in place. Mostly because if they weren't doing it in his territory, they'd be driving farther out to do the same damn thing. There'd only been one alcohol-induced death because of drunken driving since he'd been sheriff, but one was more than enough.

That didn't matter to the kids. They saw him as a representation of the Man, and they weren't going to give him any ammunition, promises not to arrest or no. It made his job a whole hell of a lot harder.

Maybe I should give Eden a crack at them. She's pretty enough to have the boys eating out of the palm of her hand, and that might be enough to get someone to talk.

He rubbed a hand across his mouth. Even if he trusted her, that wasn't a possible avenue to pursue. She couldn't be involved in any aspect of the investigation. He was already toeing the line with having her poke around out in Elysia, but his options were dwindling by the minute. Every hour Neveah stayed missing increased the chance she'd never be found.

Or never found alive.

Needing movement, he headed for Hakeem's on foot. The crisp fall evening felt damn good after being indoors all day. He paid attention as he headed down the street, but there wasn't much in the way of foot traffic. There should have been. Clear Springs might be mostly families with kids of varying ages, but there was a decent-size portion of the population past retirement age. Local fishing and hunting had brought them through the area when they were younger, and quite a few had decided to stay for good once they were out of the workforce. All that added up to folks being out and about and hobnobbing during the evening hours on the main street. The Monday-night book-club ladies usually met at the little coffee shop around this time, but when he walked past, it was deserted.

A murder does that to a town.

He walked into Hakeem's and saw the man the restaurant was named after. He was tall and lean to the point where he almost looked like he'd fold in half without warning. He offered Zach an easy smile and nod. "Sheriff."

Zach returned the nod of greeting. "How's it going?"

Hakeem shrugged. "I hear there is a murderer on the loose." He had a faint accent that turned the words beautiful despite their meaning.

"We're going to find whoever did it."

"I have the utmost faith in you." He finished tying the plastic bag around two disposable containers. "Dinner for two?"

"Business, unfortunately."

Hakeem raised thick black brows. "Times like these, Sheriff, you must find comfort where you can."

It was suddenly too easy to picture finding *comfort* with Eden Collins. She was a beautiful woman with her honeyed hair and whiskey eyes, and she had a mouth that could make a man think sinful thoughts if he wasn't careful.

At least until he remembered that she was Martha Collins's daughter and that she was more than likely connected to the murder.

He paid for the dinner. "Business."

"Whatever you say, Sheriff." But the speculative look in Hakeem's eyes didn't bode well. He'd talk to his wife, Shari, about the sheriff picking up a meal for two that a woman called in, and Shari would be off and telling her three sisters about it, and by tomorrow morning, the entire town would know. He'd always thought the prayer phone chain was more for gossip than actual prayer, and how fast news got around only served to confirm that. It was mostly harmless, but he didn't need folk focusing on his supposed romantic entanglements—especially when they were complete fiction.

There was nothing to do, though. The more he protested, the more likely Hakeem was to believe he was protesting too much. So he just took the bag and headed for the B&B. He went in the side door because Dolores was just as likely to mention to anyone who'd listen that the sheriff was heading up to her lady boarder's room. Zach loved this town. He really did. But there were days when it was damned inconvenient to live here.

He knocked on Eden's door, and she must have been waiting because it opened immediately. He stepped into the room, struck that he'd never had cause to be in the B&B's actual rooms. Dolores had several brunches throughout the year where she pulled out all the stops and basically fed whoever showed up—which was, more often than not, half of Clear Springs—but only guests used the actual rooms.

Eden closed the door behind him, and he got his first good look at her. Zach stopped short. She looked like she'd run a marathon that she hadn't the slightest bit of training for—exhausted and drawn. *If she's not involved, it couldn't have been easy to face Martha again after all these years.* It most likely would have been a combination of psychological and emotional warfare, and a person didn't walk away from that unscathed.

And I'm the reason she was there in the first place.

He didn't trust her. He couldn't with the current situation. But his gut said that while she was connected in some way, Eden wasn't responsible for Elouise's death.

Zach held up the bag. "I brought food."

She didn't move from the door. Her hair was pulled back into a tight ponytail, and she'd changed at some point into a pair of yoga pants and a loose shirt. He very carefully kept his eyes on her face. "Eden?"

"Did you have one of your people go through my stuff?"

Her question had him rocking back on his heels. "What?"

"My stuff." She motioned to her open suitcase sitting on the floor next to the bed. "I know you don't trust me, Zach, but this is a little extreme, even for this town."

He held up a hand. "Hold on. If by a little extreme, you mean highly illegal—yeah, it is. I might bend the rules on occasion, but that's crossing a very clear line." He looked around the room again. It had been child's play for him to get up here without alerting Dolores. Anyone could have done the same thing. "You kept your door locked while you were out?"

"I'm not an idiot." Though she gave him a look like *he* might be.

He actually saw the moment it dawned on her that if it wasn't one of Zach's people, it was someone else. She crossed her arms over her chest and immediately dropped them, looking everywhere but at him. *Shit.* He set the food down on the table. "What tipped you off that someone was here?"

"It might be my imagination." She hesitated, her mouth pressing into a tight line. "No, I'm making excuses. Nothing was overtly moved, but things weren't quite where I left them. I would know. I travel a lot, and I'm a creature of habit. Things were just a little *off* when I got back from the commune—and the room smells like hyacinths, though that could very well be the cleaning supplies."

It wasn't. Dolores was known for bragging that there wasn't a mess that Pine-Sol or bleach couldn't fix. If she'd been in here, the place would smell of lemons—not flowers. He frowned. "How the hell do you know what hyacinths smell like? Roses, I get. They're distinctive. Hyacinths seem a random thing to be able to identify."

Her lips quirked up at the corners, but not like anything was funny. "I was raised in Elysia. We had a significant number of greenhouses—and a whole lot of property—devoted solely to different kinds of flowers—and hyacinths are my mother's favorite."

So much of this came back to that damn cult. He set the food out and pointed to the chair across from him. "Sit. You look like you're going to keel over."

"It's not polite to tell someone they look tired—especially a woman."

"You're not a woman. You're an agent." He just needed to remember that, because it was hard to keep present in his mind with her looking so . . . human. Without her tough-as-nails persona in place, she looked softer, more vulnerable. Like someone he would have considered asking out for coffee in another life.

Eden pulled her food closer and opened her plastic utensils. "Yep, that's me. Agent. Not woman."

He couldn't shake the feeling that he'd just insulted her, but he hadn't meant to. Most women he'd come across in both his stint in the Marines and his various training exercises as a cop usually fell into one of two categories—erasing their femininity or playing it up as a piece of their arsenal. He respected both methods, though he wasn't a fan of the coquettish requests for help that occasionally came his way. Eden, though, didn't seem to fit into either category.

Or maybe she did, but being back in her old stomping grounds was throwing her far off her game, and *that* was the reason he couldn't get a good read on her.

It was possible he was looking for an excuse—any excuse—to trust her.

CHAPTER TEN

It felt weird to share a meal with someone other than Vic. Eden had spent so many nights with her partner in almost this exact same position—sitting on opposite sides of tiny tables in interchangeable hotels across the States. To do it with someone else . . . to do it with *Zach* . . . was just downright strange. It was such a silly thing to worry about, especially considering everything else going on, but she would rather deal with the man sitting across from her than with the memories dealing with her mother had brought up today—or the fact that there had most definitely been someone in her room.

Her skin broke out in goose bumps that only seemed to get worse the more she thought about it. This might be a B&B, but it was *her* space. Her things. That someone had been here, touching her stuff, moving through a space that should have been safe . . . it gave her chills.

It was almost worse that there wasn't anything she could quite put her finger on as being *evidence* of the break-in. She wasn't anal enough to have her things just so in order to function, but she'd packed and unpacked so many times, she had a system. Things had a place.

And those things weren't quite in the same place they had been this morning.

"What's wrong?"

She blinked, belatedly realizing that she'd been holding a spoonful of stew long enough for her hand to start aching. She'd eaten Ethiopian food all over the country, and Hakeem's still served some of the best. "I intensely dislike having my space violated . . . but it's a minor crime in the face of our current circumstances." And she had no *proof*. Sure, she could charge out to Elysia and make a fool of herself spouting paranoid bullshit, but that would give Martha the upper hand—and would tip off whoever had been in her room that she was aware of the trespassing.

"Yeah, maybe it is. But I get the feeling you've seen worse than Elouise Perkins."

He always did that—said the girl's full name. Like he was doing everything he could to hold on to the person she'd been instead of the body she'd become. Despite everything, it made Eden like him, just a little. "Did you know her?"

"No. Not really." He took a bite and chewed, the expression on his face letting her know that he'd registered her dodge and noted it. "Town like this, you know everyone, but there's a difference between being able to pick her out of a crowd and *knowing* her."

She was all too aware of that. "So did you *know* her dad was abusing her?"

Zach flinched, having the grace to look uncomfortable. "For someone who's been in town a grand total of three days, it's worrying that you've already heard about that."

"That's not an answer." If he had known, he wouldn't be the first good old boy to push something like this under the rug. People didn't like to admit that abuse of all varieties happened in their perfect little towns, and she'd seen local cops go to extreme lengths to cover it up and pretend it never happened. It didn't matter that doing so only did further damage to the victims.

He set his fork down and sat back. "If I'd known, Michael Perkins would be in jail. Or, if that wasn't an option, I would have found a way to get the girl out. That kind of thing is *never* okay."

No telling if he was being truthful or not, but it was hard to fake the fury that came over his entire being. Martha could have, but her mother was a master at lying with every part of her body and voice. Call her crazy, but Zach seemed pretty transparent.

Or maybe she was just trying to cling to the one person in the middle of all this mess who might actually be good.

Need to rip the bandage off this awkward conversation and get us on the same page. She mirrored his move, sitting back and crossing her arms over her chest. "I think it's time we were completely frank with each other. I'll go first. My timing for showing up here makes me suspicious, and I respect that. But I can't go into Elysia like I did today without knowing everything you do. I played the damn fool, and I don't even know what I'm looking for. Do you think the girl's father had something to do with this?"

"He was an abusive asshole, and if he murdered his daughter, I'll be the first in line to arrest him." He sighed. "Hell, my life would be a whole lot easier if he *did* do it. But, to be blunt, Michael Perkins isn't smart enough to pull it off and frame the Elysians. If he knows about the tattoos, I'm going to be really surprised."

"I'd like to be there when you bring him in."

He raised his eyebrows. "You're not officially part of the investigation."

"No, I'm not. I can't be. But I also have a unique skill set that can be valuable to you—and the investigation." She didn't say anything else. Zach had checked her out. He knew her credentials, and she'd bet he'd looked into her track record, too. They wouldn't be having this dinner if he still suspected her of having something to do with the murder. Oh, he didn't trust her, and rightfully so.

He just didn't think she was a killer.

He leaned forward and started eating, waiting until she'd done the same to start the conversation again. "You can observe, but you can't take part in the interview. We might play a little fast and loose with the rules sometimes, but when we find the killer, I need this wrapped up as pretty as a present."

It was better than she had hoped for. "Deal."

A slow smile pulled at the edges of his lips. "You don't get told no very often, do you?"

"Not when I want something." And she wanted to wrap this up as prettily as he did. "And I want this unsub found and stopped." For so many reasons.

Something cold came into his blue eyes, and it sure as hell wasn't surprise. "You don't think this is a one-off."

No, but she hadn't realized he shared that belief. Eden frowned. "You don't, either. Why?"

He hesitated, and that was all she needed to realize he'd kept something from her. She frowned harder. "Remember what I said about needing all the pieces to be effective? I think now's the time to start with that. Why the hell do you think this might happen again?"

"You wouldn't have heard because we've kept it quiet, but there's another girl who's missing."

Shock temporarily stole her voice. Part of her had been expecting that there would be another abduction and murder, but not so quickly. Serial killers, especially budding serial killers, usually rode the high of their kill for anywhere from weeks to months to *years*. Whoever had murdered this girl should be spending all their free time reliving the kill and the events leading up to it. Relishing every last detail.

But the unsub hadn't.

He—or she—had already potentially taken a second victim.

"Missing." She did some quick mental calculations. It had been only a few days since the body was found—even if this girl had disappeared on the same day, they were barely outside the required forty-eight hours to report it. "Since when?"

Zach stirred his fork through his food, then set it to the side. "Her parents reported her missing the same morning the body was found, and I'm having a hell of a time pinning down who saw her last." When she didn't say anything, he continued. "She's a little wild—likes to give her parents gray hair—and she's done things like this before. There's no reason to think they're connected."

He was too smart to really believe that. He should have been too smart to keep this fact from her, too.

She took a sip from her soda because the alternative was to yell at him until he realized that she was here to *help*. She felt as if she'd been blindfolded and was being led around with one hand tied behind her back. Part of it was being back at Elysia after all these years. Part of it was not being able to be directly involved with the investigation.

Either way, taking it out on Zach right now would be a mistake.

"You should have told me." She kept her voice even and professional, letting none of her frustration through.

He rubbed the bridge of his nose, suddenly looking exhausted. "I might not have much experience with murder like this, but forgive the fuck out of me if I don't go spilling every little detail to a woman who magically showed up—as the result of a goddamn leak."

A valid point. The truth was that she was reacting with emotion as much as he was. If they had any chance of making this work, they had to cooperate. Someone had to reach out the friendly hand first, and Zach had made it painfully clear that it wouldn't be him. "Why do you think that her disappearance is connected? And please save us both the time wasted while you pretend that you don't. You wouldn't have brought it up otherwise."

Instead of looking away, he met her gaze directly, no shame or regret to be found. "Neveah might be wild, but if you take that away, there's a girl missing who is a year younger than Elouise and fits the same basic description—petite build, dark hair, and dark eyes. Call me crazy, but every instinct I have says that girl is going to be next. And that's if she isn't already dead in a ditch somewhere."

She appreciated that he wasn't hiding under the illusion of coincidence. She just wished she had something more comforting to tell him. "If she was already dead, we'd have found her body."

He looked up. "What makes you say that?"

Being pinned in place by those blue eyes was disconcerting, to say the least. When he narrowed his focus to just her, it was hard to keep him in the neat little mental box she'd created. The man had too much presence by half. Eden set her soda down, covering up her discomfort by slipping back into work mode. "I don't have enough information to do an official profile, but the fact that Elouise was found the way she was and that she hadn't been dead more than a few hours indicates that this killer is looking for attention."

Another hesitation, but this one barely lasted a breath. She'd been trained by Britton, which meant giving her working profiles under uncomfortable circumstances was the name of the game. Years of working under him and he still intimidated the hell out of her. "She'd been running. There were cuts and bruises on the bottoms of her feet and little slices on her legs from the weeds. So either this sick fuck was hunting her, or—"

"Or she escaped."

Eden considered that, rolling it over and over in her mind. She didn't know much about Elouise Perkins and wouldn't until she got her hands on the coroner's report and sat in on the parents being interviewed, but a girl who had survived God alone knew how many years of abuse and done her damnedest to escape and start a new life in college . . . that took guts.

It still didn't jibe for her.

She tapped her fingers on the table. "Do you know when she was seen last?"

"We have it narrowed down to a window. She went through orientation at Montana State and checked into her dorm. She was in class September seventeenth—her last one ends at two—but she was marked absent the next morning. She could have skipped, but it doesn't read right. That girl did everything she could to get into that college and get the grants to pay for it. I don't see her playing hooky."

Eden nodded. She knew what it was like to throw everything into a future that wasn't certain. "She wouldn't have. When you fight so hard for something, you appreciate it more." She knew all about that. When she'd gone through training to be an FBI agent, some of her peers had thought she was over-the-top intense—and they were right. But she'd wanted it so bad, she could taste it. She wasn't going to let anything or anyone get in her way. "So it's likely she was taken that day." A little more than a week before she was killed, which meant she was kept somewhere. If the unsub had the ability to hold a captive for more than a week, what were the chances she'd found a way to escape after eight days?

Not much of a chance at all, unless he or she had made a mistake.

It was possible. If there had been murders that had these particular tattoos involved before now, Eden most likely would have heard about it. Admittedly, there were more murders in the country than a single person could keep track of, but she kept an eye out for tags that fit Elysia. There was no damn reason to think that her mother would start picking off people and endanger her power base, but once cults got to a certain point, a percentage of them fell into violence against others and even against themselves. Suicide cults weren't as common as the media would have people believe, but they *did* exist.

She tapped her finger faster. *Coming back here was a mistake.* It didn't matter. She was here now, and she'd see it through. "How familiar are you with the Persephone myth?"

"Not very. I know the basics with Martha living in my backyard, but it seemed pretty nonthreatening."

Eden almost hated to burst his bubble. "It's a Greek myth that explains the turning of the seasons—half the year when the crops are plentiful and half when they aren't, which corresponds to the time Persephone is in Hades versus aboveground."

"I read the myth. I don't see what the big deal is about bringing spring back around."

She pushed her food to the side, no longer hungry. "Variations of that myth show up across multiple cultures, and Elysia cherry-picks the pieces they want." It was hard to keep talking, hard not to fall into the past and what she'd gone through before she escaped. But he had to know. "The prevailing theme that underlies the recurrence of spring is sacrifice."

"Sacrifice." He said it like it was a dirty word.

She shared the sentiment. Eden took a deep breath because she could, because the budding pressure around her chest was all in her head and not because she was literally trapped. "Over the centuries, the methods ranged from slitting a bull's throat to killing virgins to creating a straw man and tossing him in a bonfire before an orgy." She knew. She'd done the research after she'd left. Martha didn't share the why of any particular Elysian practice, preferring to have her followers believe they originated with her.

Eden knew better.

She also had known, in her heart of hearts, that someday she'd have to come back—would be drawn back, if only to right a wrong her mother perpetuated—and she'd wanted to have every weapon possible in her arsenal of knowledge.

"Which ones does Elysia participate in?"

She'd known the question was coming, but it still took her several seconds to find her voice again. "They pick a girl from Martha's follow-ers, and after a ritual cleansing, they . . ." *God, it's been ten years. You should be able to talk about this. You lived through it.* "They bury her alive."

"*What?*"

His fury centered her, and her next breath came easier. She couldn't sit still, though. Eden pushed to her feet and started pacing, the words coming faster now. "There's no coffin to speak of. They cover her with dirt, and she fights her way to the surface. Then there's a feast where they celebrate the triumph of Demeter over Hades." The triumph of *Martha.*

Sitting at the head of that table, covered in dirt, still tasting it on her tongue and feeling the dried tracks on her face where tears had turned it to mud had been the breaking point for Eden.

She'd been gone the next morning.

Zach joined her on her feet. "I'm going to need you to go over that again. You're saying that every spring, Martha puts some girl into the ground, and she fights free, and the people out in Elysia just *let it happen.*"

She spun and nearly ran into him. "It's considered a great honor."

"That's bullshit. That's not an honor—that's torture." Something was there on his face, a memory of horror that called to the part of her where she kept everything locked up tight.

She couldn't afford to think too closely about what had been done to her while she was in Elysia's tender care, not if she wanted to be a halfway functioning adult, let alone an FBI agent. She'd been doing just fine blocking out the memories and moving on with her life. As much as anyone moved on from that sort of thing.

The truth was she used the skills Martha had taught her, inadvertently or not.

Eden didn't much like to think about that, either.

Every time she'd turned around since she'd gotten back into town, she was facing down yet another nightmare. She just flat out wasn't equipped to deal with it. She'd thought she was prepared.

She'd been wrong.

It was all too much. And here was Zach Owens, whom she'd never thought to have a single thing in common with, looking at her like he knew *exactly* what it was like to be on the receiving end of torture. She suddenly realized they were standing close—too close. She licked her lips, and his gaze followed the movement. Words came, words she had no intention of voicing, but her control had shattered right around the time she relived the moment her mother put her in the ground. "Who hurt you?"

He didn't pretend to misunderstand, which only made her like him a little bit more. "A lot of bad shit went down in the desert. Things I do my damnedest not to think about."

Everyone had their way of dealing—and not dealing. "Nightmares?"

His mouth tightened. "More often than I care to admit."

And now they were too close in an entirely different kind of way. She didn't want the empathy that flowed through her at his words, didn't want any kind of connection that might tie her to this place, no matter how fragile.

Hell, she didn't want to think at all anymore.

So Eden went and did something impulsive and downright stupid. She leaned forward, placed her hands on Zach's well-defined chest, and kissed him. It was only meant to break the moment they'd suddenly found themselves in the middle of. A distraction, and a short one at that.

Except the second his hands settled on her hips and his mouth teased hers open, it turned into something else altogether. She froze, her mind scrambling to reassign their roles, to put him back into the neat little box she'd created for him when they met.

Zach was having none of it. He took possession of her mouth, each move telegraphing a barely contained desperation that called to things deep inside her—things she didn't allow anyone access to.

It was too late to worry about that, though. She skated her hands up his chest to drag her fingers through his short hair, earning a growl that she felt more than heard. His tongue stroked hers, lighting a string of fireworks along her nerve endings and making her knees go weak.

It's just been a long time . . .

Rational thought had no place there. Then he was lifting her, turning and pinning her against the wall. Somehow her legs had ended up wrapped around his waist, but she was at a loss to figure out when it had happened.

Zach broke the kiss, his hands in her hair, his body lining up deliciously against hers. He didn't quite move back, but he gave her a moment to breathe.

To think—something she very much didn't want.

She arched up to reclaim his mouth, but he turned his face slightly to the side. If he hadn't been breathing hard, she might have died of embarrassment. Eden cleared her throat. "Let me down."

He did, but sliding against his body did funny things to the anger she was trying so hard to hold on to. From his expression, Zach knew it. He framed her face with his big hands, his calluses dragging over her sensitive skin. "I'd be lying if I said I wanted to stop."

Then why did you? She didn't give the words voice. She refused to.

His thumbs feathered along her cheekbones and down to her bottom lip, his blue eyes dark in the faint light of the room. "Neither of us can afford to be distracted right now."

He was right, but that didn't take the sting out of the rejection. She jerked from his grasp, smoothing back her hair and fighting to compose herself. "You think highly of yourself."

"Damn, Eden." He laughed, the low sound making her shake. "You need me to prove how much I want you?"

"No." She could see the evidence as plain as day, pressed against the front of his jeans. It was tempting to close what little distance remained between them and kiss him again, to press herself against that spot, but he was right. There were more important things at play than her need to forget.

If she'd been anywhere but in Clear Springs, she wouldn't have even been tempted by this too-hot-for-her-own-good sheriff.

Probably.

She turned to the window. "I think you should leave."

He was so silent, she actually glanced back to make sure he was still there. The look in his eyes stilled her breath and made her entire body perk up and take notice. Zach raked his gaze over her, but he took a step back, and then another. "You'll be okay?"

"Perfectly fine." She managed a smile, though it felt unnatural on her face. "I'm an agent, remember?"

CHAPTER ELEVEN

Neveah Smith curled into the smallest ball possible and prayed. She'd never been particularly religious in any way that counted, and in the past she'd shown up at the little church in Clear Springs only when she wanted to cause a stir. It had been so much *fun* to flash a little skin at those tight-ass boys and watch them realize what lust really was.

Those games seemed so fucking childish now.

She hadn't known what fear was.

She pressed her head to her knees and searched for some sign of the higher power her parents were always talking about. *Mom and Dad.* She missed them. Another one to chalk up to the list of things she'd never thought would happen.

Kind of like being trapped in a room without light or food or a *bathroom* for days on end. She wasn't sure how long she'd been here. Her captor didn't seem to come in with any schedule. When he'd first thrown her into the room with no windows and only one door, she'd thought it was all part of the game. A little slap and tickle. A walk on the dark side. He'd play captor and she'd play victim and he'd get his rocks off and get hers off in the bargain.

But there was no room in this dirty, dark space for pleasure.

Only pain.

It took a grand total of an hour for Neveah to realize she was in over her head, for it to penetrate that the things she'd been promised were lies. Lies that might get her killed. That's when she started begging. She'd done everything he asked and more, desperate to prove to him that she could hold her silence if he'd just let her go.

What a joke. Hours—*days*—in and she started to believe she'd never see the clear Montana sky above her again. Would her parents miss her? She'd never been the easiest kid, but who could blame her? Clear Springs might be a dream to some people, but every day that passed felt like it was choking the life out of her. She'd never meant any harm with the bullshit she'd gotten into. Mostly. Throwing herself into trouble was the only thing that made her feel alive. Some of her classmates were just biding their time until graduation and moving off to whatever college they'd picked. That was crap. Sitting around waiting for life to start was as good as a death sentence as far as Neveah was concerned. She wanted to live, and she wanted to do it *now*.

Ironic that that might be the thing that killed her. Or was it ironic? She hadn't been paying attention in English when Mr. Stigleider was talking about irony, because she was too busy flirting with John Winchester. He had dreamy dark eyes and clever hands, and she'd shown him exactly what he could do with those hands in the backseat of his car that very night. She'd even had a tinge of regret when she broke his heart a month later.

Shivers racked her body, making her grip on her shins slip. It was so *cold*. Her clothes were gone before she made it in here, taken with the promise of showing her things boys in high school couldn't dream of. She'd wanted that. She'd wanted it so much, it made her throw caution to the wind and slip away from the bonfire the Johnson boys threw Friday night.

What day is it? I don't even know anymore.

It took more effort than it should have to lift her head and stare up into the darkness. "God?" Her voice was raspy from disuse—or maybe it was from screaming—but it felt important to say the words aloud. "I'm sorry. I haven't been a very good person, and maybe you think I deserve this because of it." Her breath hitched, but she forced herself to continue. "But I'm sorry. I promise if you get me out of this, I'll be good. I'll be so good. I—"

The door opened, light spilling through the darkness and blinding her. She ducked her head back to curl tighter in upon herself. It didn't stop the soft laugh that slid through the room. "God's not listening, Neveah. But I am."

◆ ◆ ◆

The dinner with Eden Collins created more questions than answers for Zach. He wished he could blame that on the case alone, but the fact of the matter was that he could still taste her on his lips, even hours later. She was so self-assured and larger than life, but when she'd run her hands up his chest and melted into his kiss . . .

Distraction doesn't begin to cover it.

He sent Chase and Henry to bring in the Perkins parents as soon as he arrived at the station that morning, mostly so he could cross them off the suspect list. His last twisted hope that Michael Perkins was somehow involved in the death of his daughter had gone up in smoke last night, but doing his job meant pursuing all leads.

He met Eden out in front of the station. She looked . . . fuck, she looked good. She wore a fitted pair of jeans, a white T-shirt, and the same leather jacket she'd had on the day they met. Combined with the ankle boots, it gave her a certain don't-mess-with-me vibe. He couldn't help looking at her and seeing the woman transposed on the agent, her hair mussed and her eyes half-lidded with promised pleasure. Zach ran a hand over his mouth, trying to focus.

She nodded as he held the door open for her. "You're bringing them in?"

If she can put the case first, you damn well better do the same. "You were right last night—we need more information. I don't know if the Perkinses are going to be the ones to give it to us, but we have to try." He thought it was a lost cause, but he wasn't about to admit that aloud to anyone. Not even her. Maybe *especially* not her.

"Then let's get to it."

As easy as that. Except it wasn't easy, and he didn't know how the hell this thing was going to go. Zach led the way back to their two dual-purpose rooms. One was set up with the cot for the rare times when someone needed to sleep off a drunk and he wasn't in the mood to toss them into one of the three holding cells in the back of the station. The other room was a generic catchall for shit that didn't have an actual place. There weren't files or anything confidential in there, but it looked a bit like his great-aunt Ruthie's house—barely controlled chaos. "Husband or wife first?"

Eden gave him a considering look. "Wife. You're awful pretty, and she might be more likely to open up to a charming, handsome man without her husband around."

He stared. "That's some cold-ass manipulation." The exact same kind of thing he'd considered. He wasn't sure what that said about him—about what this case was turning him into—but it wasn't good.

Her hazel eyes went hard, the final piece of the vulnerable woman he'd had dinner with last night disappearing, and the hardened FBI agent taking her place. The look said that she'd seen horrors beyond reckoning. "I do what it takes to see the responsible parties brought to justice."

There was nothing else to say to that, so he led the way to the room where Ruby Perkins had been left to cool her heels. She looked so small sitting at the plain plastic table. Defeated. It was like by taking her out of her comfort zone, he'd damaged a part of her. *Is it harder to justify what Michael does to her when she's around other people?* Zach took a seat across from her, aware of Eden leaning against the door. She wasn't an imposing figure, exactly, but Ruby still watched her the way she might watch a rattler who could strike at any moment. She turned watery blue eyes on Zach. "Why is *she* here?"

"She's assisting in the investigation of Elouise's death." It didn't matter if it wasn't official—he wasn't about to spread that information around. If the locals thought he had the FBI in his pocket, it wouldn't hurt him any, and Eden seemed content to stay silent and let him lead. He sat forward and braced his forearms on the desk but immediately retreated when Ruby flinched. *Damn it.* "I'm hoping you could give me more information about that."

"I told you what I know when you came by yesterday."

She'd barely said a damn thing yesterday. Michael was the one who'd run that show. Zach tried again. "Ruby, we know. Elouise had bruises on her body that happened before she disappeared. It's been confirmed by an outside source that she admitted Michael likes to use his fists when he gets a few drinks in him." Which seemed to be his constant state of being, from what Zach had seen. He kicked himself for the thousandth time for not knowing what was going on under his nose. He'd known Michael was an asshole of epic proportions, but it hadn't ever occurred to him that he'd take that nasty temper out on his wife and child.

"I don't know what you're talking about." She twisted her fingers together until it looked downright painful. "Elouise was always a willful child. She needed a strong hand to guide her."

From what he'd learned at the high school yesterday, Elouise Perkins had been little more than a ghost who drifted through the high school's halls. She attended her classes, got good grades, and had a nearly perfect attendance record—her only absence corresponding with a broken arm from a *fall* last year. Every single one of her teachers said she was polite, if a bit distant, and kept her head down to avoid attention. From all accounts, she was counting down the days until college started and she could get the hell out of town and away from her family.

Nothing in that description fit the one coming out of her mother's mouth.

The slow-boiling anger that had been building in him since her body was found reached new heights. "That's bullshit."

Ruby flinched, her shoulders bowing as if expecting a blow. It made him feel like a monster, but he kept going. "There's no excuse to beat your child the way Michael beat Elouise, and we both damn well know it. If I'd had any idea this was going on, I would have gotten that girl out of your house and somewhere safe years ago. I missed it, and that's something I have to live with. Fuck, Ruby, you were there day in and day out, and you stood by and let him do this—that's something *you* have to live with. But neither of those things are why you're sitting in this room right now. Where were you on September twenty-fifth between two and four a.m.?"

That got her attention. "You can't possibly think I had something to do with my baby's death."

"Answer the question, please."

She straightened, actually looking him in the eye. "I was at home, sleeping on the couch, because when Michael has more than a few, he snores and I have trouble sleeping."

Zach reckoned she spent more time on the couch than in her own bed, but he wasn't dick enough to say so. He studied her, mentally mapping the trailer in his head. There was only the one door, and the windows might be small enough for a petite teenager to slip through, but he didn't see Michael fitting his gut though one. *If* she was telling the truth. "All night?"

"Yes." She looked at the table, seemed to catch herself, and raised her chin. "He passed out around midnight, and I went to bed shortly after."

Technically, she could have walked right out that front door and he doubted Michael would know one way or another once he was asleep, but Zach just didn't see it. Sometimes victims of domestic abuse fought back with violence, but it was usually against their abuser, not a fellow victim. Not to mention, there were the Elysian tattoos to consider. He ran his hand through his hair. "You ever go out to Elysia?"

Shock widened her eyes. "Why would I want to do something like that?"

The surprise seemed real enough, but he pressed anyway. "You grew up here, same as me. You know damn well that half the kids in high school went out there at one time or another."

"Well, sure." She shrugged. "I played at trespassing once with some girlfriends when I was sixteen or so, but Abram ran us off." Ruby shuddered. "He scared me half to death, and after that I refused to go near the place."

Seeing as how Abram was scary during the day in the middle of Clear Springs, Zach didn't blame her. "Did Elouise go out there?"

"She must have if Martha wrote her that letter." Some anger finally showed itself on her face. "My baby wasn't no cultist, Zach. She was getting out. I know I'm not much of a mother, but I was proud of her all the same. She was *getting out*."

And now she was dead.

It made him want to put his fist through a wall—or the one responsible. Zach studied Ruby Perkins, taking in the bags under her eyes and more lines on her face than most thirty-three-year-olds. Hell, she looked a decade older, tired and broken down. He took a deep breath. "I can get you out."

Her eyes went wide. "What?"

"I know he does the same to you that he did to Elouise—probably worse." He motioned to her long-sleeved shirt and scarf. "It doesn't have to be that way, Ruby. I can get you out, get you a restraining order, help you get your feet under you in a new life."

She looked at him for a long moment and gave a sad smile. "You always were a white knight, Zach Owens."

"What he's doing is illegal and just plain wrong. You don't beat women, Ruby." He could actually see that he was losing her, but he pressed on anyway, trying to make her *see*. "No man worth his salt would raise a hand to you. It's not okay."

She shook her head. "You're a good man, Zach. But he's my husband." She hesitated. "Can I go? I want you to find who did this to my baby, but I don't know anything else."

Fury actually stole his breath. He wanted to shake her until she saw reason, until she agreed to let him help. That wasn't his job, though. If he was really the white knight like everyone claimed, he could right wrongs like this. In reality, he was hamstrung by the law. For the first time in a very long time, he actually considered bending the rules, but the impulse passed as soon as it rose. The law didn't work if it was bent to suit his needs. To do that was an abuse of power, no matter how well meaning.

So he sat there and let Ruby Perkins stand and limp out of the room. He didn't ask why she was favoring her right leg, and she didn't look back as the door shut behind her. Zach hissed out a breath. "Fuck."

"Sometimes doing the right thing and the lawful thing aren't the same. It's really shitty when you come to a crossroads like that."

He looked up, having half forgotten Eden was there. She looked as angry and frustrated as he felt. "I want to hurt him, Eden. He's scum of the earth as far as I'm concerned, and he doesn't deserve that woman—any woman."

"The funny thing—not ha-ha funny, but sad funny—is that she probably blames herself." She took the seat next to him, a careful six inches between them. "She no doubt blames herself for not protecting Elouise, though I'd bet she took extra beatings in an attempt to spare her daughter. She's not a saint, but she's not a monster, either. People rarely are just one or the other."

A wealth of knowledge weighted those words, though her tone didn't give away much. Zach turned to face her fully. He didn't have to ask if her mother hurt her. Being buried alive sure as fuck counted as abuse, and if *that* was normal, there was no telling what else she'd endured while growing up—or had seen since she'd become an agent.

He couldn't ask, though. She'd shut him down the second he did.

"That look on your face . . . Zach, you can't save everyone—not in the present, and certainly not in the past." She touched his arm and then yanked her hand away, the move obviously involuntary. As unprofessional and straight-up inappropriate as it was, he wanted that touch again. If he concentrated, he could still feel the imprint of her hand against the fabric of his shirt, and it drove him a little nuts. Eden pushed to her feet, putting distance between them. "You gave Ruby a chance to get out, which is more than anyone can say for Elouise Perkins."

CHAPTER TWELVE

The interview with Michael was less than illuminating, but Eden hadn't expected much there. Michael Perkins was an abusive asshole who liked alcohol entirely too much for the well-being of anyone around him, but he wasn't a stone-cold murderer. And while she would place bets on whether Ruby would snap in the future or stay with Michael until *he* snapped and finally went too far, that woman hadn't killed her daughter.

If the Perkinses had something to do with the girl's death, she'd be seriously surprised.

Eden pushed through the exterior door of the police station, the clear mountain air doing nothing to sweep the feeling of sickness growing in the pit of her stomach.

You knew this wouldn't be easy. You knew it would be the hardest thing you've ever done.

The rational voice in the back of her mind didn't help a damn bit. Even though she knew better, she couldn't help seeing the similarities between herself and Elouise Perkins. Loners growing up in a town that had no use for them, keeping their heads down and going through the motions until they got to the light at the end of the tunnel. Oh, Eden had had more of a wild and rebellious streak than the dead girl.

She hadn't cared that there would be pain and punishment as a result, as long as she could stick it to her mother whenever the opportunity presented itself.

But she'd stayed until she was a legal adult, same as Elouise.

"Eden."

She realized she'd been moving fast enough that Zach nearly had to jog to keep up with her, and she forced herself to stop and take a deep breath. It didn't help the twisted feeling knotting up her insides, but nothing short of seeing the unsub behind bars would. Rationally, she knew that putting away this piece of shit wasn't going to solve any of her issues, but it didn't matter.

She wasn't okay—she was a whole hell of a long way from okay—but she could fake it.

She'd certainly had long enough to perfect the lie.

Zach eyed her like he wasn't sure if she'd take off again. "You're heading out to Elysia."

Wasting time was inexcusable, no matter how unprepared she felt every time she faced down her past. "I didn't get much yesterday. If I leave now, I can get into the commune before the afternoon worship ends and have a chance to do a little snooping without anyone looking over my shoulder." Specifically, Martha and Abram.

He should have been happy to know she was determined to get to the bottom of this, but Zach just looked concerned. "Be careful. If you go and disappear, they'll stonewall me and I won't be able to get to you. I don't know that that Britton of yours with the force of the FBI behind him could manage to get to you if Martha decides she wants otherwise."

Something in her chest loosened even as disbelief coursed through her. "Twenty-four hours ago you were sure I was part of this. Now you're worried about me?" She very specifically did *not* focus on the fact that he was right—Martha was more than capable of a standoff that would leave both innocents and cops dead.

Eden really wished it was just her paranoia making her think that.

"I never really thought you killed that girl, but I have to pursue every avenue. If you didn't kill her, and *they*"—he jerked his thumb over his shoulder to where the Perkins parents were heading for their truck—"didn't kill her, that means someone up at Elysia did. And if you're right, they have Neveah Smith, too."

She *was* right.

She didn't want to be, but there was no shaking the certainty inside her. This was all connected, though she hadn't quite figured out how. The details were too vague, the evidence not adding up to any specific conclusion. The tattoos linked up the cult with the murders, so she had a vague who, but not why. The *why* would be what brought this case to its conclusion, because she could effectively work back from there.

She just needed more information—information that could be found only in Elysia. "I'll be fine. I have training in self-defense, and I've spent more hours than I care to admit at the shooting range." She'd been at the top of her class in handgun and rifle, but saying so now felt like bragging. Not that she was carrying her gun—it was still stashed safely back in her hotel room since she wasn't technically on duty.

"That doesn't make a damn bit of difference if someone catches you when you aren't expecting it." He shook his head, hesitated, and then pushed on. "Call me when you're done. I'm going to take you out to dinner."

Shock rocked her back on her heels before reason intervened. He wasn't asking her *out*. He was looking to do the same thing they had last night—meet up and compare notes. *He doesn't want a distraction, no matter how attractive it feels to you. Have to remember that.* She smothered the disappointment threatening to raise its ugly head at the realization and managed a smile. "Why don't you just pick up something and meet me at my room?"

"No, Eden." His blue eyes were as clear as the sky above their heads. "Don't get me wrong—I want to find this killer, and we'll need to work together to do that—but dinner tonight is a date."

A date. She blinked. "I, uh . . ." What was she supposed to say to that? Her hands fluttered at her side, coming up to touch her hair and then drop down again, which only served to make her feel like a fool. She didn't do this. She didn't *flutter.* Eden took a breath, released it . . . and still didn't know what to say. So she didn't say anything. Zach walked her to her car and held the door open for her as she slid into the driver's seat.

"See you at six." Then he was gone, striding across the parking lot like a man who was in total control of his life.

She was honestly a little surprised she recognized that trait, even in another person. *This is a mistake. He was right last night when he put a stop to this whole thing.* She couldn't afford distractions when she was facing off with her mother, especially distractions in the form of Zach Owens. In another life, maybe. But in their current situation . . . it was the worst possible idea.

So why hadn't she shot him down?

The thought plagued her throughout the drive to Elysia. She finally managed to force it from her mind and focus on the problem at hand. The compound was deserted, the only sign of habitation the faint sound of singing coming from the chapel. She checked her watch. They'd be occupied for a good hour yet, which meant she had to hurry. There was no way she could search every single household in Elysia, but she didn't have to.

She was going to start at the top.

Martha was too much of a control freak to let one of her flock get away from her like this. She knew who was responsible—or at least had an educated guess. *It's just like my mother to be benefiting from this somehow, though it's anyone's guess as to what her endgame is.*

She headed to the largest house directly opposite the chapel. It was the first to be built when Martha settled here, and it had always reminded Eden of a giant hen squatting over its egg, watching every move anyone in the square made. Growing up, she'd always wondered if it was coincidental or not, but now having studied cults in all their manipulative splendor, she had all but confirmed that her mother had designed it that way on purpose. As happy and downright cheerful as the Elysians seemed on the outside, the inner workings of the cult were rife with paranoia, as well as a surveillance system that would put Big Brother to shame.

Have to wonder if those cameras have picked up something vital to this investigation.

Skirting the edge of the building, she paused by the back door and looked around. There didn't seem to be anyone watching her, but the small hairs on the back of her neck stood at attention all the same. She frowned, giving the surrounding area another sweep. There shouldn't be anyone out and about. If anyone dared miss chapel this morning, Martha would have sent Abram to bring them in—and ensure they never missed again.

Her favorite way to bring members of her flock to heel was to use the torch so vital to Persephone and Demeter. There were few injuries more painful than burns, and there were ways to burn a person that didn't scar afterward. Eden rubbed her wrist, almost able to feel Abram's uncompromising grip as he forced her to hold it a few inches above the candle on the kitchen counter. Many people didn't realize that *that* spot was the hottest, not the flame itself.

The pain . . .

Most people weren't subject to the private sessions. For them, Martha performed her *cleansing* ritual in the chapel, in front of the rest of her followers. Her mother claimed that fire was pure, devoid of any of the sin of this world. Eden didn't think ancient Greeks figured sin the same way Martha did, but the memories of those burns on strategic parts of her body when she acted out against her mother were more than enough fodder for her nightmares, even without the rest of the shit that went on.

She exhaled and let the past go. Or tried to.

Nothing moved in any of the windows of the houses facing her, and there wasn't even the slightest breeze to sway the wild grass growing between them. *Must be my imagination.* But she couldn't shake the feeling she was missing something.

She couldn't afford to waste any more time. Eden crouched next to the lock—one of the only set of doors in the entire compound with a lock on it—and took her lock-picking kit out of her jacket. It had been a long time since she'd had to use one of these things, mostly because breaking and entering was the slightest bit illegal and she was a law-enforcement officer, but she'd gotten good when she was in the midst of her teenage rebellion. She'd kept up the skill over the years, no matter how impractical, because you never knew when you'd have to get yourself out of a tight spot.

Or into one.

The lock clicked open, and she moved into the house and shut the door behind her. *So far, so good.* It took a grand total of three steps into the main hallway before what she was seeing registered, and Eden stumbled to a stop. She looked around, blinked, and looked around again. "Impossible." It was identical to when she'd lived here, right down to the tear in the rug on the stairs where she'd fallen down the last three steps one night when she was trying to sneak out. The keys in her pocket had ripped clean through the old carpet. But that was thirteen years ago. She could understand Martha not fixing it while Eden was still here, but after all this time?

She walked through the first level on silent feet, every room increasing the feeling that she'd knocked her head a little too hard yet again and the last ten years hadn't happened—that she was still a seventeen-year-old kid staring through the bars in a cage.

Eden shook her head. It didn't matter that not one thing—from the faded blue paint on the walls to the position of the decorative bowls on the table—had changed in the last decade. That was eerie and uncomfortable, but it wasn't why she was here. The information she was looking for wouldn't be downstairs. It would be up in the bedrooms.

She climbed the stairs, avoiding the squeaky one out of a habit she'd thought she was long past. The first door on the left was her mother's room, and she slipped through, holding her breath against the familiar floral perfume that lay in the air like a distant memory. A memory that tasted both bitter and comforting, all wrapped up into a toxic present.

Just like the rest of the house, the room was identical to when she'd last been here. She stared at the bed. Somewhere around when she was thirteen and won the fight to attend public school, she'd realized that not all girls had relationships with their mother like hers and Martha's. With Eden and her mother, there were no late-night gossip sessions or movie dates or any of the many other mother-daughter bonding activities that normal teenagers had in between hating their parents. No, all she had was Elysia and the role Martha insisted on casting her in.

Persephone.

Her throat tried to close, but she took a deep breath in through her nose, held it, and then exhaled. It took five more breaths before her heart rate dropped down to something closer to normal, and another five more before she could force herself to move past the giant four-poster bed. The bed she'd so often been tied to and lashed on as a form of punishment. Martha couldn't take *her* out into the square like she sometimes did with someone who really stepped over the line, so she'd always kept those sessions private. Just her and Eden—and Abram to observe.

No matter what Eden did in rebellion, Martha maintained the fiction that she was heir to everything. That someday she'd step up and take on the mantle of leadership that was just waiting for her.

Eden snorted. Even if she'd been fool enough to believe the lies, her mother would give up power when it was pried from her cold, dead hands. She'd grown to suspect she might have suffered an unfortunate accident if she'd ever tried to actually follow her mother's plans.

Demeter was most powerful while grieving, after all.

She went into the closet and pushed the clothing back to reveal the little panic-room door, the one she wasn't supposed to know about. It seemed beyond impossible that *this* would be the same, too, but Eden plugged in the code, holding her breath. She hissed when the error message scrolled across the little screen. *Damn it.*

It doesn't matter. I know where she stores the code, so I just need to get into her office alone soon and then make another trip back here and . . .

God, it seemed so impossible. She meandered through her mother's room, but there were no state secrets hidden among the jewelry littering the top of the dresser. She hadn't really thought there would be. Just to cover all her bases, she checked beneath the bed, and her breath rushed out at the sight of the cedar box stashed there. She knew that box, knew every groove carved into its side—and not just because it depicted the many tortures Persephone supposedly suffered at the hands of Hades. Throughout her childhood, that box coming out had signaled that Eden had once again stepped out of line. That she needed *purifying*. She knew exactly what that box contained—a whip, and candles, and padded cuffs that could restrain a person without leaving bruises.

It took more effort than it should have to push up to her hands and knees, the very gravity seeming to increase in an effort to keep her pinned in place. Her mind oh-so-helpfully supplied her with the memory of her shirt being ripped down her back, of the snap the whip made just before contact, the breathless moment of numbness before the pain hit. She managed to push herself up a few inches. Of the green candles with their pretty red flowers on the side, so innocent-looking despite the pain their flame inflicted. Over and over again. Her fingers dug into the thick rug, scrambling for purchase even as the past threatened to drag her under.

Move, move, move. The only other option was to lie here and wait to be found out, which wasn't an option at all.

She staggered into the hallway, desperate to keep moving so she could get out of this nightmare. She bypassed the room that had always been hers. The thought that nothing in it had moved since she'd left, that it had stood against time as a shrine to her, was too much to bear. *They probably held vigils praying for me to come back. It seems like something my mother would do.*

She hated the guilt that spawned in her chest—*hated it.* There was absolutely nothing to feel guilty for, but logic had no place in Martha's house.

It never had.

The next room made her hesitate, instinctive fear holding her back from pushing open the door. She gritted her teeth and turned the doorknob. The blackout blinds kept the room like some kind of vampire's crypt—or maybe that was her opinion of Abram coloring her perspective. She had to be careful about that. She was too close to this whole thing—so close that if Britton knew, he would have yanked her back to Virginia the second the information reached him.

Except he does know, because Zach called him to check up on me.

She hadn't received the call demanding she explain what the hell she was up to, and she wasn't about to call *him* and bring more attention to herself. It didn't matter if she was too close, because there was no one else as uniquely qualified as she was to investigate Elysia. Maybe he knew that, and *that* was why she hadn't heard from him. Britton couldn't give explicit approval, but as long as they didn't speak about it and she was on her own time, he could claim no knowledge of what she was up to.

Stop stalling. You're running out of time.

It didn't take long to search his room. Abram had some kind of military in his background—something she'd always suspected—because she'd never seen anyone but retired military do corners on their bed quite like he did. She poked through the nearly empty closet, finding a few jackets and pairs of boots caked with mud, but there wasn't any collection of serial-killer trophies or a conveniently signed confession letter. She did a cursory search of his dresser and shook her head at the immaculately folded shirts. Even his *underwear* was folded.

But then, she'd always known Abram was a control freak. This was just further evidence to support that truth.

As much as she wanted to find evidence that he was the killer, the truth was that he was just too damn anal-retentive to kill someone so sloppily. If Abram was the killer, the victim would have been dispatched with a garrote around the throat from behind, or maybe a neat little shot to the back of the head, execution-style, and then buried in the woods where no one would find them. There would be no body, and Elouise's parents would have spent the rest of their lives believing that she'd moved off to college and maybe finally been happy.

Call her cynical, but that would have been almost preferable.

Except then there would be no justice for Elouise, and that wasn't right. Eden shut the drawer carefully and checked her watch. Another fifteen minutes of worship, which wasn't that long at all. There were two other bedrooms to search, but they'd always stood as empty guest rooms when she lived here, so she didn't expect to find much. Still, she was here, so she might as well check them out. She frowned when she opened the first door. After the entire house being the same, she'd assumed this would be, too.

Except it wasn't.

The color scheme used to be tasteful neutrals with a few pops of blue, but now it looked like . . . Eden toed the pile of dirty clothes on the floor. It looked like a teenage boy lived here. She moved farther into the room, skirting more clothes of dubious cleanliness, and froze in front of the dresser. It had a few pictures in frames propped up on top of it, every single one showing Martha and *Joseph*.

Eden swallowed hard, looked again, and gagged. *That is so incredibly wrong.* Joseph had been proprietary when she'd run into him yesterday, but she hadn't actually paused to think about the fact that he was *living* here. There had always only been Abram, and she'd kind of assumed that always would be.

Guess I can't assume a damn thing anymore.

It was something she should have remembered, but she'd been so caught up in how identical everything was, she'd gotten herself and her instincts all turned around. She couldn't take anything for granted.

But . . . Joseph?

He was pretty, she'd grant him that, but she would have thought her mother would look for something beyond physical attractiveness for her inner circle. *Maybe he's good in bed.* She gagged and shoved that thought into a dark little corner of her mind where she hoped it would never see the light of day again.

Eden went through the drawers, finding clothes stuffed in haphazardly. The last drawer made her pause. The bottom of it wasn't where it should be. She frowned and pressed carefully around the edge, finding a little gap where she could wedge her finger and pull it up. *What do we have here?*

Eden started to reach in, thought better of it, and yanked on one of the gloves she'd stashed in her pocket. She was seriously glad she did when the carefully placed black cloth came away to reveal porn. *What the hell?* The girl on the top one looked to be all of sixteen, which lined up with the BARELY LEGAL! headline running right over her crotch. Eden thumbed through the drawer, finding about a dozen magazines, all featuring petite brunettes that had probably seen their eighteenth birthday in the last month.

Coincidence?

Hard to call it that with a petite brunette found dead and a second one missing.

Outside, the bell tolled, signaling the end of worship. "Shit." She dumped the magazines back into the drawer, put the cloth over the top of them, and replaced the fake drawer bottom. There was no telling if things were exactly the way he had them, but judging from the rest of the room, she doubted Joseph would notice. Or at least she hoped he wouldn't.

She shut the bedroom door behind her and hurried for the stairs. The chances of her making it to her car without running into someone was slim to none, but she could say she was taking a walk. Martha would know she was snooping, but she wouldn't know *where* she was snooping. If there was one place in this commune not covered in cameras, it was *this* house.

Eden thumbed the lock over on the back door and shut it as she left the house, breathing a silent sigh of relief when she didn't see anyone. *Safe.* She hurried down the back porch, heading for the parking lot.

She barely made it three steps when rough hands turned her around and slammed her face-first into the side of the house.

CHAPTER THIRTEEN

"You're not supposed to be here." Abram's voice, so cold and detached, had the years of memories surging, threatening to drown Eden in fear. So she fought back the only way she'd ever known.

With rage.

She slammed her foot into Abram's instep, but he didn't budge. "Get off me!"

"Breaking and entering is a crime. You of all people should know that."

He knows. She pushed back, which he allowed only to slam her back against the house. Her breath left her in a rush, and black dots temporarily danced across her vision. She blinked once and then again, things finally falling back into place. "So is assaulting an FBI agent."

"According to code 45-3-102, I am fully entitled to defend myself and my property."

He *would* start quoting Montana law at her. Martha and Abram had no use for the law except when it benefited them. In this case, he might actually be right, since she *was* breaking and entering. She huffed out a breath, changing tactics. "Martha invited me here."

"You're lying." His grip tightened on her arm, wrenching it higher between her shoulder blades. "Your mother didn't invite you into her home. I would know."

She couldn't bluff him on that, because he was right. When Eden was a teenager, nothing went on with Martha that Abram didn't know about, and she didn't think that fact had changed much in the intervening years. "You know why I'm here."

It was a calculated bet, but she couldn't have Abram dragging her out to face the firing squad and potentially shut down anyone who'd be willing to gossip with her. The Elysians were already going to be reserved because she'd been gone for so long, and one thing these people didn't abide was outsiders. Eden didn't quite fit into that category because she'd been born and raised here, but she wasn't one of them, either. If Abram publicly set her apart, she'd have no hope of talking to anyone.

"You think someone here had something to do with the killing of Elouise Perkins." He finally let her go, and she paused for a full second to get her game face on. It didn't matter how much being around Abram made her want to curl up into a ball and rock until the monster went away. It flat out wasn't an option to show weakness. It would be like cutting her wrists and then going swimming with sharks.

A death sentence.

He stared at her with those cold blue eyes. "It wasn't one of our people." He said it with no more inflection than he'd said anything else since he'd caught her. Abram could be commenting on what a warm fall day they were having and his tone would be exactly the same. It was possible he was lying. It was equally possible he was telling the truth. She just couldn't tell.

"Then help me prove it." It didn't matter if he believed she was in Elysia to prove the cult's innocence or if she was here to prove otherwise—if Abram truly thought the people here were innocent, he wouldn't stand in her way. She hoped. It was a gamble. God, everything she'd done since catching the flight back into Montana had been a gamble. She didn't think Martha believed she was considering coming back into the fold any more than Abram did, but both of them were willing to play along for their own reasons.

He jerked his chin in the direction of the chapel. "Talk to Lee. The sooner you satisfy your curiosity, the sooner you are gone and the less pain you'll deal your mother."

Everyone was so goddamn concerned about Martha's pain. No one really cared that Eden had been walking around feeling like an exposed nerve for the last few days. *No one made me come back here. I chose this.* The problem was that it was getting harder and harder to remember that the longer she was around these people.

She couldn't shake the feeling she'd been drawn back here.

It sounded paranoid. Hell, it *felt* paranoid in the extreme, but that suspicion sat in the back of her mind all the while.

She frowned, trying to get herself back on track. "Lee. Why does that name sound familiar?"

"He joined our number a few months before you left."

Ah, *now* she remembered. He'd wandered through the gates one day, which wasn't abnormal exactly, but most people were bused in with the recruiters after a carefully intricate vetting process. She'd been surprised at the time that they'd let him stay, but Eden had been too consumed with her plans to get out to pay him too much attention. All she remembered was a black guy with sad eyes.

She raised her chin, fighting back a flinch when the move pulled at her back. "I'm going to tell him you sent me his way."

"Do that."

There was nothing more to say. She took a careful step back and then another, uncomfortable with the thought of presenting her back to him. How her mother went to bed with this man was beyond her. If Abram had a softer side, Eden hadn't seen it in all the years she'd known him.

But she couldn't scoot all the way to the edge of the house without looking like a damn fool, so she turned and walked away, the skin on the back of her neck prickling the entire time. She could *feel* his eyes on her, and it made her want to take the hottest shower she could stand.

Later.

Right now you have to focus.

Easier said than done.

Though chapel had let out a good fifteen minutes earlier, people still gathered around the entrance, chatting in small groups. Martha liked to crow that everyone was welcome and then some, but the group's skin tones definitely tended toward the lighter end of the spectrum. It was child's play to pick out the tall, attractive man with dark skin in the midst of the others.

She approached, mentally comparing him with what she remembered of the guy who'd come when she was a teenager. He couldn't be more than a few years younger than she was, and though he smiled at the pair of women in front of him, he still had sad eyes. She stopped a few steps away and cleared her throat. The women took one look at her and scattered like chickens seeing a fox in the henhouse.

Lee didn't seem all that bothered to be facing down Martha's wayward daughter. He took her measure, looking her up and down, but in a strangely respectful way. She responded in kind, but her first impression stuck—attractive with an underlying sorrow that would bring people in like catnip. She cocked her head to the side. "I don't suppose you're in recruitment?"

This guy would have moved through colleges across the United States and made friends wherever he went. He was just good-looking enough to draw people to him, but not so attractive that he would intimidate women or make men jealous.

He flashed a smile, though it didn't reach his eyes any more than his other had. "What makes you say that?"

"Call it instinct." She looked around, noting the blatant eavesdropping going on. Most of the people around them weren't even trying to pretend not to listen. "Is there somewhere we can speak privately?"

"I really don't think that's wise."

He could think that all he wanted. She had the only information that mattered. "Abram is the one who gave me your name." Part of Eden hated that she was playing the game, using the big, bad monster beneath the bed to scare this man into submission. The rest of her didn't give a damn as long as she walked away with much-needed answers.

Just like that, the careful smile on Lee's lips disappeared. He looked over her shoulder, and she didn't have to follow his gaze to know the man himself was behind her, silently giving permission. She hadn't really expected Lee to take her at her word, but it still rankled.

He sighed. "I have to relieve a shift."

"I'll walk with you, then." Maybe if she got moving, she'd get rid of the feeling making her skin crawl. Eden rubbed her hands over her arms, realized what she was doing, and dropped them to hang at her sides.

Of course you're being watched. You're standing in the middle of a crowd.

It wasn't just being watched, though. It was the little voice inside her screaming that she was being hunted. She turned a slow circle, studying the faces around her, but they held nothing but blatant curiosity. A flash of pale hair caught her eye, and she waved at Beth, mentally reminding herself that she planned on talking to the woman when she had a chance. It wouldn't be today, but soon.

Lee motioned. "After you."

They walked away from the chapel, Lee carefully leading her north toward the pastures. Martha kept everything going on the property that they would need to survive without outside resources, including cattle and various gardens and crops. It was part of her back-to-nature preaching, and with the way the world was going these days, she'd drawn in more than a few people with the promise of being able to survive in the event of any kind of government meltdown. People were scared. The media had a lot to do with it, but in truth, they *should* be scared. Global warming and too-big government and corporate corruption abounded. And in the midst of it all, Martha stood, offering a simpler way.

Even though she knew it was a sham, Eden understood why so many people ended up at the gates of Elysia.

The place was nearly 100 percent self-sufficient. Martha had no problem importing what she needed to run her businesses, but most of the food they ate was grown in Elysia, the clothing sewn there, even if the fabric came from elsewhere. The people had nearly every one of their needs met, and most chose not to take advantage of Martha's allowance for them to travel into Clear Springs or Augusta whenever they wanted. They'd rather go without certain luxuries than have to interact with noncult members.

Lee stopped in front of the closest garden. It had high fences designed to deter deer, and through the chain link she could see neat little boxes about two feet tall lined up in perfect rows. It was hard to tell at this time of year, but they appeared to be herbs rather than produce. *Just like they were when I was here.*

Eden waited, but Lee didn't seem all that inclined to start talking. *Fine. I'll go first.* "Why did Abram point me in your direction?" She suspected she knew—that Lee was the man who'd stepped in on behalf of Elouise—but she was curious if he'd tell the truth.

"I guess it's because you're looking into Elouise's death." He frowned at her carefully blank look. "He didn't tell you? She and I were . . . close."

Close. There were so many ways that small, innocent word could be interpreted. Eden wasn't inclined to make any guesses in general—and that rule went double for dealing with anyone under her mother's control. *Close* went beyond saving a girl from her abusive asshole of a father. "Explain."

He hesitated, and she could almost see him weighing the benefit of defying Abram. She could have told him it was a lost cause, but he seemed to come to that conclusion all on his own. Lee dropped onto the low wall surrounding the taller fence. "I was the one who originally brought her here. Back in July, I was in town doing an errand for Martha, and I heard a scuffle. I went to investigate and found Elouise on the ground and her father standing over her with his fist raised." Anger flared in his brown eyes, temporarily chasing away the sadness. "I intervened. It wasn't my business, but I didn't have it in me to walk away." He shot her a look. "I got a little physical with Michael Perkins, which I'm sure he'd be all too happy to report if you ask him. He took off, and I brought Elouise back here."

That was interesting. She took a seat next to him, a carefully considered foot between them, angling her body slightly away from him. Some people revealed more information when they were crowded and against the wall. Her instincts said Lee would clam up if she pushed too hard.

She casually asked, "Martha was okay with that?" Even having heard the same story from her mother, she just didn't see it. Martha took the term *control freak* to a neurotic degree, and Lee bringing back some local girl she didn't know from Adam couldn't have sat well.

His lips twitched. "She wasn't too keen on it at first, but I insisted. She had a one-on-one talk with Elouise, and after that said she could come and go as she pleased, within reason."

Reason being they didn't want her wandering around and finding things outsiders weren't supposed to know about. Eden reached down to pull up a couple of blades of the long grass that grew in the area, shredding each one slowly, still keeping her voice casual and low. "That was months ago. From what I understand, Elouise had no intention of joining Elysia."

"She didn't." He shrugged, the move too controlled. "She might have come back, though—after college when she got out of Clear

Springs for a few years and realized the world out there isn't any better than what she left behind. *Who* she left behind."

Who . . .

Just as I suspected. Except his tone when he said that word was too full of angst for someone who was merely sleeping with the victim. She flicked the shredded grass off her leg and turned to face him, studying his expression. *Definitely more than sex.* "You were in love with her."

He looked away, his expression full of naked pain. "What I felt for her is irrelevant. I offered her a refuge when she needed it, so that's why she spent some time coming and going here. But she left for college. Abram put her on that bus out of town and watched it leave. He told me so." His breath caught, but he kept talking. "She texted me when she got there. She was *safe*, damn it."

Eden didn't tell him that no one in this world was safe. He'd learned that the hard way, and driving the point home now would just be cruel. She stretched her legs out and crossed her ankles, considering him. For all his obvious angst, there was one glaring truth she couldn't quite let go of.

Elouise had willingly chosen to leave him behind. He obviously had strong feelings for her, and even if she'd returned them, she'd still put college before him. Before Elysia.

People had killed for less.

She uncrossed and recrossed her ankles, keeping her body language relaxed and her tone vaguely interested. "Were you mad she left?"

He frowned. "Mad? No. I mean, I was disappointed, and I'm not going to lie and say I didn't try to convince her to stay. She promised she'd consider Elysia once she had her degree. That was good enough for me."

So he said. No way to determine if he was telling the truth.

She'd pass the information on to Zach, but she wasn't sure what to think of Lee. On the one hand, he'd obviously cared very deeply for the girl. On the other, there was the whole thought process of *If you're not with me, then you won't be with anyone.* He could both kill her and grieve her with that mind-set.

She'd seen it happen before.

But for now she had enough information to get rolling, and she'd get confirmation of what he'd told her independently to verify it was the truth. She couldn't take his sorrow at face value—she couldn't take *anything* here at face value.

Eden pushed to her feet. *I won't get anything else out of him right now. Better to circle back after I've talked to a few other people.* "If I have more questions—"

"I'll hear from you. Got it." He raised his head, his eyes shining, just a little. "I don't like you on principle. I don't get you. You left this all behind, and for what—to rub elbows with the worst humanity has to offer? I don't get how you stand it." He took a deep breath. "But I'm glad Elouise has someone—someone who understands—looking out for her."

Eden didn't have to ask what he meant. Someone who understood Elysia. Someone who'd seen the worst the world had to offer and who could come back swinging. Lee was right about one thing—she *had* seen the worst humanity had to offer. He was just wrong about where she'd seen it.

She made her way back to her car, not having the energy to go another round with her mother. They weren't anywhere near close to finishing this hunt, and if she had to deal with the passive-aggressive pokes and questions on a daily basis, she might lose her mind.

By the time she made it back to the courtyard, it was empty, everyone having gone off to their varying duties. Martha might be a monster of a particular variety, but she had a well-run establishment. *But then, she would. Keep her people too busy to stop and wonder about some of the insane shit she preaches.* That saying about idle hands didn't originate with the Greeks, but her mother had never been shy about incorporating whatever dogma she found most useful. No one questioned it.

No one but Eden.

And she'd paid for every question she'd asked.

She stopped next to her car, slowing her movements, because if she didn't exert total control, she was going to fling herself into the driver's seat and tear out of here as fast as the car could go. She wouldn't stop in Clear Springs. She'd just keep driving until she put a few states between her and Elysia.

Not an option. You made damn sure of that.

She noticed the door was unlocked and frowned. Had she locked it when she got here? Eden couldn't be sure. She'd been so rattled and practically bursting with adrenaline and dread that it was entirely possible she'd headed for her mother's house without pausing to lock the door.

But she didn't think so.

She opened the driver's door cautiously, half expecting something to explode. She only had cursory bomb training, so even if she swept the vehicle, she couldn't be sure she'd find something. If there was even something to find. *Hello, paranoia, my old friend.* She turned a slow circle, trying to figure out if someone would have had enough time to plant something. If a person had the know-how, setting up a bomb in a half hour was cake.

Way to be reassuring.

She leaned back into the car, a flash of white and yellow catching her eye. Frowning, she leaned in farther and used the pen in her cup holder to hook the circular wreath of daisies lying on the floorboard of the passenger side. It looked like the kind of thing she'd made when she was a kid and bored out of her ever-loving mind during the summer. She'd weave together the flowers that grew in the fields of Elysia into something very similar to this and wear it while she pretended she was Persephone, just waiting for her Hades to appear and whisk her away to be his queen. Eden dropped it like it'd caught fire. She'd completely forgotten about playing that game. Hell, *no one* knew she'd done it. She'd always been alone out there.

Or so she'd thought.

She wanted to throw the flowers away, to rip the wreath apart and grind it beneath her boots. But it was most definitely some kind of evidence. Even if there was no trace on there to find whoever had left it, it was proof that someone *had* been watching her when she got here.

Apparently my instincts aren't as ravaged as I thought.

She wasn't sure if that was comforting or terrifying.

CHAPTER FOURTEEN

Zach didn't take a lunch, spending the hour he would have been eating on the phone with the cops up in Augusta. They'd seen neither hide nor hair of Neveah, and they'd pulled her in often enough for various petty offenses to know her by name. His friend up there, Jared, had promised to keep an eye out for her, but three days since she'd been reported missing—and most likely closer to six since she'd actually *been* missing—and Zach was starting to lose hope. In the best scenario, she'd taken off for good, and that was that.

His gut said she wasn't gone for good, but he was starting to suspect they wouldn't see her alive again.

"Sheriff."

He looked up and mentally cursed at the panic in Chase's brown eyes. It could mean only one thing. The man went and confirmed it when he looked over his shoulder and lowered his voice. "The Smiths are here. I tried to talk them down, but they want an update, and they want it from you specifically."

He had nothing to tell them. Fuck, he had less than nothing to tell them. But Zach knew those folk—they would park themselves in his waiting room and terrorize anyone who came in until he saw them. *Now, that's not charitable. Their daughter is missing, and they're scared shitless. If you were in their position, you'd be doing the same thing.* He knew that. Damn it, he really did know that. But their showing up randomly to corner him made it harder to do his job. There was nothing for it. "Bring them on back." He eyed Chase. Whatever rest the man had gotten that had recharged him this morning was gone, leaving him looking drawn and downright haggard. "After that, take a break to eat something."

He gave a halfhearted smile. "Yes, Mother."

At least some of Chase's snarky attitude was back. It had been missing since he'd found Elouise's body, and the lack of sleep and running himself ragged hadn't helped. But hopefully the worst had passed.

Somehow, he didn't think any of them had seen the worst yet.

But the rest-and-recovery time he'd forced on Chase obviously hadn't worked. He didn't blame the man. Every time he'd closed his eyes last night, he'd seen Elouise's face. How much worse would it have been if he was the one who'd found her? Some things a person didn't just get over, and despite working the homicide beat back in Seattle, Chase obviously hadn't developed much of a thick skin. Which was probably why he'd gravitated to Clear Springs—for the peace and quiet.

Not much of that going around these days.

Robert and Julie rushed into Zach's office like they thought he was going to sneak out a window while they weren't looking. It didn't seem like too shabby an idea from where he was sitting. Julie immediately sank into the chair across the desk from him while Robert took up a position at her back. His hands came down on her shoulders, and he glared at Zach. "Where is our daughter?"

He tried to hold on to his impatience, reminding himself yet again that they were concerned parents and had every right to be bashing down his door at every available opportunity. "We're still doing our best to search for her." *Which isn't made easier by the fact that no one wants to answer our questions.* He couldn't tell the Smiths that, though. They were already in danger of going around him and starting a search of their own.

In fact, it was time for that.

He hadn't wanted to go there, but they couldn't afford to wait any longer. Zach scrubbed a hand over his face. "I'm putting together a search party."

"A search . . . *oh.*" Julie pressed a hand to her mouth, her eyes going wide. "You don't think she's lost out there? Neveah might not be an outdoors kind of girl, but she knows the area. She wouldn't wander into the mountains, especially at this time of year when the nights get so cold."

He knew that. He also knew that Elouise hadn't tattooed herself, stripped naked, and then wandered out into the night, either.

Robert's eyebrows slanted down. "You're looking in the wrong direction, Zach. I told you once and I'll tell you again: Martha Collins has our girl."

If he didn't handle the situation carefully, they'd have their church organized into a well-mannered lynch mob and be out there beating on the gates of Elysia by nightfall. Zach kept his tone mild. "I have someone searching the commune as we speak."

"Eden Collins." Julie practically spat the name, which told him all he needed to know about her opinion of *that.* Folks in these parts had memories that went back a long time, and they tended to view Eden as the daughter of the devil. He'd been the same way if he was going to be perfectly honest, though his opinion had changed the more time he spent with her. She was smart and capable, and if she was under Martha's spell, he'd seen no evidence of it.

"Word does travel fast in these parts."

"Don't try that aw-golly-gee-shucks bullshit with us, Zach." Robert drew himself up, stretching to all six feet three inches of his height. "If you're going to focus on that other girl instead, then we'll take matters into our own hands."

What the hell is he talking about?

It came to him all at once. "Other girl." He looked at Julie and then at Robert, taking in the stubborn set of her chin, the defiance in his eyes. Yep, he'd heard the man correctly. He spoke carefully, doing his damnedest not to lose it. "You don't mean you want me to walk away from Elouise Perkins's death to put every resource I have on chasing down Neveah." If it hadn't occurred to them that the two things were related, he sure as hell wasn't going to be the first to voice his suspicions.

"Elouise Perkins is trash." Robert tried to shush her, but Julie was having none of it. "No, I'm going to say it. Our girl might be a little misguided at times, but she's a good girl. She was raised right, and she's got big plans for her future. God might strike me down for saying it, but Elouise Perkins most likely put herself in a bad position with some boy and got herself killed as a result."

Zach opened his mouth, but words failed him. It wasn't only that Julie had that poor girl's number so damn wrong. It wasn't that she put her daughter above some other teenager she'd probably seen around town only here and there. It wasn't even that she was coming across as a judgmental monster, either. "That girl is dead, Julie. *Dead.* She's not coming back, and she sure as fuck didn't do a damn thing to bring that on herself." He pointed at his door. "Get out. I'm doing my best for both those girls, because that's what they *both* deserve. I'll remind you kindly to remember that."

He waited until they were in the doorway to say, "And if I hear about you riling up the church folk to go after Martha Collins, I *will* arrest the lot of you for trespassing."

The look Julie sent him was downright lethal. "I always knew you had a soft spot for that cult, Zach, but you're going too far this time."

"I'm upholding the law, which is more than I can say for whatever is going through your head right now." Until he had genuine proof that Martha or one of her flock had something to do with either Elouise Perkins's death or Neveah Smith's disappearance—or, heaven help him, *both*—he'd do everything in his power to bring them to justice. But he wasn't going to start handing out pitchforks and torches.

Not yet, anyway.

There was a proper way to do things, and he was already crossing that line by enlisting Eden in his investigation. He waited for the Smiths to leave before getting up and closing the office door. He thumped his forehead on the thick wood a few times, but nothing changed.

So he started making calls. It was too late to start the search today, but if they got going early tomorrow morning, they'd have all day to comb the surrounding area. The boys up in Augusta had already volunteered to be brought in on it, and the state troopers were ready whenever he was.

He just hoped like hell that taking this step wasn't going to spook the killer into killing again.

It took two hours to coordinate everything, and part of him resented the time spent. He didn't think a search was going to do a damn bit of good—the Smiths were right on that count. Neveah might be wild and uncontrollable, but she wasn't stupid enough to wander into the mountains and die out there.

On a whim, he called down to the Greyhound office and, with a big of finagling, was put through to the driver who'd been working their circuit this weekend. The man had picked up only a single passenger in Augusta—an old man—and hadn't seen anyone matching Neveah's description. Zach thanked him and hung up, dread curdling his stomach.

It was time to change tactics.

He called Eden.

She answered almost immediately, the background noise making him think she was driving. "Yes?"

"How'd it go?" *How are you?* He couldn't ask that, though. He'd been the one to draw the line in the sand about distractions and then promptly go and break his own damn rule. The least he could do was keep them focused on the case. *It's more important than dwelling on how good she tastes . . .*

She sighed. "About as well as can be expected. I have some information, but I didn't get as much snooping done as I wanted to before Abram caught me."

His chest tightened at the thought of her facing off with Abram. Zach had seen some scary motherfuckers in his time in the desert, but Martha's right-hand man put them all to shame. He'd seen some things—done some things, too, if the lack of emotion was anything to go by. As far as Zach could tell, there was only one thing the man cared about, and that was Martha. If he thought Eden was a threat to her mother, he wouldn't hesitate to take action.

Permanent action.

He gripped the phone tighter. "You promised you'd be careful."

"I was careful."

"Funny, but getting caught by Abram doesn't count as careful in my book."

Another pause, longer this time. Finally Eden said, "Did you call to lecture me, or are you canceling for tonight?"

He couldn't figure out if she sounded hopeful or disappointed. Hell, asking her out had been an impulse he couldn't deny, no matter how questionable an idea it was. Everything she'd said was correct—this was the worst possible timing for him to start having potential romantic interest in anyone, let alone Eden Collins. But he couldn't help wanting to know more about her outside the case.

That wasn't why he was calling now, though.

"I'm still taking you out to dinner, but I'm about to head over and see if I can get some information out of Neveah's best friend." Chase had tried yesterday, and Zach had talked to Rachel at the high school, both to no avail, but he got the feeling someone of the feminine persuasion might have a better chance with her. "Want to tag along?"

"As if you have to ask." Her voice brightened right up. "I can be at the station in fifteen."

"Perfect. See you then." He hung up, mentally going over everything he knew about Rachel Carpenter. She wasn't a wild child like Neveah, but she didn't quite fly under the radar, either. The few times he'd talked to her, she'd nearly jumped out of her skin, which he'd chalked up to her being intimidated by the focus of the sheriff. Now, he wondered. With Neveah still missing and the mental clock ticking down in his head, he was grasping at straws, and he knew it. It didn't matter.

Either Rachel Carpenter was irrationally terrified of cops . . . or she knew more than she was saying.

Eden was almost pathetically grateful for the distraction Zach offered her. She had too much stuff circling her head, over and over again, and sitting in her hotel room would only make it worse. After parking in front of the station, her gaze was drawn once again to the flower wreath lying in the passenger seat. It looked so innocent there, not sinister in the least. There was no proof that it *was* sinister.

Except her gut said it was exactly that.

It was too late in the year for daisies. She hadn't touched them yet, but a few of the petals had fallen onto the car seat itself, and they looked like they'd been dried, which indicated that someone had woven this wreath a while ago—probably last spring—and then hung it to dry.

Someone planned this.

But that was impossible. It *had* to be impossible. There was no way anyone could have known that she'd come back to Elysia *ever*, let alone be able to pinpoint the season well enough to plan in advance.

Unless that someone was the unsub.

She shook her head, but the thought wouldn't dissipate. Martha knew she'd joined the FBI. Her mother liked to keep track of her over the years, and what Martha knew, Abram knew—possibly Joseph, too, since apparently he was in the inner circle now. But her mother wasn't going to go advertising that fact to anyone else.

Eden had a solid record since she'd joined the BAU, but she hadn't handled any cases that had made the national media. Even if she had, the Bureau tended to try to foster goodwill with local law enforcement by stepping out of the limelight as much as possible. Sometimes it worked better than others, but Eden had no interest in people knowing her face or name. If they did, they might track her back to her mother and Elysia, and *that* potential scandal would be a nightmare, as far as she was concerned.

It wasn't a secret that she was with the FBI, but it wasn't exactly advertised, either.

If she was smart, she would have changed her name before she joined. But doing so felt like giving in, like hiding something she refused to feel ashamed about. She hadn't joined a cult. Her mother ran one. It felt like the first choice she'd made was to leave, and she wouldn't back down and hide once she was free.

So she'd kept her name.

She huffed out a breath. "It's entirely possible that I'm being para-noid. This place does that to me—in addition to making me talk to myself like a crazy person." She needed a second opinion, but everyone here was so freaking close to the case. If she told Zach she was starting to suspect someone had killed a local girl with the intention of drawing her home . . .

It sounded insane, even in her head.

Especially since there wasn't *proof.*

Except that someone had gone through a lot of trouble to send her a photo of the dead girl. It was practically an engraved invitation back to Clear Springs.

Back to Elysia.

I'll call Britton. I hate to put him on the spot, but he, of all people, will have a clear, unbiased view of this. If I'm nuts, he won't hesitate to tell me. And if I'm not . . . if I'm not, then I'm in over my head, and I'm going to need help in a big way.

Already feeling more in control, she turned off the engine and climbed out of the car. Eden double-checked and then triple-checked that she'd locked it before heading into the station. If someone was breaking into her car—and potentially her room at the B&B—she wanted to make sure it was actually happening and not a figment of her imagination.

It's not my imagination.

It's probably not my imagination.

God, it might be my imagination.

Zach appeared in the doorway, the sight of him stopping her in her tracks. It didn't matter that she'd just seen him this morning. He was just so *solid*, like he could hold the weight of the world on his shoulders and not miss a beat. Like maybe he could even shoulder her problems for a little while and give her the pillar to lean on that she desperately craved.

It's not his burden to bear. Asking him to do so is a dick move.

He frowned. "When's the last time you ate?"

"I don't know." She wasn't much of a breakfast person, and knowing there was the chance of a confrontation of the maternal sort upset her stomach too much to think about food. She wasn't particularly hungry now, but she recognized the look in his eyes.

Britton sported it from time to time. Her boss took it almost personally if the people under his charge weren't taking care of themselves. *And I haven't been.*

"Rachel can wait."

She held up a hand. "No, she can't. We don't know for sure that Neveah and Elouise are connected, but if they are, our timeline for finding her alive is shrinking by the hour. I have some snacks in my purse. I'll eat while you drive."

He looked like he wanted to argue but finally gave a short nod. "Let's go."

The snacks were a sleeve of peanuts she'd tossed in there before her flight because sometimes her stomach got upset while in the air. Knowing where she was headed had only made that feeling worse. Eden climbed into the passenger seat of Zach's cruiser and pulled out the peanuts, though she wasn't sure she could tolerate even that.

She looked over to find Zach watching her again. "What?"

"We're going straight to dinner after this. That isn't a meal, especially if you haven't eaten since last night." He sounded so grumpy about it that she laughed despite the circumstances, which only made him frown harder. He turned out of the small station parking lot. "Between you and Chase, you're turning me into a nagging fishwife." Zach glanced over. "You wouldn't have known him back when you were a kid. He moved here a few years ago from Seattle. He worked homicide over there."

"That's a big change." She could understand, though. When it came to law enforcement, a lot of cops washed out, leaving them to seek solace where they could. A small town like Clear Springs offered stability and the ability to keep on being a cop, but without the constant emotional turmoil of seeing the worst humanity had to offer day in and day out.

Usually.

"His uncle used to bring him fishing near here when he was a kid. He kind of washed into town one day and stayed." He sighed. "He moved here to get away from all that bullshit, and then *this* happens."

She still hadn't seen the coroner's report that he'd promised to bring, but she'd gleaned enough facts to know that one of Zach's deputies had been called in on a trespassing report and found the body. If it hadn't been Henry, that only left Chase.

"He blames himself. There's nothing he could have done, but he still thinks if he'd shown up sooner, she might have had a chance."

Eden knew about guilt like that. So often, her cases were a matter of waiting for the next victim to show up, to tell them more about the unsub and bring them closer to bringing the bastard in. Guilt from that knowledge could break a person—it *did* break agents on a regular basis. From his tone, she got the feeling that Zach understood. "He'll get through it. He has you in his corner, and it sounds like you're doing a good job of keeping an eye at him."

"I try. Fuck, I try." He hesitated and then cursed. "You should know the Smiths came to see me this afternoon. They're half a second from forming a mob and heading out to Elysia to demand your mother deliver Neveah into their waiting hands."

"It wouldn't work." She popped a few peanuts into her mouth and watched the houses roll by—well-maintained, picture-perfect little snapshots that hid a myriad of sins. Not everyone was a murderer or abusive, but she'd given up on the idea of a perfect childhood, free of trauma. The world was an ugly place. Unfortunately for so many, the most dangerous predators were often sharing space beneath the same roof.

"I know."

He didn't, though. She ate a few more peanuts. "No, you don't understand. Martha's power is all tied up in her followers' belief that she's above the rest of us basic human folk. It is, at its very heart, an us-versus-them sort of thing—*us* being the Elysians and *them* being every other person on this planet. It's why she doesn't have to instill rules forcing them to stay on the commune grounds—they view the outside world as foreign and deplorable. They don't *want* to leave. If a mob shows up, they will shut the gates, and it might push Martha and her inner circle into doing something regrettable." She ate some more peanuts. "As in six feet beneath the ground regrettable."

CHAPTER FIFTEEN

Eden and Zach didn't talk about her taking the lead, but when they climbed out of his cruiser, he fell a half step behind her. *Smart.* The adults of Clear Springs might see her as a threat to one degree or another, but she was still fresh-faced enough to approach the teenagers like a peer. Without the uniform and in her white T-shirt, jeans, and leather jacket, she only perpetuated that illusion. Eden pulled her hair out of its ponytail and mussed it a bit, ignoring Zach's questioning look. The style made her look younger, and that was what they needed right now. If Zach and his men had struck out with this girl before—and she doubted he would have extended an invitation if they *hadn't*—it meant a different tactic was needed.

He paused a few feet down the walkway. "This isn't official. I can't question a minor without a parent present."

"I'm not questioning her. We're just going to have a chat." She said it aloud so he could have plausible deniability. *Skirting close to the line with this one.* But she was willing to do that and more if it meant bringing Neveah Smith home to her parents.

Eden approached the door, aware of the man at her back, aware of the way his gaze rested on her. *Put it away. It's not relevant to the present, and it'll only distract you.*

Easier said than done.

She gave a purposefully tentative knock and checked her watch. Though the high school had let out an hour ago, it was still too early for most parents to be off work if they had a normal day shift. Eden glanced at Zach. Did he do that on purpose? *I just bet he did.*

The sound of footsteps echoed on the other side of the door two seconds before it cracked open, a pair of dark doe eyes peering through the space. "Yes?"

"Rachel?"

"Yes." She didn't open the door any farther, but Eden noted her long dark hair and petite frame—what she could see of it. Having seen pictures of both Neveah and Elouise, this girl could have been their sister.

Or Eden's.

She gave a practiced innocent smile. "I have a few questions, if that's okay?"

"Who are you?"

Suspicious little thing, isn't she? "I'm Eden. I'm with the FBI, and I'm helping out Sheriff Owens with the search for Neveah." She withdrew her badge all the same and showed it to Rachel. "You're not in any kind of trouble—I promise." *And I'm not here officially for all that I'm flashing my badge around. Britton is going to kill me if he finds out.*

"You can't talk to me without my mom around, and she won't be home for another hour."

Zach had *definitely* timed it like this on purpose. She shot him a look and lowered her voice, slipping half a step closer to the door. "The truth is, I'm only helping out unofficially. The only thing we care about is finding Neveah." She motioned to Zach, moving out of the way enough so the teenager could get a look at him. "He'll even stay outside if that would make you feel better."

Rachel hesitated, but Eden knew she had her. The girl brimmed with nervous energy. All kids that age had more energy than they knew what to do with, but from the way she kept looking around as if she expected assassins to burst from the trees, she had a secret. A secret she wanted to tell. It was only a matter of applying the right pressure. Finally Rachel nodded. "You have to leave before my mom gets home."

"Of course." She turned to Zach. "This won't take long."

He raised his eyebrows and gave a short nod before ambling back to the cruiser. Eden considered him. *He really is too smart by half. He knew exactly what he was doing when he invited me along.* She followed the girl into the house, taking in every detail she could as they walked down the hallway to the living room.

It was a cozy house, with an obvious amount of love that had gone into the decorating. But everything had most likely been purchased secondhand, and the tendency toward frilly things and pink made Eden think there wasn't a man in the house.

Rachel stopped in the kitchen. "Do you . . . do you want something to drink?"

Polite. Good girl, from all appearances. Her nervousness makes it unlikely she's ever been in real trouble. Eden smiled. "No, that's totally okay."

She started wringing her hands, pressing her lips together. "I—"

If she let this go on too long, the girl was bound to have an anxiety attack. Eden moved around to the fridge and took in the pictures. They were all of Rachel and a woman who looked similar to her, though she had more lines around her mouth and eyes—lots of laugh lines, but there were sad ones there, too. The reason why most likely had to do with the man in uniform right at eye level. "How long has your dad been gone?"

"He died ten years ago."

Right in the midst of all the wars overseas. Eden ignored the pang in her chest. She knew what it was like to grow up without a dad, though it would appear Rachel's relationship with her mom wasn't as problematic as Eden's own. "I'm sorry."

"It was a long time ago."

Not long enough for your mom to move on. But that wasn't why she was here. She kept her gaze off Rachel, who wandered over to adjust the fresh flowers sitting in the middle of the kitchen counter. *Yes, this is a house filled with love.* "Do teenagers still go party out on the Parkinson property like they used to? There's a great place for a bonfire down by the creek, and for all the old guy's love of waving around that damn shotgun, he can't see or hear the parties down there."

"How did you—?" Rachel seemed to realize she was about to admit to something and clamped her mouth shut.

Eden kept her smile gentle and her words quiet. "The adults of this town don't like to admit it, but when they were your age, they did the same thing. Even the old-timers snuck out and drank moonshine and hooked up in the woods, though old-man Parkinson *was* one of those kids back in those days. It's a rite of passage, which is why I get the feeling Sheriff Owens doesn't bug you kids about it too much as long as you're not wrapping your cars around trees."

Rachel hesitated, then finally whispered, "My mom doesn't know. It'd kill her if she knew."

"I see no reason anyone has to tell her." It wasn't Eden's business if Rachel indulged in a little underage drinking. Finding out what happened to Elouise—and potentially Neveah—*was*. "You were out there Friday?"

"I went with Neveah." She made a face. "She said high school boys were lame, but that didn't stop her from wanting to go."

"I knew girls like her when I was in high school." Though she hadn't been friends with them, mostly because she'd grown up perpetually on the outside. Back then, her peers had either taken a note from their parents' book and looked at her with suspicion—or they'd wanted to be friends with her so they could walk on the wild side. She hadn't had a use for either type of person. Eden eyed the way Rachel readjusted the flowers. "Did she take one of those high school boys out into the woods?"

"More often than not." She spoke so softly, it was barely more than a whisper. "Friday it was . . ." Her voice hitched. "God, this is stupid. *He's* stupid. If he really liked me that much, he wouldn't have chased after Neveah and hooked up with her. That's not how people act when they're actually into you."

Eden narrowed her eyes. "Which boy?"

"Christopher Jackson."

She made a mental note. "Did you see her afterward?"

"No. I"—she took a deep breath—"I left after that. I didn't want to cry in front of everyone, and I was upset."

"That's understandable."

"It's just so *wrong*. Neveah's supposed to be my friend. She's the one who said I should text him and ask him to the Sadie Hawkins this year, and then she turned around and hooked up with him just because she could. Why? She's beautiful and she could have any guy in school. Why did she have to have *him*?" Apparently the quiet support was all she needed to keep talking. Eden understood. Even if Rachel and her mother were close, some things were still hard to talk about.

It wasn't really her place to give this kid relationship advice, but she sounded so anguished, Eden couldn't help it. "I'll tell you something it took me a long time to figure out—people like that, both him and her, aren't worth your time. If she was really your friend, she wouldn't have hurt you like that. If he really was worthy of dating you, no other girl would do. It's not going to make you feel better right now, but it's the truth." What *really* wouldn't make the girl feel better was if her friend turned up dead.

Shit.

"Did you two ever go out to Elysia?"

Rachel blinked. "How did you know?"

Oh, fuck. Eden worked to keep her expression placid. "Let's call it an educated guess. And I'd bet it was Neveah's idea." Rachel might be prime picking for Martha and her people, but not yet. Then again . . . timid or not, the girl seemed to have a pretty legit support system, even without a father. *She'll do okay if given half a chance.*

"She wanted something *exciting.*" Rachel made a face. "I don't get what's so exciting about that place. It was a whole lot like going to church, though they weren't teaching stuff like any church I've been to."

Yeah, well, most churches didn't cover Persephone's fall. She made a sympathetic noise. "It's not as exciting as most people believe." At least not where civilians could witness it.

And sure as hell not the kind of exciting it seemed Neveah had been looking for.

"Neveah was sure there were other things—*secret* things—going on. She even made me go back a second time because she said one of the cute guys was sending her the look."

"The look?"

"You. You know, the *look.*" Rachel wrinkled her nose. "The one that says he wants to take her somewhere alone and, well, *you know.*"

The poor kid. She looked like she might die of embarrassment right then and there. "Got it." With the picture Rachel was painting, Neveah appeared to be rather free with her charms. Eden didn't particularly condemn her for that, but there were plenty of people who would.

Maybe Elouise had turned down the same man Neveah had seduced and then abandoned.

Women had been killed for less.

She tucked the thought away, focusing on the girl in front of her. "Did she happen to tell you the name of this guy?"

"No, but she said he was, well, black."

Lee.

◆ ◆ ◆

Zach knew something was up the second Eden walked out the front door. That little line had appeared between her brows, and though he found it charming, it meant nothing good. He waited until she'd slid into the passenger seat and he'd put Rachel's house in the rearview to ask, "Well?"

"What do you know about Lee?"

Not enough. "His name is Lee Whitby. He's not a bad sort, as such things go. I believe he rolled into town right around the time you left—that is, if I haven't misremembered."

"You haven't."

He waited, but she didn't give him any more. She just stared out the window like the forests edging up to the road held all the secrets of the universe. So Zach searched his memory for everything he knew about the man in question. It wasn't much. "He's not like Abram, or even Joseph. He seems to fly under the radar in town. I believe Martha sends him out for recruiting, though I couldn't begin to tell you where."

"The colleges. He's got soulful eyes—I bet the girls just eat it up, and the boys would want him to be friends, though they wouldn't understand why. I bet he's the reason recruitment is at an all-time high. I knew it the second I saw him today." She rubbed her eyes. "There are men and women like him in every cult. They're trained to push the right buttons to play on people's fears and dreams—and then manipulate them into joining up. He's got more raw talent in that department than training, but I could be wrong."

He didn't ask how she knew that. Eden seemed to know a lot about her mother's operations that she had no business knowing. Originally, he'd thought that meant something about her involvement with the cult. Now . . . now, he suspected that she'd been watching and waiting for the moment Martha stepped out of line, solely so she could bring Elysia crashing to the ground. He didn't fault her that, especially with some of the information she'd let slip. *Buried alive . . .*

He pushed that away to focus on the present. "Why are you asking about Lee?"

She finally turned to look at him. "He's got connections to both girls. He has a thing for Elouise, to the point where he was the lure Martha used to try to get her to stay. She ultimately didn't, but maybe he didn't handle it well. And apparently Neveah had her eye on him, and he indicated enough interest in her to get her back out to Elysia a second time."

Zach frowned. "Out of all the people out there, I'd think Lee would be the least likely to bring violence to the table."

"Do you know how many times I've heard a variation of that same thing?" She ran a hand through her hair, making the setting sun glint off the golden strands. The beauty of the view was dimmed by her next words. She pitched her voice so that it sounded like someone completely different. "'I had no idea. He was so normal. We played poker every Friday night. He was always there to help out when I needed it.'"

"From what I understand, a lot of people say that about serial killers."

"Organized ones, yes. And all facts point to this killer being exactly that." She pinned him in place with her dark eyes. "I need to see Elouise's body, Zach—or at least the coroner's report. I know you've gone over it, and I'm not saying you missed something, but there isn't another person in this investigation with my knowledge of Elysia and what goes on there. There might be some evidence or *something* that no one would notice but me."

He knew that. There was no real reason to keep that vital report from her—not now that he was reasonably sure she was on the up-and-up. But part of him still hesitated. "After dinner."

"Fine." One clipped word, leaving him with the feeling she didn't really want to see that report any more than he had. Something had happened out at the commune, something that had shaken her up.

He needed to know what. "You talked to Lee."

"I talked to Lee." She sighed. "I don't know. My first instinct is that he's innocent, but I can't trust my instincts when it comes to anything that has to do with Elysia. He's been there for a full decade, and in that time he's worked his way up the ranks enough to be as accomplished a liar as my mother is."

She doesn't know. Zach opened his mouth, then reconsidered. Ultimately, though, Eden had to know. "He's one of your mother's inner circle. Him, Joseph, and Abram."

She turned a narrow-eyed look on him. "There are *three* of them?"

Yeah, she most definitely hadn't known. "I'm not sure when she added the younger two, exactly, but about five years ago Joseph started doing some of the talking on Martha's behalf down in town, talking Abram used to take care of." He drummed his fingers on the steering wheel. "Joseph likes to brag, even to us lowly outsiders. He never goes into details, but it's clear that he's the third in command now. Lee is next."

"That's . . ." Eden shuddered. "Sorry, I'm having issues with the fact my mother is apparently sleeping with two men my age in addition to Abram, which is a mental exercise all its own. Hold on while I process." It took a grand total of thirty seconds before she gave another shudder and ran her hands through her hair. "That's . . . wow. I knew she'd added Joseph, but I hadn't realized Lee was as well. That changes things."

"How so?"

She sat back and then straightened, the very picture of nervous energy. "If Lee is in Martha's bed, that means she'd see both Elouise and Neveah as potential competition, especially if he's telling the truth about having a thing for Elouise. My mother does *not* take competition well."

Martha might be aging well, but she was still aging. It wouldn't be easy to see one of her personal men chasing after a girl almost young enough to be her granddaughter. Zach turned away from Clear Springs onto the highway. "This isn't narrowing the suspect pool any." Because if those girls were killed because of some wrong done to Martha, that didn't mean Martha was the one who pulled the trigger, so to speak. Or that she even knew it had been done on her behalf.

Though he had a hard time believing that anything happened in Elysia without her knowing about it.

"No, it really doesn't." Eden sighed, sounding so damn exhausted that he wanted to hug her. She looked up as he turned onto a dirt road leading deeper into the trees. "I don't suppose you're taking me out into the woods to kill me."

"Hardly." The forest parted, revealing the little patch of land that had been cleared, occupied by a small house with a massive porch. *His* house. "We need time to unwind and process all the information, so I'm going to cook you dinner, and we're going to spend an hour or two talking about anything except the case." She didn't look convinced, and he couldn't really blame her. He'd more or less steamrolled her into this meal, and he wasn't the least bit sorry about it. "Come on, Eden. You've got to eat. And, right now, your brain is running in circles like a rat on a wheel. It's not doing anyone any favors."

"I don't know what to think of you, Zach Owens."

Hell, he didn't know what to think of himself right now, either. This was a bad idea—possibly the worst idea—but he couldn't give two fucks.

CHAPTER SIXTEEN

Eden surveyed Zach's house. She was used to filing away information and using it to form opinions about the person who lived in a particular place, but it felt different with this man. The house was small, but it was charming and filled with character, from the shutters framing the windows to the hunter-green front door to the exposed timbers of the porch. That porch created the image of long summers spent lounging in the shade, and from the dual chimneys coming from the roof and back of the house, she could imagine curling up in front of a fire pit watching the snow fall.

This wasn't just a house.

This was a home.

"Eden?" From his tone, he'd said her name a few times.

She tried to paste a smile on her face, but it was nearly impossible with her heart trying to beat its way out of her throat. It wasn't like the fear she'd felt earlier. No, this was something infinitely more dangerous. "It's a nice house."

"Eden, I'm going to cook you dinner. You're looking at the place like you think I'm going to toss you in the oven and have *you* for dinner." He grinned when she finally looked at him. "Though maybe another time we can talk about it."

"Talk about it . . ." She blinked, his meaning hitting her like a freight train. He meant . . . *Oh, good lord.* She closed her eyes, trying to center herself, but she was assaulted with images of Zach on his knees before her, parting her legs and kissing her. Of him using his mouth to drive her out of her mind. Of her pulling him up her body to . . . *Stop it. This is not why you're here.*

But it was so hard to remember that when she opened her eyes to find him staring at her, blatant awareness written all over his face. He wanted her. "Zach." She started to tell him that this wasn't why she was here, that she had no interest in jumping into bed with *anyone*, but the words wouldn't come.

Because they were a damn lie.

"Come on." He turned, breaking the moment, and headed up the stairs to the front door.

She almost laughed when he opened it without unlocking it. *Of course* he didn't lock his front door. Eden followed, shaking her head. "You know, there's a killer on the loose. You might want to consider upping your personal security."

"I've got it covered." The sound of paws on the hardwood floor stopped her cold as two giant mastiffs raced down the hallway to throw themselves at Zach. She was shocked he didn't topple over under their combined weight, but he just laughed and took turns greeting them. Once that was done, his tone changed. "Down, boys."

He held out a hand. "Come here."

She took his hand before she could talk herself out of it, allowing him to tow her over to the giant animals. From their distinct brindle coloring and boxy heads, they looked like English mastiffs, which was where her knowledge of the breed ended. She swallowed hard. Eden wasn't *scared* of dogs, exactly, but they were each as large as she was. "Hello."

"This is Spot and Biscuit."

She froze. "You . . . you named them . . ."

"No." He laughed softly. "My nephew was here when I brought them home, and seeing as how he was three at the time, he had strong opinions on what a dog's name entailed."

It was all too easy to picture Zach with a small child. He had that feel, the one that said he'd make a great family man. That was, if one ignored the sharper edges lurking just beneath the surface. She gave each dog a careful pat and straightened to look around the house. The exposed-beam style of the porch carried over into the interior, which would have overwhelmed the rooms if not for the sharply pitched ceilings. The furniture all looked sturdy enough to hold a football team if one wandered in, but there wasn't much in the way of personal effects.

The mantel held a handful of pictures, but Zach was already moving into the kitchen, so she held off on her curiosity and followed him. The kitchen . . . *this* was the room that felt the most like Zach. If she didn't miss her guess, the cabinets were all custom-made, and the gas stovetop and double oven were definitely high-end. She watched him pull out well-loved pots and pans. "You love to cook."

"I love to cook." He went to the fridge and pulled out a pair of beers. "Want one? If you're more into wine, I think I have a bottle or two stashed for when my sister visits."

"Beer is fine." *But only one.* She was having issues around Zach while in complete control of her facilities, so she didn't like her odds if she drank too much. No, she needed her wits about her in order to not make an ass of herself. She accepted the bottle and sank onto the bar stool he pointed to at the island. It gave her a full view of the kitchen.

A full view of *Zach.*

Like every other time she'd been around him, he seemed perfectly at home with his surroundings. The only difference was that some part of him seemed more . . . relaxed . . . in his house. She studied his body language, trying to figure out what gave her that impression, and finally decided there were fewer tension lines bracketing his mouth. But that gave her entirely too much time to look at his mouth and remember how good it had felt on hers.

In an effort to keep herself on track—a losing battle if there ever was one—she said, "Do you have much family in town?" She seemed to remember a father who'd been the sheriff before him, and a sibling or two, but a lot could change in a decade.

"My dad and mom moved a bit farther out into the mountains—for the fishing, he says—and my brother took off for California a few years back to do some sort of independent contracting with computers. He makes it back for holidays, which is about as much as you can ask of Joe. My sister settled here, though. She's married and has three kids." He paused in the middle of tossing butter into a skillet. "Three kids and one on the way. Christ, the woman keeps breeding." For all the exasperation in the words, he had a smile on his face. The man obviously loved his family.

What would that be like?

Eden shut down the thought as fast as she could, but it didn't stop the stab of pain from hitting her in the chest. The *longing*. Family life hadn't been for her growing up, and she didn't think it'd be for her moving forward, either. She traveled three weeks out of four, and that wasn't even taking into account that Bureau divorce rates—that *any* law-enforcement divorce rates—were through the roof. It wasn't fair to chain herself to someone when she couldn't put the time and effort into actually making a relationship work. For fuck's sake, she didn't even know *how* to make a relationship work. She'd failed at every one she'd attempted.

It's not like she'd had a role model when it came to that sort of thing. Though Martha seemed capable of holding down whatever passed for a relationship with Abram, she hadn't stuck it out with whomever Eden's father was. And, call her crazy, but she had *no* interest in emulating what her mother and Abram had going on.

She tightened her grip on her beer, forcing herself back to the present. "That sounds nice."

"It is. And frustrating and infuriating and mostly great." He shrugged, piling up enough food on the kitchen island to feed a small army. "How do you feel about stir-fry?"

"Works for me." She wasn't sure she could eat anything at all, but she didn't think he'd appreciate her saying as much.

He started working some sort of voodoo at the stove. Eden wasn't exactly a whiz in the kitchen, and when she was on a case, her meals were usually found in a drive-through or a room-service menu. She hadn't had a home-cooked meal in . . . She took a quick drink of her beer. God, she wasn't even sure when the last time was. Ramen in her tiny apartment in Quantico didn't count. Not really.

Zach passed over a plate of cheese and crackers that she hadn't noticed him putting together. "Dinner's going to be a bit, and you didn't have lunch."

He really was a mother hen. It was . . . kind of nice.

Eden paired a cracker with a slice of cheese and nearly moaned. She'd expected Ritz and cheddar, and this was most definitely *not*. "Oh, my God."

Zach's grin had her fighting back a moan of a different sort. "Glad you like it." He turned back to the stove, leaving her staring at his wide shoulders that tapered down to a waist his jeans seemed designed to show off. She'd never been an ass woman, but for him, she might be willing to make an exception. He was like some golden god who'd wandered into this strangely domestic scene, and she didn't know how to reconcile the two conflicting impressions.

That's not why I'm here . . . except it kind of is. The problem was that she didn't know much about him beyond the superficial. He might be the golden boy of Clear Springs, but it was the shadows in his eyes that intrigued her—the shadows that were akin to her own. "Why did you join the Marines?"

"Because I was young and stupid, and it seemed a glorious thing to be part of." He glanced at her over his shoulder, eyeing the plate until she took another bite. "Don't get me wrong—I loved being part of the Marines. It's not something you ever really leave behind, you know?"

"I know." Every single Marine she'd met, no matter how long out of the Corps, still identified as a Marine, present tense. She doubted he was any different. That didn't explain the darkness, though. "But?"

"But war is ugly and monstrous, and I wasn't prepared. I don't know if you *can* be prepared. I didn't realize how much I valued what Clear Springs had to offer until I was out in the world, seeing how horrific people act toward one another if given half the chance."

It was a different side of human nature than the one-on-one or small-group violence that she usually experienced with her job. War was . . . something else altogether. "And now it's happening here."

He transferred meat—chicken, she was pretty sure—to a cutting board and started chopping it up. "And now it's happening here. I'm taking it too personally, and I know I'm taking it too personally, but it doesn't seem to matter, because this is *my* town, and some monster is hurting *my* people."

"Do you often collect people you consider yours?" The joke fell flat, full of things she wasn't sure how to put into words.

He shrugged. "Call it a habit I've never been able to escape."

Would you collect me *if given half a chance?* She wasn't sure how she felt about that. The very thing she'd initially resented about him—the fact that he fit here—was a strength in its own way. No matter how striking the chemistry between them, she and Zach were as different as a circle and a square. They just didn't *fit.*

She needed to remember that.

CHAPTER SEVENTEEN

Zach wasn't sure what he'd said to make Eden shut down, but she spent the rest of prepping and the meal itself steering the conversation to safe, meaningless topics. He didn't mind, exactly. Small talk had its time and place, and he'd promised her a night when they could tune out the case and relax as much as possible. He couldn't very well start demanding she share her deepest secrets with him that same night. He finished his last bite, watching her closely. "You don't seem to have much of an appetite."

"No, I don't." She stopped playing with her food and set her fork to the side. "Some people stress eat, but I'm usually the exact opposite. Spending any amount of time with my mother does that to me."

He sat back. "You don't live in this town as long as I have and not hear rumors about what goes on up in Elysia once they've cleared out all the folk who don't actually live there. From what you've said, it's worse than people think. You don't have to tell me more for me to know that."

She blinked those dark eyes at him. "How generous of you."

"Not really." It didn't *feel* generous. He felt like he had back when he was in his early twenties and had gone hunting with his old man. He was a bit out of practice with both, but being around Eden reminded him of being out there, the cold biting through the layers of his gear, the bow heavy in his hand, and having to hold his body perfectly still to avoid startling the deer that was just out of range.

The only difference was his end goal.

He kept his voice pitched low, his words steady and slow. "I figure you've seen a thing or two that's enough to give anyone a lifetime of nightmares, and I'm not the kind of man who would ask you to break yourself open for my curiosity. There are things that happened in the desert that I have no desire to think about, let alone talk about. I expect it's the same for you."

"Then why bring it up at all?"

That was the damn question. He lifted his hands and let them fall in a half shrug. "I don't know. I want to know more about you."

Eden picked up her fork and then set it down again. "You have a strange way of going about it."

"It's a strange situation."

A small smile pulled at the edges of her mouth. "That it is." It was a great mouth. The kind of mouth that could tempt a man to thoughts of things best done naked and in the dark. He jerked his gaze to her eyes, and the knowledge there threatened to take his breath away. She was as aware of him as he was of her, and she wanted him, too. *Fuck, that's going to make it hard to keep control.*

She pulled her hair over one shoulder, braiding a small lock without looking down. It was the first nervous move he'd seen her make. Nothing seemed to faze the woman—not facing down one of the scariest motherfuckers Zach had ever come across, and not blazing back into a situation she'd fought tooth and nail to get out of. It was downright astounding.

What if you were ever called back into action?

He'd go. He didn't even have to think about it. But it would be hard, and he'd face things he never wanted to face again. Zach scrubbed a hand over his face. "Do you watch movies? Read? Listen to music?"

"No, yes, yes."

He opened his eyes. "That was very specific."

Eden's smile widened, her eyes lighting up, just a little. "I'm a fan of immersive experiences. With the work, well, you're getting the idea with this case. It can take over everything, until you're obsessing every moment that you're awake, and then you go to sleep and you dream about it. I almost burned out my first year." She made a face. "I would have, too, if my partner hadn't stepped in. Vic. He's a good guy, and he'd been there. So I started taking time and reading, listening to music. I got back into the habit of playing."

"Playing?"

She dropped the braid and started on another lock of hair. "I can play a mean fiddle when provoked."

As soon as she said the words, he could almost see it, her fingers dancing across the strings, her eyes closed in concentration, that little line present between her brows as she became a conduit for the music. Zach leaned forward. "How long have you played?"

"Since I was nine. It was one of the extracurricular programs offered in school."

"I remember." He'd thought about it, but getting up early to be driven to the high school to learn an instrument had seemed like too much sacrifice. "I'm surprised Martha allowed it."

"She didn't want to. As far as she's concerned, the violin is the devil's instrument—or Hades', as it were." She shrugged, her expression becoming shuttered again. "I didn't give her a choice. I was a terror even at that age."

There was tension beneath the words, and he got the feeling that Martha might have given in publicly, but she'd punished Eden for it all the same. The woman didn't like to be contradicted, and though she might cover that fact up with smiles and sweet words, Zach had seen the hard glint in her eyes enough times that he'd second-guessed joining up back when he'd been interested. He didn't like liars much, and there wasn't another word for presenting one personality to the public and a completely different one in private.

Needing to steer them back to safer territory—if there even was such a thing—he said, "I'd like to hear you play sometime."

"Sure. Maybe." It wasn't quite an agreement, but it wasn't a no, either. Eden pushed to her feet and stretched her arms over her head, the move making her T-shirt ride up and revealing a sliver of pale skin. There were tattoos there, too, though he got only the barest hint of blue-black ink before she lowered her arms. It didn't matter. Zach was pretty sure that image was permanently tattooed on the inside of his brain, his body surging to attention and his brain temporarily checking out. He jerked his gaze to her face, and the awareness there only made his control slip through his fingers faster. "Eden."

"Zach." Just that. Just his name. But it felt like she'd reached across the distance between them and touched him. She smiled, the expression a little wistful. "You have a bed in this place?"

Shock temporarily stole his breath. "I didn't invite you here for that."

"No, but you invited me here for a distraction." She raised her eyebrows. "I think taking me to bed would qualify."

He didn't feel like *he* was taking her anywhere. Then there was the fact that he didn't particularly like serving as a distraction and nothing more to Eden. Damn it, he *liked* Eden. He didn't know what was going on between them, but he knew it was worth more than a quick fuck.

Zach took a deep breath, reining in his desire. He got the feeling that if he took her up on what she was offering tonight, he would never get a real shot with the woman. He stood. "Eden."

"I know that tone of voice. You're about to let me down gently." Her smile this time looked definitely more sad than wistful. "It's okay. Really."

That wasn't it. He pushed to his feet and circled around the table to stand in front of her. "Let me tell you something."

"I'd rather you not." But he wasn't going to let her get away that easily. Zach waited, watching her closely, and she finally sighed. "I'm listening."

This is definitely more similar to hunting with Dad than I'm used to. He closed the last of that distance between them, until their chests brushed with each breath. Her scent, something warm and summery, wrapped around him, more intoxicating than the best kind of whiskey. His gaze dropped to her mouth, the only part of her that seemed soft, no matter how cold her expression.

It's not cold right now.

No, she looked hot enough to burn the house down around them. She blinked dark eyes at him, her blonde hair a tumble around her shoulders, her breath coming too fast, and for one eternal moment he put serious consideration into throwing caution to the wind and taking her up on her offer. Only the truth that he'd never get a second shot stopped him.

Mostly.

He cupped the back of her neck. "Both of us deserve to be more than a conveniently timed distraction in the middle of a shitshow case."

"Sweet of you to make excuses, but—"

He kissed her. It was meant to shut her up and stop her from making excuses he didn't need, but the second his mouth made contact, it developed into something else entirely. *I should stop. I'm the one putting the brakes on this, but . . .*

He didn't stop.

He held her closer, tighter, as if the contact would center him. It did the exact opposite, shredding what was left of his control and setting fire to his world. Her tongue stroked his, her hands fisting the front of his shirt. She pulled back enough to say, "Zach, please." Just that, but there was so much more beneath the words.

Please don't stop. Please help me forget.

He knew all about wanting to forget. There had been weeks on end without sleep when he got back from the desert, weeks when he slept on the floor because the thick mattress was too foreign to him, weeks when he disappeared into the woods because he wasn't sure if he could tell friend from enemy with the shit going on in his head.

He'd gotten past it.

Looking down at her now, he recognized a kindred spirit. There had been layers beneath her comments earlier. She'd gone through more shit than just growing up in Elysia. He didn't miss the two years unaccounted for between her leaving Clear Springs and enrolling in the FBI academy. She'd done what it took to survive. She didn't have to tell him details for him to know that.

What would it do to him if the military came calling? To walk off the plane into the dry desert heat and know that he was going to a place where an enemy could take the form of anyone, no matter how inconspicuous?

What lengths would he go to escape that reality, even if only for a few hours?

I can't deny her this.

I can't deny either one of us.

"I want more from you than just sex."

Her smile was more than a little bittersweet. "Sex is the only thing on the table."

For now.

He might not know everything there was to know about Eden Collins, but he knew enough. He wasn't willing to pass that up without exploring what might lie between them, but he understood her enough to know that if he said that aloud, she'd be gone before he finished his sentence.

Zach kissed her again, drawing her against him, offering the distraction she craved. Reality would be there in a few hours. Right now there was only her and him and how good she felt in his arms.

"Come on." He led the way out onto the back porch, closing the door between them and the dogs. The night had cooled to just this side of warm, the crisp fall air not doing a damn thing to clear his head. Eden was more intoxicating than the best alcohol, and he wasn't about to let go of her.

She looked around, raising her eyebrows in question, but he didn't give her a chance to comment, pulling her down to straddle him on the porch swing he'd installed against the back of the house. Eden glanced over her shoulder to where the woods were shadowed in encroaching darkness. "Anyone could be watching."

"They'd have a hell of a hike to get out here, and the dogs would bark if they sensed anyone." He coasted his hands up her sides and back down again. "The fresh air makes it easier to think."

She laughed softly. "Thinking is not high on my list." Eden leaned down and captured his mouth, and he wasted no time lacing his fingers through her hair and holding her in place while he explored her thoroughly. If he'd hoped the change of venue would calm his need for her, he was so wrong it wasn't even funny. She was fire in his blood, a temptation he couldn't afford, but he didn't care.

Time lost meaning. There was only her body against his, his tongue stroking hers, his hands on her body. Every time he touched her, she made a desperate little sound that drove him wild.

He couldn't stop.

He didn't want to.

Zach pulled her shirt off and dropped it on the bench next to him, and then sat back and just looked at her. Her tattoos traced down her chest, framing her breasts without encroaching on them, and then descended down her ribs to tease her hip bones. He traced a line, a phoenix in the midst of a flame. "You have a lot of ink."

"Call it compulsion. I couldn't . . ." She shuddered. "Let's not talk about this."

He heard what she didn't say—she couldn't stand the thought of the only ink on her body being from Elysia.

He kissed her sternum, and then first one collarbone and then the other. "You're beautiful."

"And you talk too much." She pulled his shirt off, lightly dragging her nails across his chest. The sensation made his cock jump, and from the look in her eyes, she felt it. Eden stopped just north of his jeans. "You're not going to do the noble thing and try to put a stop to this, are you?"

"You say stop, we stop."

Once again, the smile she gave him was so bittersweet it made his chest ache. "You are the real thing, Sheriff Owens, white knight extraordinaire."

He didn't argue with her, because what was the point? There was nothing wrong with wanting to take care of his people—to take care of *her*. Eden might not see it that way, but then it was obvious she'd been taking care of herself for her entire life.

She leaned down, her lips brushing his ear. "I'm about to take advantage of you, Zach. So stop thinking so hard and just enjoy it."

"Hard to do otherwise when you put it like that." He huffed out a laugh, the sound dying in his throat when she slithered down between his thighs and went for the button of his jeans. "Eden—"

She already had the button undone and his cock free before he could figure out how to finish the sentence. The sight of her on her knees before him, gripping his length with one hand, a wicked amusement in her eyes . . . it flat out did it for him.

And when she took him into her mouth, sucking hard, he was pretty damn sure he'd died and gone to heaven.

Eden was the kind of woman who took no prisoners in life, and apparently that mind-set transferred to sex as well, because she didn't bother teasing him. She stroked him with one hand while working him with her mouth, using her tongue and lips to drive him to the edge in record time. *"Eden."*

"I like the way you say my name." She licked the underside of his cock, flicking him with her tongue. "Do it again."

It struck him that he might be on the far side of out of control, but she was fully aware. *That won't do.* He hooked the back of her neck and towed her up his body, taking her mouth even as he started on her jeans. Getting them off was impossible, but he settled for pushing them far enough down her hips that he could dip his hand into her panties. She was soaking wet, and she moaned as he slid a finger into her, using the palm of his hand to rub her clit with each stroke.

She took his cock again, resuming her pace even as he pushed her closer and closer to orgasm. The quiet of the night was broken only by her gasps and his harsh breathing. It was good, too damn good. He broke their kiss, nibbling his way down her neck to the sensitive spot where it met her shoulder. "Come for me, Eden. Let go." He twisted his wrist, flicking his fingers over that sensitive spot inside her.

"You, too."

That wasn't going to be an issue. He was hanging on by a thread.

Zach kissed her again, losing himself in the feel of her, her body twining tighter and tighter until she cried out his name as she came.

Even in the midst of her pleasure, she never lost her grip on him, stroking him, driving him crazy. He came with a curse.

Eden laid her head on his shoulder. "Not going to lie. I feel better."

Hell, he did, too. Zach rearranged them, using his shirt to clean himself up, and then tucked her against his chest. It felt good to have her here, in his house and in his arms. Too damn good.

CHAPTER EIGHTEEN

Eden stared at the coroner's report, her mind a million miles away. No, not a million miles—just across town with the man who'd rocked her world not an hour ago. Her body still pulsed with remembered pleasure and he hadn't even gotten her pants all the way off. If he could do that with his hands, what would it be like to have access to his entire body?

She wanted it. She wanted it desperately.

Eden knew all too well that sex would only further complicate things between them because she couldn't just catch a flight out of town the next morning. They had to work together until they figured out what the hell was going on with the cult, and adding the awkward morning-after conversations that inevitably arose would just waste time no one had.

But if he'd so much as crooked his finger after that insane orgasm, she would have been naked and in his bed, no questions asked.

It stung that he hadn't, but his response . . . She shivered, a small smile pulling at the edges of her lips. *What a response.* She allowed herself a few more minutes of reliving the way his body had felt against hers, the way he'd taken charge without being pushy, how freaking good he'd tasted . . .

And then Eden set it aside.

As good as it had been, there were more important things to focus on. Zach had Chase watching Elysia to ensure Lee didn't sneak out, but he was right that everything they had was circumstantial and secondhand information. They *could* bring him in, but it would antagonize Martha and show their hand before they had anything that could stick. As he'd said when he dropped her at the bed-and-breakfast, making eyes at a teenager wasn't illegal—if it had even happened. While she agreed that Lee didn't seem the type, stranger things had happened.

And maybe I just want to pin this on Martha and her flock so badly, it's coloring my perception.

There was nothing else to do tonight but read through the report and see if anything popped out at her. Tomorrow, she'd go back out to Elysia and see if she could corner Beth into giving her the information the woman obviously had. She'd approach it as trying to get back in contact, but she didn't like her odds of a second visit to Elysia without Martha insisting on some time together. Eden's stomach lurched, but she muscled the instinctive response down. She'd faced Abram and Martha multiple times since she'd been back in town, and she hadn't been threatened or kidnapped or even turned away. There was no empirical evidence to back up her physical and emotional responses.

But then, each victim deals with things in their own way. Facing down their abusers is the single hardest thing most victims deal with.

She didn't like to think of herself like that—as a *victim*. She'd fought long and hard to take control of her life, to stop free-falling and reacting and start being *proactive*. To admit she was anything other than in charge of her own destiny felt like admitting failure.

But she'd be an even bigger fool to ignore the reaction she had to being back in Clear Springs.

Her past was like any other injury—she needed to take it into account because there was a chance she might freeze up, or mix up her fight-or-flight responses in a conflict, or react in some unexpected way. Ignoring the issue wasn't going to make it go away, no matter how much she wished it was so.

And you're most definitely stalling.

She picked up the mug of instant coffee she'd made the second she walked into the room. She was too riled up to sleep, and even if she tried, all the markings were there to indicate that nightmares would chase her through her dreams. Better to just skip it altogether. She couldn't do that indefinitely, but one night wouldn't kill her.

Still stalling.

She sank into the love seat that backed up against the bay window in her room, coffee in one hand and the coroner's report in the other. It was time. She hadn't been so tweaked about the thought of reading the report before she'd gotten her little present today, and part of Eden kept saying she was as narcissistic as her mother if she really thought these murders had anything at all to do with her. What were the odds?

Better than I'd like.

She opened the report and began to read. Zach had gone over the basics with her, so she wasn't surprised at the long list cataloging Elouise Perkins's many bruises and healed broken bones. Fury stole Eden's breath at the pain and suffering this girl had gone through even before the killer set his—or her—eyes on her. *Him. Definitely him.* She swallowed hard at the detailed description of the evidence that the girl had had sex within twenty-four hours of her death. No, not sex. It appeared there had been nothing consensual about it.

Damn it.

Eden set the report down carefully and took an equally careful drink of her coffee. She'd read worse reports in her years in the Bureau. Reports concerning children or torture or any number of things that gave her nightmares plenty of fodder—as if she didn't have enough already. But none of those other victims had been connected quite as closely to Eden.

Steeling herself, she picked up the report and started reading again. She froze at the description of the newly inked tattoos. She'd known they existed—the ones in the picture were what had brought her back here in the first place—but she hadn't realized there were *four.*

She flipped through the pictures beneath the written report, setting each of the tattoos out and tracing them with her gaze. The picture that had brought her back to Clear Springs in the first place had been at a distance—close enough to identify the newly inked tattoo, but the dirt and bruises had kept her from seeing it clearly.

Now that she could, she picked out differences between the tattoos on the dead girl and the ones Martha gave each cult member. They weren't particularly clear to the untrained eye, but there were hesitation marks throughout the lines. Eden traced the bat with her finger. The differences could have been because the victim fought. That would make sense.

But Eden didn't think so.

I fought every single tattoo my mother gave me, and there still weren't hesitation marks like this.

She turned to the key. It had the same hesitation marks she'd seen on the others, but that didn't change the fact that it existed at all. No one had that tattoo except Eden, Persephone to her mother's Demeter. No one even *knew* about that tattoo.

She dropped the pictures and surged to her feet. *Maybe I'm just being paranoid. Or maybe I'm* not *paranoid, but I'm so used to being paranoid that I'm ignoring evidence because I really, really don't want this girl to have died to bring me back here.* She walked to where she'd tossed her phone onto the middle of the bed and dialed numbly. It wasn't until she heard her boss's answer that the time registered. *It's one a.m. on the East Coast.* Not that she could be certain Britton was in Quantico—he traveled nearly as often as his teams did.

"Eden."

She took a deep breath. "I'm in trouble."

"Tell me." No recrimination, no telling her that coming to Clear Springs in the first place was a bad idea. Just a calm order for more information.

Some of the tension bled out of her shoulders. "You're familiar with the case."

It wasn't quite a question, but he answered all the same. "I'm up-to-date."

She didn't ask how that was, since Britton made a habit of knowing things he couldn't possibly know. It was just one of those things people started taking for granted after a while. When she'd first become an agent, she'd harbored half a dozen theories on how he knew the things he did, ranging from a complex network of informants to a crystal ball, but she'd stopped questioning it. He was just that good.

Eden's gaze tracked back to the photos. "I'm more connected than I first thought. I share a tattoo with the dead girl—I'm the *only* one who shares that tattoo. Before you say coincidence—"

"Eden, I would point out that you sharing such a prominent trait with the victim—in addition to the superficial similarities *and* the connection with the Elysians—is unlikely to be a coincidence."

"I know that. *You* trained me to know that." She sank onto the sofa, her heart in her throat. "Someone left me a present today. I'm reasonably sure I left my car locked, but it's possible I didn't, because this place messed with my head."

Britton was silent for a beat and then another. "You need to convince Sheriff Owens to officially ask for BAU assistance. Once he does, I'll send in Vic."

"Britton—" She stopped her instinctive denial that she needed help. If she was in his position, she'd do the same thing. "You're right."

"Bring me up-to-date."

"We have one girl dead, and another who could be her sister in the looks department missing. Every point of the way, there is evidence linking up to me—to my past." She went over the case one point at a time. "The cult is centered around the very idea of the prodigal daughter—I fit the bill. I had no intention of ever coming back, and everyone associated with Elysia during the time I was there knows that, so I have to assume the new recruits would know as well. Both the girl killed and the girl missing are petite with dark hair and dark eyes. I'm blondish now, but as a teenager my hair was the same color. The girl who was found has the same tattoos I do, and I think it's safe to say she wasn't any more consenting to them than I was." She clamped her mouth shut. She hadn't meant to say that last bit aloud. When Britton didn't say anything, she straightened and continued, "Add to that the fact that someone has left me a present, and I'm reasonably sure there was someone in my room while I was gone, and it's hard to think I'm *not* connected to this somehow."

"You know as well as I do that psychology and profiling are vital components to what we do, and everything you've just told me leads me to believe it's personal. If it's personal, Eden, that means you're somehow involved, whether you want to be or not." He sighed. "Frankly, I wish it weren't. You're too close to this case because of your mother and your history, and if I could get you out of town right now, I would."

"It wouldn't matter." The truth held her immobile, but she had to get it out. "If we're right, the killer will come after me. It's only a matter of time."

"It is."

It was almost a relief to acknowledge that—to have it confirmed by a person she trusted. She turned and looked through the crack in the curtains to the darkness beyond. "Good."

"Except . . ." Her relief faded before it could take hold, the truth making her sick to her stomach. "Neveah is still missing. If I'm right, then I'm the endgame. The unsub isn't through with whatever he or she is planning."

Which meant there would be more victims.

CHAPTER NINETEEN

Neveah couldn't breathe. She clawed at the loose dirt, panic making her movements jerky. How long had she been holding her breath? It felt like an eternity. She fought harder against the weight pressing her down, dragging her body toward the surface.

What if it's not the surface? What if I'm clawing deeper into the earth?

Before that thought could take root, her hand shot into the air. She renewed her efforts, gasping and choking as her head cleared the ground. It was hard to pull the rest of her body to freedom, harder than anything she'd ever done in her life.

But the thought of what might happen if *he* found her helpless like this kept her moving.

She pushed to her feet, weaving. Before her, the hills rolled east, gravity pulling at her, demanding that she run screaming into the night. Clear Springs was *right there*. She'd never been that good at eyeballing distances, but it couldn't be more than a few miles. She took a step, and then another. A hand came down on the back of her neck, holding her in place. "Not yet, Persephone."

No, no, no. I was so close! She bit the cry back, the truth sinking into her chest, heavier than his hand against her skin. She'd never been free.

She'd never even had a chance. It was just a sick game he was playing with her for his own amusement.

The woman was even worse.

After each beating and . . . Her mind shied away from the things he'd done to her. The moment she'd curl in on herself and listen to his footsteps across the dirt floor, *she'd* come sit next to Neveah and stroke her hair and tell her how beautiful and important and *vital* she was.

Neveah preferred the beatings. At least they were honest.

He moved closer, and she couldn't stop herself from cringing away from him. The soft feminine laughter behind them told her all she needed to know. After all, the woman liked to watch. The man's grip tightened. "It's time for you to earn your place. You never were much good at that before now, but it's your chance to change that—to change *everything.*"

She didn't know what the hell he was talking about. The two times she'd been out to the cult, she hadn't paid much attention to what that bitch was going on about. Maybe if she had, she wouldn't be in this mess to begin with . . .

A mess she wasn't sure she was going to make it out of.

She'd seen the movies. If these two were holding her for ransom, they would have taken a picture with a newspaper or something to show proof of life. They wouldn't have hurt her for fear they wouldn't get paid—not that her parents had much money, but there was her college fund to think of. A sob worked its way up her throat, bursting from her mouth. *College.* She'd taken it for granted. All of it. The future. College. Boys. That she'd live to see eighteen, twenty-one, even the much-distant thirty.

She looked at the sky, the imprint of the man's hand digging into the sensitive skin of her throat.

I don't think I'll live to see tomorrow.

"Run, Persephone." His lips touched her ear, his breath unnaturally hot against her cold skin. "If you can make it home, you will be free."

Neveah Smith ran.

Eden started awake, a nightmare she couldn't quite remember leaving her breathless with fear. She winced when the sudden move jarred her back muscles, out of whack from sleeping half curled on the sofa. She cursed and rolled her shoulders, trying to relieve the tension. A quick glance at the clock made her curse again. *Nine a.m.* "How the hell?"

The answer lay on the nightstand, blinking at her incessantly. "Oh, no, I didn't." She snatched up her phone and had a moment of wishing she'd melt into a puddle on the floor. *I don't even remember putting it on silent.* She never did, and sure as hell not while on an active case, officially or not. Eden thumbed through her messages, finding a text from Vic saying he was catching a flight out that evening as soon as he wrapped up a few things in Michigan, another from Britton repeating that information, and four from Zach of increasing worry.

A knock sounded on her door, and she jumped half out of her skin. "What the hell?" She stumbled to the door and opened it, blinking at the big brunet on the other side. It took her sleep-plagued mind precious seconds to connect name with face. "Chase."

Zach's deputy looked her up and down, but more like he was searching for injuries than checking her out. "The sheriff was worried."

He shouldn't worry about me. She bit the words back at the last moment. The truth was shaping up to be that Zach *should* worry about her. And she hadn't answered her phone, so he wasn't exactly out of line to send someone to make sure she was okay. "I'm fine."

"I see that." He stepped back, as if aware he was looming. "Owens says you'll want to be there for the interview."

She blinked. "What interview?" Damn them both, why had she let him talk her into that whole *break* thing last night? If they'd gone over the case, she'd be up-to-date instead of finding this crap out now. She glanced at her phone. Then again, if she hadn't overslept, she would already be at the station.

"Sheriff brought in Lee Whitby this morning."

"*What?*" Hadn't they just talked about how there wasn't enough evidence to do exactly that?

Chase nodded. "He got a call this morning from little Rachel Carpenter's mom—turns out she left out a pretty important piece of information yesterday when she talked to you."

Eden wasn't surprised. The kid had been as skittish as a cat in a room full of rocking chairs. In fact, she'd had half a thought to talk to the girl again to see if she could pry loose any more information. While Chase watched, she grabbed her keys and phone. "What did she say?"

"Turns out Neveah did more than make eyes at Lee. She told Rachel she, uh, got up close and personal with both him and Joseph Edwards."

She froze. "Say that again." He did, and the words didn't make any more sense to her the second time. "*Both* of them?"

"That's what Owens is going to try to figure out." He relayed all the information with a reserve that she'd seen before. Deputy Chase Moudy didn't believe they were going to find Neveah alive, and he was already trying to distance himself from her memory, albeit subconsciously.

Eden didn't blame him, and she didn't call him out on it. She just shrugged into her jacket. "Let's go."

"Forgive me for pointing it out, ma'am, but you're wearing the same shirt you were yesterday."

"Damn it." She almost said *Screw it*, but the fact was, she didn't need any more marks against her as far as Clear Springs went. They already thought she was as dangerous as her mother. She didn't need them thinking she was loony, too.

"Seems like you're having a rough time, being back here and all."

She started to shut him down but paused. There were a grand total of three cops in Clear Springs—alienating one-third of them would be a mistake. Still, she hesitated. She wasn't inclined to rip herself open just to appease his curiosity. "It's an adjustment—though it sounds like you've had one yourself."

His mouth tightened, just a bit. "Came out here for a change of pace. The city and I didn't get along all that well." Something in his tone discouraged questions.

Fine by her. She was already tired of this conversation. She nodded at him. "Give me five minutes to change."

"I'll be downstairs in the cruiser."

It took her three to change her clothes, throw on some deodorant, and drag a comb through her hair. It went up into its customary pony-tail, and she paused long enough to check the truly attractive circles forming beneath her eyes. They'd get worse before she was through with this town, so she might as well make her peace with them. Hell, the only reason she checked at all was because of Zach, and that was stupid beyond belief. She had bigger things to worry about. She needed to remember that.

By the time they made it to the station, Zach was closeted with Lee, and a grim-faced Henry stood outside the door. He shook his head as they approached. "He's grilling the kid up good. Anyone going in there is going to break his flow."

Eden peered around him through the tiny window to see Zach bent over the table, his hands braced, his face expressionless. He didn't appear to be yelling, but Lee cringed repeatedly, his head down and his shoulders bowed.

It's not him.

She didn't realize she'd spoken aloud until Henry answered her.

"Evidence says otherwise."

"I haven't exactly put together a fully comprehensive profile of the unsub, but there are certain traits that he *has* to have to fit this type of killing. This guy is a dominant personality, and when confronted by an authority figure, he wouldn't be able to hide his derision. He thinks he's superior, and if he bows to anyone, it's not going to be someone in law enforcement."

Henry frowned, the lines across his face seeming to fold in on one another. "You sure think you know a lot about a guy who's little more than a ghost."

Except he wasn't. A ghost didn't kill, and a ghost sure as hell didn't break into cars to leave presents. These killings weren't murders of opportunity. He'd stalked Elouise. He'd created a place to hold the girl for more than a week, and then he'd most likely allowed her to run to fulfill some kind of twisted fantasy of his. Was he sick? Beyond a shadow of a doubt. But organized. Cold. Not the type of personality to be shaken by a single cop, no matter how strong Zach's personality was. She lifted her chin. "He wouldn't cower. I'd stake my badge on it."

"He could be faking." This from Chase, who'd taken up a post a little farther down the hall, though he hadn't stood still for more than a heartbeat. *Nerves and a whole lot of anger.* He seemed to take Elouise's death personally—more personally than anyone else she'd come across, except maybe Zach. *He blames himself, though part of him must know it's bullshit. If push comes to shove, he's going to be a loose cannon.*

She wanted to snap back but forced herself to respond calmly. "He could fake for only a little while. Interrogation rooms are designed to break people. Yeah, there are criminals who can sit in there for days on end and not be the least bit ruffled, but Lee isn't one of them. If Zach's to be believed—and I don't see why he wouldn't be—the guy hasn't so much as stepped up to the line, let alone over it, in ten years. Even if he was into all sorts of trouble as a kid, a decade is enough to kill any habit. And *even if* it wasn't, *that* is not how a hardened criminal—or a sociopath—acts." She pointed at the window again.

But Chase wasn't backing down. *Loose cannon.* He stalked from one wall to the other and back again, never taking his gaze off her. "Then how does a hardened criminal act?"

Once again, she tried to stay calm. It was a legitimate question, and getting snappy with the man wasn't going to do either one of them any favors. *No wonder he didn't last in homicide. They deal with murder day in and day out. A cop can't be tipping over the edge of the deep end after the first one.* "Calm, cocky—take your pick. They don't *cower.*"

Or maybe Britton was right and she really was too close to this case to do anything but cause problems.

CHAPTER TWENTY

Zach knew the moment Eden showed up, though he didn't acknowledge her presence on the other side of the door. Lee Whitby was seconds away from breaking, and he wasn't going to give the guy a chance to recoup his control—or for Martha to show up and start causing problems. "Walk me through it again."

"We've gone over this ten times." There wasn't any anger there—just wretched defeat. Lee dropped his head into his hands, his voice muffled but still clear. "I asked Elouise to stay. We spent a lot of time together after I stepped in with her dad."

"After you threatened him." He didn't really blame Lee for the threat—Zach wanted to do that and more to Michael Perkins. The difference was that Zach wouldn't take that step, and if Lee had done that, it was possible he was capable of much worse.

He lifted his head. "Yes. I liked her. She was a good girl in a bad situation, and I know a thing or two about that."

"Right. From your past." He'd done some digging last night and made a few calls to the precinct in Detroit, which was where Lee originated. He had a sealed record from when he was a minor, but Zach had gotten in contact with the detective who worked the case all those years ago. Nothing much memorable about it, but the man had been able to confirm that it was breaking and entering. It was a far cry from holding a girl hostage for days on end, torturing her, and then ultimately strangling her in a field a few feet from a road, but it was something.

He just wished it didn't feel so much like he was stretching.

"I have a past. Everyone does."

This was his opening, clear as day. So far he'd danced around Lee's relationship with Elouise. As Eden suspected, it was clear that the man had strong feelings for the girl, though he maintained his story that he'd stood back and let her go. There wasn't any anger, apparently—only grief. It didn't mean it wasn't there, simmering deep, though. Zach just needed to find the right button to push.

"You have a past with Neveah Smith."

Lee blinked at him, frowned, and blinked again. "I don't . . ." He shook his head as if trying to clear it. "I know that name. Neveah. Isn't she a local teenager? I think she's been out to Elysia a few times."

If he was acting, he deserved an Oscar. That didn't stop Zach from pressing. "Cute that you're playing dumb, but I hear you know her in more of a biblical sense."

Lee went stock-still. "That's impossible. I think I met the girl once."

Still no anger. Only shock. Either he's that good or we've got the wrong guy. "Her best friend says Neveah snuck off Friday night to meet you for sex." He barely waited a beat. "Where is she, Lee? Her parents are out of their minds with worry, and the whole town is up in arms. They just want her home. They don't care about anything else." He did, but he wasn't above misleading the man if it meant Neveah would be returned safely.

Lee shot to his feet. "I don't know what you're talking about. I think I might have said hello to her, but I do that with any outsider who visits Elysia. That's my *job*. I wouldn't have been alone with her under normal circumstances, not with her being a minor, but I especially wouldn't because of Elouise." He ran his hands over his face, then dropped them to his side with a defeated sigh. "I loved her." There was no mistaking the *her* he meant.

Zach opened his mouth, but the creak of the door distracted him. He turned to cuss out whoever had disobeyed the order not to interrupt, but the look on Henry's face stopped him cold. The older man's skin was gray, and the haunted look in his eyes told Zach what he needed to know before the man opened his mouth. "The search party found Neveah Smith."

It didn't take a genius to understand they hadn't found her alive.

He headed for the door and then spun on his heel. "You: don't move."

For his part, Lee looked just as shocked as if he'd had no idea the girl would wind up dead. He held up his hands. "I want to find Elouise's killer, the same as you. I'll help in whatever way I can."

"We'll see." He walked out of the room and closed the door softly behind him. "What do we know?"

It was Chase who spoke, his voice unnaturally hoarse. "Hakeem Ahmed's team found her. She's off Prairie Road, in the ditch. They almost stumbled over her."

Just like Elouise, though she was a whole lot closer to town than the other girl had been. He hesitated when he drew even with Eden. "You're not officially part of the investigation."

"I know." Her mouth was tight, but she didn't show any other signs of distress. He wanted to reach out to her, to hug her, to tell her this wasn't her fault, but he didn't do anything. This wasn't the time or place. She pulled at the end of her ponytail. "I'm going back out to Elysia. If Lee didn't know I'm here, I'm just going to play dumb and see if anything comes of it."

The last thing he wanted was her out there again, but short of locking her in her room or sending a deputy to escort her out of town, there wasn't a damn thing he could do. Still, he stepped closer, closer than was strictly polite. "Be careful."

"I always am."

"Eden."

She stopped in the middle of stepping back and raised her eyebrows. "I'll keep my phone on me. I'm not planning on kicking any hornets' nests while I'm out there."

And yet it seemed like every time he turned around, shit was starting, always with her at the center. He couldn't say that without sounding accusatory, so he didn't say a damn thing. "Text me when you're on your way back."

"Sure." She turned and strode down the hallway, every move filled with purpose. She seemed to do everything like that—with purpose, no wasted movements.

He braced himself and turned to Henry and Chase. "Henry, keep an eye on our suspect." Lee was less a suspect than a potential source right now as far as Zach was concerned, but he wasn't about to share that information. Depending on when the coroner placed Neveah's time of death, Lee's alibi might be Zach himself. *Talk about ironclad.*

He could be working with a partner . . . but what are the odds?

No use in speculating until he had more information, and he wouldn't get that until he got a look at the crime scene. *Shit.* He pointed at Chase. "Call the coroner. Get him out there as soon as possible and meet him there. If Hakeem is still at the scene, he needs to make sure no one tampers with the evidence." He hesitated, not liking the wild look in his deputy's eyes. "If you're not up to this—"

"I'm fine."

There wasn't time to argue. He nodded. "Okay. Do you know which search party the Smiths were part of?"

Chase's brows lowered. "They're out west. Just south of the compound."

Of course they were. They'd want to keep as much of an eye on Martha's people as possible. Even as the thought crossed his mind, he hated that it had occurred to him. They'd lost a daughter . . . and he was going to have to be the one to tell them. He grabbed his keys off his desk. "I'll be out there as soon as possible."

"I'll get in contact with the other search parties and call it off. Then I'll meet you out at the crime scene."

"Do it." Zach headed for his cruiser, wishing he could delegate this job. It wouldn't be right to. The Smiths had come to him to find their daughter and bring her home safely, and he'd failed them. There was no recovering from that.

There was no forgiveness.

It took simultaneously too much and too little time to get out to the fields where a line of people worked their way east. They combed the area with efficiency, and even from the distance he could see the mask of concentration on their faces. There was no bracing for this, no preparing, so he got out of his cruiser and started for the couple in the middle of the line. He was ten feet away when Julie Smith glanced up, took one look at his face, and wailed, crumpling to the ground. Her husband was at her side instantly, gathering her to his chest. His eyes demanded Zach make this right, but nothing would.

Zach shook his head. "Robert. Julie. I'm so sorry."

"No!" Julie covered her ears with her hands, shaking her head. "I don't want to hear it."

"I'm sorry." He said it again, but it didn't make their daughter any more alive. "You're going to want to go home. I'll have more information soon."

By now the other search-party members had realized something was going on and had come to gather around. Zach turned to the rest of the group, picking out Lucas Winchester. "I need you to get them home. Call Julie's sister and her mother." He didn't know that the two women would be much help, but at least there would be people there for support.

Julia thrust herself out of her husband's arms and pointed a shaking finger to the west—in the direction of Elysia. "It was that woman, Zach. She took my baby away from me."

"Julie—"

She spoke right over him. "You either make her pay, Zach Owens, or I'm going to." With that, it was like all the fight went out of her, and she sank back to the ground. Robert scooped her into his arms, for once not having a single thing to say, and strode toward the parked cars.

Zach stood in the field and watched them go, waiting until the last car pulled out onto the road before he turned and looked in the direction of Elysia. Eden would be almost out there by now, walking right into the lion's den with no backup to speak of. It made his skin twitch. They couldn't keep going like this. Not without help.

He pulled out his phone and scrolled through his contacts until he found the one he was looking for.

It barely rang once. "Britton."

"Sheriff Zach Owens."

"I was expecting your call."

He wasn't sure what it was about the man's calm voice that irritated the fuck out of him, but he had to rein it in. There were more important things afoot. "I think I have a serial killer on my hands."

"Three victims."

"I'm sorry?"

"Technically, there have to be three victims before a killer can be termed serial."

He didn't throw his damn phone across the field, but it was a near thing. "I have two dead girls in the space of less than week, and judging from the ritualistic aspects of the killings, whoever did this isn't done." He didn't know there were ritualistic aspects in Neveah's death, but he didn't believe in coincidences. If she was found *just like Elouise*, then she was found naked in a ditch with new tattoos on her body and evidence that she'd run—or been chased—before she was killed.

"I happen to agree with you."

Then why all the circling? It didn't matter. What mattered was getting someone in town who could watch Eden's back—someone she'd *have* to let watch her back. "I'm officially requesting assistance from the BAU. I know there's some formality involved, but frankly, I don't have time for that shit right now. This killer held both Elouise Perkins and Neveah Smith for eight days, which means it's likely he or she has already chosen their next victim. Eden Collins is here, and her help has been essential, if off the record, but I need someone here officially." He searched his memory. "Vic. She said his name is Vic."

"He's on the next flight out."

He blinked. "That was quick."

"I had hoped I'd hear from you." There was a rustle of papers on the other end of the line. "Vic's flight lands this evening, so I suggest you have as much evidence in hand as possible before that happens."

"Thanks." He hung up and immediately dialed Eden.

"I told you I'd text you when I was leaving."

The relief at hearing her voice nearly sent him to his knees. He hadn't considered that there would be a next victim until he'd said the words aloud. *The victim might have already been taken.* "Come back to Clear Springs. You can snoop around out there once your partner is in town."

She was silent for a beat. "You called Britton."

"You should have told me."

"I've been a little distracted." In the distance, the car engine shut off. "I'm here, so I've got to go. I'll text you when I'm done. Promise."

"Eden—"

But it was too late—she'd already hung up. He cursed and shoved his phone into his back pocket. Short of driving out to the commune, there wasn't a damn thing he could do to keep Eden safe. Hell, if he went out there and tossed her into his cruiser, he might be painting an even larger target on her back.

More than that, there was the body of a girl who'd been alive a few short hours ago waiting for his attention. Zach let his shoulders drop for one long moment, the sheer knowledge that *he* was responsible for catching the killer making him sick to his stomach. He let himself have that moment, but no more. Wallowing would do nothing but make sure he wasn't capable of the job he was required to do.

So he took a deep breath and started for his cruiser. Whether he liked it or not, they were at war. It made no difference that the enemy was a single person rather than an entire army. He'd held it together in the desert. He'd hold it together now.

He had no other choice.

CHAPTER
TWENTY-ONE

Eden tucked her phone into the pocket of her jacket and triple-checked that she'd locked her car door. At the very least, if someone left her something again, she'd know they were capable of breaking into a car without leaving a trace. That had to narrow down the suspect pool . . .

She turned and surveyed the mostly empty square, the gates that had been left open as if in personal invitation. *Then again, maybe not. It's not like I can run background checks on every cult member, especially when some of them don't even go by their real names.* Even fingerprints wouldn't help if they weren't already in the system, and she highly doubted Elysia was filled to the brim with criminals who'd been charged at some point. It was an impossible task.

She marched to the main chapel and pulled on the doors, only to find them locked. Eden frowned and yanked harder. All she managed to do was rattle the wood a little. "What the hell?"

"It's closed."

She bit down a sharp reply and turned to face the male voice behind her. Shock dropped her jaw. *There's been a lot of that lately.* "Jon!"

He gave a soft smile. "Hey, Eden."

She hugged him before she could think better of it. She and Jon hadn't been as close as she and Beth, but he was still one of the only kids who'd been near her age in Elysia. Back then, he'd had a chip on his shoulder to rival hers, not that she could blame him after his mother abandoned him to Martha's tender care. He'd always had his eye on the horizon, vowing to get the hell out the first chance he had. She still couldn't believe he'd changed his mind about that.

But apparently that had changed, because he was still here, and he'd married Beth at Martha's behest. *Because of a dream. What a crock of shit.* "How have you been?"

"Good. Really good." He hugged her tightly enough to squeeze the breath from her lungs and set her back on her feet. Jon had never been a large guy, and time hadn't changed that. In her boots, they were exactly the same height. He'd filled out a little, though, in the same way most guys did once they hit twenty-five, his muscles apparent beneath his plain gray T-shirt. *Lucky Beth.* She shut the thought down *real* fast. It had never been like that with her and Jon—with her and *anyone* at Elysia.

His smile widened. "Are you doing anything right now? Beth's got lunch going, and it'd make her day if you came over."

She *had* wanted a chance to talk to Beth a bit more. Eden turned to glare at the doors. "I'm here to talk to my mother."

"You might be waiting awhile. She's holed up with Joseph and Abram. She had nightmares last night, so she's seeking counsel to determine their meaning."

She eyed him, but there wasn't any cynicism to be seen. He actually believed that her mother's nightmares were prophetic visions, and that if she had time to "get counsel" she would be able to determine the future. *How does a grown man of generally sound mind fall for that kind of thing?* Jon had had most of his life to get inoculated into that sort of thought process, but he'd always been the one Eden went to when she was furious and questioning everything about her life and the beliefs of her mother's flock.

A battle for another day.

At least she wouldn't have to sit here and wait at the door like a kid in time-out. She forced a smile. "Lunch would be great."

"Awesome." Jon led her out of the square and into the second circle of houses. They all looked more or less the same, but there was a charming potted-plant arrangement by the front door that screamed *Beth*, and when he opened the door, the smell of fresh-baked bread wafted out.

Inside was more of the same. There were the expected Elysian elements—a print of the same mural that was in the chapel hung over the fireplace, and the bookshelf in the living room was filled with nothing but Martha-approved texts—but there were also pictures of Jon and Beth together, alone or in small groups, smiling at the camera. As if they were really happy.

Maybe they are. Just because I was miserable here doesn't mean everyone is.

That didn't make it *right*, but it was something she needed to remember. If she came crashing in here and demanding everyone see reason, the very people she was trying to save would throw her out faster than she could say *clusterfuck*.

They rounded the corner and walked into a cozy little kitchen. Beth was frowning down at a plate of sandwiches, but she broke into a smile when Jon said, "Look who I found."

"Eden!"

She was once again engulfed in a hug. Eden had been hugged more in the last few days than she had been in the last few *years*. Beth smelled of strawberries and practically bounced on her toes when she stood back. "I'm so happy you're here."

"I didn't get you into trouble the other day, did I?"

She frowned in incomprehension and then laughed. "Oh, of course not. Everything is fine. I just got a little uppity in one of our small groups. You know how it is."

"Uh . . . okay." She wasn't sure if she believed the other woman, but she wasn't in the position to call Beth a liar. Or to point out that getting *uppity* wasn't enough to justify hours spent scrubbing a floor. But Eden was so damn tired of fighting and being on her guard every second of every day. She took a seat at the island, letting some of the problems of the current situation fall away. She could question Beth and Jon; then she'd corner her mother and head back into town to talk to Zach about the body.

I hope someone's with Rachel when she hears about this.

She shook her head. She had enough to worry about without adding a teenager to the list, but there was something about the girl that she identified with. Rachel's relationship with her mother was obviously light-years better than Eden's, but she seemed to kind of stand just outside the circle. Neveah had drawn her in, and she'd put up with some serious crap in her effort to maintain that contact.

And now Neveah is dead.

She accepted the lemonade Beth set in front of her. "Thank you."

"You'll have to tell us everything you've been up to the last ten years. I bet it's so exciting." Beth loaded up two sandwiches and passed them to Jon. "Is it true you're in the FBI?"

"Word gets around fast." She was surprised Martha had advertised that fact. Her mother despised the feds, though her ire was usually directed at the white-collar crime division. They were the ones who'd given her such grief about taxes back when Elysia was first becoming a force to be reckoned with. She'd won that war, but she was a smart woman. She knew that most cults were brought down because of fraud.

Eden imagined her mother knew a thing or two about fraud, though she hadn't been caught yet.

"Well, you know how it is. This time of year, all anyone can talk about is the crops." She lowered her eyes, her voice dropping to just above a whisper. "That and Persephone being taken."

Call her crazy, but Eden had forgotten. She sat back. "That's in"— she did some quick mental math—"a week."

"Yeah." Jon wasn't really looking at her, either. "This year Martha chose Beth to play the role of Persephone."

She searched for the right response and came up short. "That's . . ."

"A great honor." Beth's smile never wavered. If anything, it brightened. "It's not without its challenges, but the reward is more than worth it. I've worked very, very hard this year to prove to Martha that I'm worthy of stepping into, well, into your role." She fidgeted. "I know it's customary to pick a girl right on the cusp of womanhood, but we don't have many that age in Elysia these days. There are younger children, of course, but that would hardly be appropriate."

Younger children going through that torture . . . She shuddered. If she concentrated, she could still feel the loose dirt beneath her fingernails as she clawed, desperate for air. She hadn't gone into the grave willingly, but most of the girls did. Elysia had never had a plethora of underage kids, but there were always at least a few.

But Beth is my age. Or was that significant, too? "I . . ." *Damn it, Eden, you can do better than this.* "Congratulations." The word came out choked and unconvincing, but neither Beth nor Jon seemed to notice.

"Thank you." Beth hesitated. "Though, since you're back, it should be *you* playing Persephone again. Martha always intended for that role to be yours and yours alone."

Eden's breath stalled in her lungs, and a buzzing sounded in her ears, drowning out Jon's response to Beth. Her body broke out in a cold sweat, and she had to clamp her mouth shut to avoid screaming that she'd be put back into the ground over her dead body. *Someone would probably like nothing more.* She swallowed once, then again, trying to work away the dryness in her throat. "I'm not back."

Beth's face fell. "Right. You said that. It's just that our generation is finally reaching a point where we have a little power. Think of what we could do if you took the role Martha has set aside for you—and I was your right-hand woman." She cleared her throat, her cheeks flushing.

"It's okay." It wasn't, but the fault didn't lie with the couple in front of her. It fell firmly into the lap of the woman who birthed Eden. She accepted the sandwich Beth had put together for her, though the last thing she wanted was to eat anything. "Hey, since I have you two here, I have a question."

"Sure. What's up?" Jon slipped an arm around his wife's waist and pressed a kiss to her temple.

She briefly considered not asking them any leading questions, but she wasn't going to get any new information by playing nice. "Do you guys know anyone who would have left a garland of daisies in my car?"

Jon shook his head. "Wrong time of year for those."

"Yeah, I know."

Beth nibbled her lip. "Those are Persephone's flowers—or at least one of them."

She knew that, too.

Beth looked at Jon and frowned. "Maybe someone thought the same thing I did—that you'd be playing Persephone in the ritual? The avatar wears the garland during it."

Shit. She'd forgotten about that. Eden fought down a shiver. She'd thought every second of her time in Elysia was imprinted on the darkest recesses of her brain. She hadn't anticipated that she'd forget anything, let alone so much. She didn't like the idea that someone—possibly the killer—wanted to bury her alive. This time the shiver couldn't be repressed. To cover up the involuntary reaction, she changed tactics. "Did you guys ever see Neveah Smith or Elouise Perkins out here?"

Beth smiled. "Elouise spent some time in Elysia. It was a blessing that Lee was in the right place at the right time to be able to rescue her."

That wasn't how it had happened at all, especially since the girl had gone back to her home many times before she finally left town, but Eden wasn't about to argue. "He seems to really care about her."

Jon shrugged. "Lee's a good man."

"Oh, honey." Beth laughed. "Men." She looked at Eden. "He has no idea. Lee asked Martha to release him from the inner circle so he could pursue a relationship with Elouise. She really made an impression on him, and from what I witnessed, it was mutual."

Jon turned a disbelieving look on his wife. "He'd give up his position for a girl who was leaving with no intention of coming back?"

Beth shrugged. "Love does funny things. Look what it did for us."

Eden didn't comment on the fact that from Beth's own account, it had been Martha who paired the two of them up—love had no place. Obviously they'd found it along the way, and that was better than most people managed. Better than *Eden* had managed. She took a bite of her sandwich because it would have been rude not to, and stood. "Thank you so much for catching up. I've got to go see if I can get in with Martha."

Jon nodded. "Good luck."

It wasn't until she'd left the house behind that she turned her thoughts to what the couple had revealed. It might not seem that daunting on the surface—she'd known Lee had strong feelings for Elouise—but having strong feelings and actively trying to *leave* Elysia and Martha were two different things. And if Elouise had similar feelings and encouraged him to come with her?

Her mother had done awful things in the past to keep her flock from wandering. She'd turned peer pressure into a weapon, effectively creating an environment where speaking up was policed by the very people she abused. She'd tortured individuals—though God alone knew they didn't *call* it torture—in front of her entire flock. She *buried* a teenage girl alive every single year.

Who's to say she wouldn't commit murder?

Eden stopped next to her car and peered inside. There didn't seem to be any gifts, but her time in Elysia today wasn't over. She squared her shoulders and headed for the chapel doors again. If they were locked, she'd circle around back and climb in the low window to the ladies' bathroom. Very little had changed around here if her mother's house was anything to go by, so she had her doubts that the lock had ever been fixed.

But this time when she yanked on the door, it flew open, almost spilling her onto her ass. Eden cursed, looked around to see if she had an audience, and cursed again. What were the damn odds? She didn't like this. She didn't like it one bit. But the only other option was rushing to her car, so she headed inside. "Hello?" With the lights down low and her footsteps echoing from the walls, she felt like she'd mistakenly been cast in a horror movie.

Not so much a mistake as a predestined role.

"Mother?" The word tasted bad in her mouth, but they all had their roles to play. No one had more answers about this cult than Martha, so Eden would jump through whatever hoops the woman set up for her. "Are you here?" She turned the corner, heading deeper into the building, unable to shake the feeling that there was a second set of footsteps echoing in time with her own, though if they were ahead of her or behind her, she couldn't begin to guess.

The small hairs at the back of her neck rose, and she glanced over her shoulder. The hallway was empty, but she could see a grand total of only ten feet of it. Someone could be standing just on the other side, holding their breath the same way she was, waiting for her to start walking again.

This is crazy. There's no one there. No one even knows I'm here.

Except you announced yourself the second you walked through the door like an idiot.

Oh, yeah, except for that.

Instinct demanded she run, but if she did, she was little better than prey. She reached for her gun before remembering she didn't have it on her. It didn't matter. She'd been trained not to be defenseless while unarmed. Eden moved as silently as possible and then burst around the corner, ready for anything.

It was empty.

Movement farther down the hallway caught her eye, the slightest shift of a door closing. Eden almost let it go, but the very instincts that demanded she flee before now had her rushing down the hallway and through the door. There *had* been someone there.

Someone who just might be the killer.

It didn't occur to her that pursuit was a shitty idea until she rounded the corner, got an eyeful of metal, and was knocked onto her back. Blackness sucked her down, taking everything with it.

CHAPTER
TWENTY-TWO

Zach cursed long and hard at the sight of a dozen cars gathered around the spot where Chase's directions had led him. Despite the police tape—which he never thought he'd have to use while he was sheriff of Clear Springs—cordoning off the crime scene, there was a small crowd of townsfolk gathered, staring avidly at William and Chase where they crouched next to a cloaked form.

Neveah Smith.

He searched the familiar faces, picking out Hakeem and a few others, but no Robert or Julie. He didn't think for a second they'd gone home to process their loss like he'd instructed—it was only a matter of time before they either showed up here or on Elysia's front doorstep, demanding answers. He couldn't help thinking of Eden and what she'd said would happen if they did. *Nothing good.* Even if he wasn't motivated by the deaths of two teenagers in his town, the potential of an armed conflict between the Elysians and townspeople was enough to have his blood pressure rising. They needed this case closed and peace restored—sooner rather than later.

Ignoring the questions a few people lobbed at him, he ducked under the police tape and walked over to the two men. "Chase. William."

William seemed to have aged ten years in the last week, something in common with everyone else involved in the case. "Sheriff." He nodded to the tarp on the ground. "Chase here took pictures of everything in the area of the body—pictures that will *not* leak this time. I've told my staff in no uncertain terms that a repeat will mean their jobs. Though I still can't figure out who sent it in the first place." He glared at the gawkers. "But we couldn't leave the girl like that with *them* around. It wasn't right."

No, it wasn't. He didn't like the potential of mucking up evidence, but Zach didn't fault his reasoning. This wasn't some random drifter who'd wandered into town, unconnected to anyone. This was a girl who'd been born here, who'd grown up around them, who'd lost her chance to ever reach adulthood. It was wrong on so many levels that he didn't know where to start. He crouched down and carefully lifted the edge of the tarp.

Even knowing what he'd find, it still rocked him back on his heels to see her like this. He tried to take a mental step back, to look for evidence, rather than remembering the girl she'd been—trouble, sure, but so full of life.

It was impossible.

He gritted his teeth at the bruises on her wrists—clear rope burns that hadn't been on Elouise—and the sliver of tattoo peeking out. It would be a sheaf of wheat, just like all the cultists had. Where there'd been some question over Elouise potentially joining before she left for college, there was no doubt in his mind that Neveah wouldn't have submitted to the tattoo, let alone Martha's ruling with an iron fist. The girl had never met an authority figure she wasn't eager to give the middle finger to.

Never again.

Her hair was a tangled, dirty mess, hiding her face, and for that he was grateful. He didn't want to see her brown eyes vacant in death. Elouise's murder had felt personal. Neveah's was even worse.

William came to crouch next to him. "I won't know more until I get her on my table, but the markings on her neck indicate strangling." He paused a beat. "Though it's hard to tell, I think there are layers of bruises there."

Zach shot him a look. "You think she was choked before she was killed."

"Several times, possibly long and hard enough to make her lose consciousness. You don't get this rainbow of bruises from a single event, especially since I doubt she's been dead long enough for the killing marks to show this clearly."

He couldn't tear his gaze away from the bits of her neck he could see through her hair. *She must have been terrified. Being choked to unconsciousness is enough to break grown-ass men, and she was just a seventeen-year-old girl. She probably went looking for a little fun and got* this *as a result. Fucking unforgivable.* "How long do you figure she's been gone?"

"I can't say for certain, but less than six hours."

He checked his watch. It was noon. Zach frowned and pushed to his feet, turning to survey the road behind them. "The killer moved the body."

"What makes you say that?"

"If she died after six a.m., then someone would have found her before now. There's a ton of traffic on this street, but even if you discount cars not being able to see her in the ditch, the Abbotts walk their dogs around seven every morning down this stretch of road. The dogs would have sniffed out a dead body if they came within a hundred yards of it. There's no way they missed her."

"The other girl wasn't moved."

"I know." He wasn't sure what it meant, but if she was dropped here after six in the morning, that took Lee right out of the suspect pool.

He nodded at William to put the tarp back into place. "You need help moving her? We're not going to get anything done with the audience."

"I've got it."

While William went to work, Zach once again surveyed their surroundings. Like so much of the land outside Clear Springs, it was miles of open ground running right up to the mountains. There were homes and farms scattered, but most of them sat on at least a handful of acres, if not significantly more. A person could walk for hours without seeing another person.

Except Neveah didn't walk—or run—here. At least not the whole way.

He turned like a toy on a string, looking west, ever west, to Elysia. It didn't matter that he couldn't see the compound. He knew it was there, the shadow the cult cast finally too long and dark to ignore. If Lee wasn't the killer, it was someone else who answered to Martha.

Or Martha herself.

He couldn't rule it out. There was nothing saying there couldn't be two killers, and he and Eden had discussed how unlikely it was that someone at Elysia was operating without her say-so. He still didn't like the idea that Martha could be somehow responsible. He didn't much like her, but it was a big jump from conning people out of their money to murdering two girls in cold blood.

Then again, maybe it isn't that big of a jump. And that bastard might have already taken another victim.

That snapped him out of it. He looked up at Chase. "Henry has Lee secure." For all the good that would do. Lee had been in the interview room when Neveah was killed. "In the event that Lee and/or a partner *isn't* guilty, we need to get in contact with every teenager who fits the same physical description. This monster isn't through, and I want our girls safe." Clear Springs wasn't large enough to have its own high school, so the kids were bused over to Augusta, but he figured there were a good hundred kids of roughly the right age group, half of them girls. Off the top of his head, Zach couldn't count many of them who fit the victim profile. Clear Springs didn't exactly have an unlimited number of teenage girls, and most of them had features that would set them apart from the victims—blue eyes, not petite, too young. That said, he wasn't about to gamble that the killer would stick to that if his chosen prey was removed from his hunting grounds.

Chase nodded and grabbed his phone.

"Wait." Zach glanced at the crowd and lowered his voice. "Take the call in your cruiser. I don't want to start a panic." Clear Springs was a ticking time bomb and would only become more so once word of Neveah's death got out. One strike of the wrong match and they'd have bigger problems than the Smiths riling people up. It was his job to keep people safe, and if someone pulled the metaphorical trigger, they'd turn to the outsider and start stringing people up. It would start with the Elysians, but he didn't think it would stop there, especially if Martha closed the gates. People would sniff out someone—*anyone*—to blame.

They'd come for Eden.

Lee aside, he couldn't discard any suspects. Fuck, he couldn't even discard Lee, because if he opened up the possibility of it being more than one person, that demolished the man's alibi. It was enough to have a headache spiking behind his left eye. "What a fucking mess."

He needed more people on this, but he couldn't deputize any of Clear Springs's citizens, because they couldn't be trusted to be cool and collected in the face of someone who potentially killed their people. He didn't blame them for that, but it made his job that much harder. Augusta was already understaffed as it was and couldn't spare any men for him, especially when he didn't have a time frame for when they'd be back.

The FBI . . . well, Eden couldn't afford to be officially connected. This guy coming—Vic—wasn't going to be enough.

We'll make it work. We have to.

In the meantime, he needed to change up his strategy. There was no doubt Lee had more information to be delved into, though he needed the right pressure points to push. Of Martha's inner circle, he was the weak link. They'd get nowhere with Abram. If Zach didn't miss his guess, the guy had been in worse than interrogations a time or two, and the only way to ruffle him was to go after Martha—something Zach wasn't prepared to do without strong evidence. It would bring the entirety of Elysia down around his head, which would spark animosity with the Clear Springs residents.

He pulled out his phone and called Eden. He wanted to run his plan past her and see if she thought it had merit. But the phone just rang and rang before finally clicking over to voice mail. *What the fuck?* She'd promised him she'd be careful, but that didn't mean she had to take his calls. They'd just talked half an hour ago. *She's probably in with Martha.*

But that didn't stop him from worrying.

He put it out of his mind as much as possible. Eden was a grown woman—and a federal agent—so out of everyone involved in this case, she was the most capable of taking care of herself. He had other things to keep him occupied. Zach called Henry. "Get the second interrogation room prepped. I'm bringing Joseph in." He couldn't crack Abram, and he wasn't ready to take Martha on, but Joseph was a cocky little bastard. Even if he couldn't get under the man's skin, he could use the loudmouth to get Lee talking.

Adrenaline surged. They'd figure this out, and they'd put a stop to this fucking killer.

He froze when Chase bolted over, skidding to a stop on the other side of the police tape. "Zach." The man was so damn pale, he looked like he was about to pass out. His breath came too fast, and his eyes were too wide. "Zach, it's Rachel Carpenter. She's gone."

CHAPTER
TWENTY-THREE

"Eden? Eden, honey, wake up."

Eden opened her eyes and immediately closed them when the light assaulted her. She concentrated on breathing and took inventory of her body. It had been a long time since she was knocked out cold. The last thing she remembered was chasing down someone who'd been following her. It could have been the unsub, but then she was in Elysia, so it could have been *anyone*. She reached up and gingerly touched her face. *That's going to bruise up real pretty.* It hurt—good lord, it hurt—but nothing seemed to be broken. Thank God. She'd broken her nose on her first case with Vic, and he'd never let her live it down.

Probably because it had nothing to do with chasing down an unsub and everything to do with a drunk girl with too much strength and too little coordination.

Not her finest moment, though this was shaping up to be one for the record books. The familiar scent of hyacinths wrapped around her, as if she needed more than the sound of Martha's voice to confirm that she was kneeling right beside Eden.

As tempting as it was to lie here and pretend to be unconscious for a little bit longer, it wouldn't serve any purpose but delaying the inevitable. *I can use this. Think clinically.* It was hard, so hard, with her head pounding in time with her heartbeat. All she wanted to do was lie there for a few more minutes, or maybe a few more days, and just wait until this all passed her by.

But Eden had never lived her life passively, and she wasn't about to start now.

She opened her eyes, but more slowly this time. Her surroundings solidified around her, and they were *not* the hall she'd run down. She started to sit up, but the room spun, forcing her back to the ground. "Where am I?"

"Honey, you're in Elysia. You don't remember?" Martha exchanged a glance with someone, and Eden twisted to see Abram looming against the doorjamb. That got her moving. She'd be damned before she lay supine while *he* was in the room. She managed to sit up, but making it to her feet wasn't possible without potentially passing out again, and that would be even worse than lying on the ground. She gritted her teeth, but that just made the pounding in her head worse.

"I know I'm in Elysia." The last thing she needed was for Martha to jump on the idea that she had amnesia or some nonsense like that. "I mean why am I here?" She motioned to the entranceway of the chapel. Eden knew for a fact she hadn't been knocked out *here*, head injury or no.

"This is where we found you." Martha reached out to smooth her hair back but aborted the move halfway through when Eden flinched. Her mouth tightened. "I was told you were in Elysia, and since you didn't deem your mother worthy of seeing last time you were here, I was on my way to see you."

She ignored the passive-aggressive jab and tried to focus. "You didn't see anyone else?"

"There was no one else to see. We walked around the corner and here you were." Martha's dark eyes lit up with concern. "It appears you weren't paying attention to where you were going and walked into the post."

Eden eyed the post. That thing had been there since she could walk. No matter how distracted she was—and she'd been *very* distracted more than a few times walking down this hall—she'd never made contact with it. Martha knew that. She knew there was no way in hell Eden would run into the damn thing, let alone run into it hard enough to knock herself out cold.

She's hiding something.

What's new? If there's one constant in the universe, it's Martha Collins hoarding secrets.

Call her crazy, but a small secret part of her had been sure her mother wouldn't do anything to put her in direct danger. Even with girls dropping dead around her, she'd somehow held out hope that Martha wasn't involved—that her mother didn't know what was going on under her nose.

That belief turned to dust in the face of Martha creating this lie that seemed solely designed to gaslight her into . . . she didn't even know. She couldn't think, couldn't focus. Eden touched her face again. The pain was centered around her left brow, where the weapon had made contact. *A shovel, maybe. Something hard and flat.* She checked her watch. She hadn't been out long—maybe ten minutes—but it was long enough for whoever hit her to move her here and for Martha and Abram to find her.

That's not very long at all.

Either they knew exactly who hit her . . . or one of them was the one who'd done it.

She looked at Abram, but he gave her as little to work with as normal—which translated to nothing. The man was a blank slate, always had been. And her mother was far too adept at manipulation to give away something by accident—she'd had years and years of practice, after all. The realization left Eden cold. She searched Martha's face. *Tell me you didn't do it. Tell me you're not responsible for those girls' deaths. Tell me you didn't do it all to lure me home.* But all she said was, "You're probably right. Can you help me up?"

"Are you sure you should be standing?"

No, but that wasn't going to stop her. She started climbing to her feet, and Martha rushed to assist. "Mom, I need to ask you a few questions." The words left a metallic taste in her mouth, but she forced them out all the same. There was no time for pride. A clock ticked down in her head. She wasn't sure exactly what would happen when it hit zero, but it wouldn't be good no matter which way she looked at the situation. Another girl dead, or the unsub coming after Eden personally.

I know which I'd prefer. I'm better equipped to deal with anything this bastard has to throw at me.

She touched her face again. *Though if anyone's keeping score, we're at unsub: three; Eden: zero.* Zach was going to lose it when he saw her, let alone dealing with Vic once he got into town.

Martha was already nodding. "Of course. Let's go into my office. Abram, would you be a dear and get an ice pack for Eden? I do believe that's going to bruise up something fierce." She headed off without waiting for him to reply, but then she had no reason to think he wouldn't obey. He always seemed to in the past.

Eden shot him a look over her shoulder as she followed her mother, her mind going a million miles a minute. She didn't think Lee was guilty of murder, but that didn't mean his actions hadn't indirectly brought the unsub's attention to both Elouise and Neveah. Martha wouldn't take too kindly to being passed over for younger girls, and all she had to do was make an offhand comment and Abram would see it done.

Abram wouldn't flinch under interrogation. She doubted he'd flinch under actual torture. He'd just sit in that uncomfortable chair and stare at Zach with those dead pale eyes and say nothing. *Sociopath* was too nice of a description in her opinion.

Martha opened the door to her office and closed it once Eden had taken a seat. She didn't immediately move around to sit at the desk, once again looking like she wanted to touch her, to offer some of the comfort she was so good at. Eden worked very hard to keep her body language as closed off as possible, and after a few long moments, her mother took the hint and sank into her seat on the other side of the desk. "Now, what questions, baby?"

Don't call me that. She didn't say the words, couldn't afford to, and hated that her mother managed to silence her protests even now, even though it was Eden's choice. It didn't *feel* like her choice. She took a careful breath. "I need to know about the key." She touched her sternum, though she doubted Martha misunderstood the reference.

Sure enough, her mother's brows slanted down before she smoothed her expression out. "I'm not sure what brought this on, but unless you're planning on being reinstated, I can't share that information with you. It's for Elysians only."

"You didn't share that information with me when I *was* an Elysian." *I was never one of you. If I had any choice, I never would have set foot in this place, let alone been raised here.* There was no telling if her nameless father would have been any less a monster, but *anything* would have been a better choice than Elysia. A better choice than Martha.

But he was gone before Elysia started. Her mother had birthed that damn cult mere months before she birthed Eden herself. As far as she knew, her father had never come looking for her, but there was no telling the truth. Maybe he'd come for her and been run off.

Or maybe she was just reaching for impossible dreams, like she had when she was too young to know better.

"You were a child." Martha gave a sad smile. "Some mysteries aren't meant for children."

"That didn't stop you from tattooing it on my chest against my will." She tried to get control of her anger, but the pain radiating from her brow outward made it so damn difficult. "No one else has this mark. The other three, yes, but not this one."

But her mother just gave her that pacifying smile. "If you want to talk about coming home—"

"You're impeding an investigation and withholding what could potentially be vital evidence."

Martha's gaze sharpened. "What does the key have to do with a dead girl in Clear Springs?"

Damn it. She'd said too much. She worked to keep her expression bland. "You tell me." She already knew it had something to do with Persephone and Demeter, but Martha had borrowed from other myths, too. There was no telling how she'd twisted the story to suit her needs.

"Don't be difficult, Eden. If you're in danger, you need to tell me."

She stared. "You can't have it both ways. Either I'm walking into columns or someone is out to get me. You can't pat me on the head and then tell me you're concerned for my safety. That ship sailed too many years ago to count."

"You're being dramatic."

She opened her mouth, but the door behind them cut off her response. It was just as well. For all her pleas and words about offering support, Martha hadn't changed. She still cared about her secrets and her power more than she cared about anything else. Eden accepted the ice pack Abram handed her, ignoring the childish impulse to throw it at his feet. The look on his face gave her pause, though he had eyes only for Martha. "There's trouble."

Her mother was on her feet immediately, following him out of the room without a backward glance. It was just as well. Eden took half a breath to consider following them, but she couldn't ask for a better opportunity than she'd just been handed. She pushed to her feet and hurried around her mother's desk, knowing it was only a matter of time before Martha sent Abram to escort her out. Daughter or not, if something was happening to make the Elysians close ranks, Eden wouldn't be welcome in the commune.

She opened the top drawer and felt around, allowing herself a small smile when she found the catch for the false bottom. Her mother thought she was so clever, but Eden had found this particular hiding place when she was thirteen. She lifted the panel out and ran her finger down the list of passwords, stopping at the one marked CAMERAS. *ABRAM. Didn't see that one coming.*

She started to replace the panel but stopped, a flash of metal catching her eye. Frowning, she slipped her hand farther into the drawer and pulled out a revolver. Eden blinked. *What the hell is my mother doing with a gun?* Martha was renowned for her hatred of the things, and she didn't even allow Abram to carry one when they were in Elysia. In the outside world, he insisted for her safety, and she'd agreed to it only under duress.

It was the only time she'd seen her mother give in.

That still didn't explain what one was doing *here*, in Martha's personal desk. *As if she's afraid of something. But what could she possibly have to be afraid of?* She *is the monster under the bed in Elysia.* She hesitated, but there was no time. After replacing everything exactly as she'd found it, she put the false bottom back into the drawer and arranged the things that had been on top of it. She'd just started for the door when Abram appeared, suspicion clear in ever line of his body. "What are you doing?"

"I got dizzy." She touched her face and winced. "Head injuries are tricky, you know."

He pointed her out of the room and then locked the door behind her. She started for the exit, and instead of melting off into the shadows, he followed. Goose bumps broke out over her arms as his footsteps echoed hers, just like what had happened earlier. Eden watched him out of the corner of her eye. *Was it you?*

The sneak attack didn't seem like his MO, but stranger things had happened. She rubbed her arms. Coming home had been a mistake. She was so wound up that she was jumping at shadows, and paranoia was starting to get the best of her. *Is it really paranoia if they're all out to get you?* She preferred to think of it as well-earned caution.

Abram held the door open for her, and she sidled past him and outside. To distract herself—and to distract *him* from thinking too much about what she was doing in Martha's office—she said, "So, what was the big emergency?"

It was Martha who answered her. "They took my boy. They took *both* my boys."

She frowned at her mother, taking in the way she clutched her dress and the wild look in her eyes. Eden didn't believe for a second that it was genuine grief. Sure enough, there were a handful of people around, all watching with varying stages of anger and disbelief.

Eden didn't have time for that shit. "What are you talking about?"

"Sheriff Owens just arrested Joseph." Abram's voice was too close behind her, and she jumped, feeling like she'd been shocked. She turned to glare, but the anger on his face stopped her. He continued on, pitching his voice too low to carry. "And I suspect you already know where our Lee has gone missing to."

Zach arrested Joseph. She grabbed her phone, but there were no missed calls or texts. *What the hell?* If he was going to come out here and start arresting people, the least he could have done was give her a heads-up. She pressed the ice pack more firmly against her face. Right now she needed a handful of Advil and some time to sit and *think*, but it didn't look like she was going to get either.

Martha swayed as if faint. "We have given the police in Clear Springs our utmost support, and this is how they repay us—with treachery. We will not stand for it!"

Her mother wasn't going to be slowing down anytime soon. If anything, she was picking up steam. Eden sighed. It didn't really matter.

Martha had more than proven that she wasn't going to be *cooperative*, no matter how many times she claimed otherwise. The key tattooed on Eden's chest had something to do with all this, and she was just going to have to find out on her own.

The fact that she'd already spent a not-inconsiderable amount of time researching it didn't bear mentioning.

She headed for her car, relieved beyond measure to discover that it was still locked and there weren't any new presents sitting around. Without looking at her mother, Abram, or the gathering crowd, she slipped into the driver's seat and started the engine. A knock on the window took several years off her life. She sighed when she recognized Beth on the other side of the glass, and Eden pushed the button to lower the window. "I can't really talk."

"Oh, Eden, look at your face." Beth pressed a hand to her mouth, her blue eyes wide. "Are you okay?"

"I'm fine." *Possibly lightly concussed.*

"Oh, well, good." She hesitated and seemed to steel herself. "You've got to do something about the sheriff."

Eden blinked. "What exactly do you expect me to do?"

"He arrested Joseph *and* Lee." Beth bit her lip. "Joseph might be unkind sometimes, but Lee is a good man. He couldn't possibly have done anything to deserve being arrested."

Technically, Zach hadn't arrested either of them. She'd bet her badge on it. He didn't have enough evidence, and bringing someone in on a trumped-up charge would undermine any trial that happened once they found the unsub. Explaining that to Beth, though, would take time and effort, and Eden had neither. "I'm not in charge of the investigation."

"But you could talk to him, couldn't you? This is all just some horrible misunderstanding, I'm sure of it."

Eden's gaze dropped to the handful of people standing just within earshot, and then back to Beth. *For fuck's sake, it's just as much a ploy as my mother's wailing and clothes clutching.* For all that, her former friend was rather transparent. Eden was so damn tired, tired of the manipulations, tired of the politics, tired of everything.

Even so, she just didn't have it in her to slap the other woman down. It wasn't Beth's fault this was happening. "I'll talk to him." That, at least, was true. She wanted to know what the hell was going on. She couldn't deny that Joseph topped her list of suspects, but she couldn't be sure if that was because of her personal dislike for him or not. *Zach must have found something out.*

Time seemed to be moving fast, skipping forward to an inevitable end. She didn't know where it would stop, but there was violence in the air. It was only left to figure out who would fall next.

CHAPTER
TWENTY-FOUR

Zach's relief at seeing Eden's car pull up outside the station died a terrible death when she climbed out and her face came into view. He shoved through the door and out into the crisp afternoon air. *It's going to be a cold one tonight.* The completely unnecessary observation did nothing to calm him. He stopped in front of her, not touching her but close enough that he knew damn well he was crowding her. "What the fuck happened?"

"I could ask you the same thing. I thought we were waiting to pull anyone in until something changed."

He couldn't take his eyes off the bruise blossoming down the side of her face. "Didn't you get my messages?"

Eden looked like she'd been about to rip him a new one, but she froze. "You didn't leave any messages."

"I left three." He shook his head. "You're dodging the fact that you have yet to explain *that*." It looked like she'd gone one too many rounds with a boxer, and she'd be sporting one hell of a black eye before too long. "You said you'd be careful."

"I was careful." She touched her bruise and winced. "I was mostly careful. I didn't get anything useful, but someone was following me, so I chased them down and caught what feels like a shovel to my face for my efforts. Knocked me out cold."

The bottom of his stomach dropped out. Anything could have happened to her while she was unconscious. If it was the killer who'd attacked her, he could have taken her to wherever he'd been holding his victims, and likely the next time Zach saw her, she'd be in a ditch. The mere thought stole his breath. He jerked Eden into a hug he had no business demanding.

She tensed, but then released a pent-up breath and relaxed against him. It was only then that he registered how her body shook. He rubbed her back, holding her closer. *Just a minute. Just another minute and I'll let her go.* "It's okay. You're safe."

"It's nothing. Adrenaline letdown."

He didn't believe that any more than she did, but if she needed to tell herself that she hadn't been scared shitless, he wasn't going to be the one to poke holes in that belief. They each told themselves the lies necessary to get through this situation. And what he was about to tell her was going to shove her day from horrible right over into nightmarish. "He took Rachel."

She pulled away enough to look up at him. "Say that again?"

"Whoever's doing this—they took Rachel. She was home alone while her mom was working swing shift, and she wasn't in her room this morning. Lisa Carpenter went straight to bed when she got home, so we're not even sure how long she was missing."

Eden took a step back, and he could actually see her putting her emotional armor back into place. It was both wondrous and terrifying. She took a deep breath, and when she exhaled, the woman was gone, replaced by the fed. "Do we have a time of death on Neveah Smith yet?"

"She was killed between two and four a.m." He ushered her into the police station, heading for his desk. He'd left Joseph in the second interrogation room, and Lee was still in the first, so there was a little time to bring her up-to-date. Zach flagged Henry down. "Can you grab one of the ice packs from the freezer? And then you need to get out of here for a little bit—go eat a hot meal and grab a nap. You've done enough for today." He knew it killed his senior deputy to babysit Lee while shit was hitting the fan with another body and Zach was storming Elysia to bring in Joseph.

"Yes, Mother." Henry took the order with more grace than Chase had, but then, he was older—he'd been around the block enough times to know that running himself ragged without the end in sight was a recipe for disaster.

Once Eden had the ice pack, he got back to the case. "The death doesn't clear Lee, but the time the body was dropped does."

"Dropped." Her dark eyes sharpened. "Elouise Perkins wasn't dropped. She was killed where she was found."

"There's a lot of traffic down Prairie Road between six and seven in the morning, and no one saw anything." He knew. He'd made a couple of calls while driving out to Elysia. He hadn't really expected someone to have seen the body and *not* called him, but he couldn't take anything for granted these days. "There's no way she was killed and left there."

Eden shook her head. "That doesn't make sense. Why change things up now?"

"Trying to confuse the trail? I don't know. But I plan on finding out." Starting with Joseph. The man had been nothing but belligerent since he'd put him in the back of the cruiser, and Zach was hoping he could play on that arrogance and get him to reveal something. "William will be ready for us in a little over an hour, so I'm going to take a shot at Joseph before then."

"He's arrogant." Hearing his thoughts come out of her mouth was disconcerting, to say the least. Eden dropped into a chair and tipped her head back, the ice pack firmly against her face. "If you can get him to start bragging, he might let something slip. Just don't threaten

Martha—or even bring her up, if that's possible. Lee's loyalty to her might be in question because of Elouise, but Joseph grew up in Elysia. If he thinks you're threatening her or the cult, he'll shut down."

Zach filed that away. "Do you need someone to look at that? Concussions are no joke."

"I'm fine. It sent me for a loop, and I have the headache from hell, but it's not going to affect my performance."

It wasn't her performance he was worried about. It was *her*. Britton had said Eden was too close to this case, and Zach couldn't help but agree. His concern wasn't that she'd be biased—though he guessed that was a very real possibility. It was that she'd push herself to the point of exhaustion and beyond chasing this down.

Because she felt responsible.

It didn't matter that she hadn't done anything to bring these murders on. Logic had no part of what she was no doubt feeling right now. He knew, because he was feeling the same thing—at least to some extent. *I should have known something was wrong earlier. I should have been smarter, faster, better organized. I should have known the killer would go after Rachel.* There was no way he could have done better than he was doing, but that didn't make a damn bit of difference. He couldn't protect her any more than he could protect the teenagers who'd gone missing and died under his watch.

The only thing he *could* do was find and catch the killer.

Joseph sat exactly where Zach had left him, lounging in the chair and chewing on a toothpick he'd had with him when they brought him in. Zach was tempted to take the stupid thing away, but right now he was going to play nice guy and see where it got him. It was much easier to ramp up the aggression than it was to take back harsh words. He just didn't have *time*.

He dropped into the opposite chair. "Howdy, Joseph."

"Sheriff."

"Don't suppose you know why I brought you in for questioning."

"Don't suppose I do."

So that's how we're going to play it. He should have known this man's cage wouldn't be easy to rattle. A man didn't make it to the top tier in Elysia without a degree of ambition and cunning. *I've been underestimating Joseph all along. Letting my dislike for him color my views.* He leaned back in his chair and laced his fingers behind his neck. "How long were you sleeping with Neveah Smith?"

Joseph started, the tiniest movement that Zach would have missed if he hadn't been zeroed in on the other man. *I'll be damned.* He'd thrown that out on a whim, chasing a gut feeling he hadn't known to put into words until they were out of his mouth. But that was the one part of Rachel's story that didn't quite line up. Neveah had been bragging about sleeping with Lee, but if she'd actually gotten to that point with the man, he would have reacted differently. Lee was a goddamn open book, no matter how he tried to hide it, and Zach doubted he was capable of lying on such a fundamental level.

Which had raised the question—if Neveah hadn't been with Lee when she'd sneaked away, who *had* she been with?

Now he had his answer.

He reined in the rushing anger snapping at his nerve endings, demanding he move, demanding he do something to punish the little shit across from him, sitting in this room while Neveah and Elouise were dead. It took work to keep his voice calm and his words offhand. "How does that work, exactly? You get off on sleeping with kids, looking at borderline underage porn, and then close your eyes and bear it with your woman?"

Joseph's eyes flashed with white-hot anger, but then his face slid into his usual cocky smile. "Don't know what you're talking about, Sheriff. What Martha and I do in the privacy of our home is no one's business."

"You mean what you two do in *her* house."

There was that anger again, quickly doused. "Even if I did what you're accusing me of, the age of consent in Montana is sixteen. Correct me if I'm wrong, but isn't Neveah Smith seventeen?"

"Wasn't."

Joseph drummed his fingers on the table. "What?"

"You said 'isn't,' and you meant 'wasn't.' She's dead." Zach watched him like a hawk.

For the first time since he'd walked in the room, Joseph's face went completely blank. No shock, no anger, no arrogance. Nothing. Joseph drummed his fingers again. "You don't say. That's a shame."

If he hadn't liked the man before, he sure as fuck wouldn't with him sitting here, cool as a cucumber while being dealt the news that a woman—a *girl*—he'd slept with was dead. *Unless he already knew because he's the one who did it.* He had to keep control. The goal was to make *Joseph* lose it. Not Zach.

It was harder than he could have dreamed. "You know, you say *your* home, plural, when you talk about Martha, but I don't see it."

"I don't really give a damn what you see, Sheriff."

He ignored that. Eden had said to keep Martha out of it, but the only time he'd gotten a response and made the other man's mask slip had been when he'd brought her up. "Martha doesn't really share—not power and not men. Don't suppose she knew that you were knocking boots with Neveah Smith."

"Don't suppose she did."

He gritted his teeth. "Woman like that, one of her younger men—well, both of them—dicking around with girls closer to their own age. That's got to be a blow to the ego. She's got Abram, sure, but that woman doesn't share."

Joseph leaned forward, every line of his body reading as lazy arrogance. "I know you're not suggesting Martha killed those girls in a jealous rage. That's ludicrous."

Zach couldn't exactly argue that, but it was motive all the same. That was the problem with this case—there was more than their fair share of motive to go around. He nodded as if agreeing with Joseph. "You're right. Martha's too smooth for something like that. If she wanted those girls to disappear, easy enough to make it happen without leaving a trail and dumping the body on my back doorstep. You, on the other hand, aren't nearly as smart or as smooth as she is."

"Me? Sheriff, you must really be hard up for leads if you're looking in my direction. If I fucked Neveah—and that's a big *if*—then it was a little fun between two consenting people. That girl wasn't looking for something serious any more than I was. She had her plans set on the horizon—same as the other one."

The other one. "You spend a lot of time with Elouise Perkins?"

Instantly, Joseph shut down. "Don't know what you're talking about."

Zach pressed and circled and nearly ground his teeth to dust, but Joseph never changed his story or offered up more information. An hour later, since he was about to lose his mind and commit assault, he pushed to his feet. "Make yourself comfortable. You're not going anywhere."

Joseph looked at his watch. "Only for another twenty-three hours. Unless you're planning on charging me with something?" His shit-eating grin told Zach that the man knew exactly how little evidence they actually had on him. *Fuck.*

He walked out of the room without another word. The man might be right, but that didn't mean Zach would allow him to bait him. Because that's all the entirety of the interview had been—Joseph playing hard to get and sending him in circles. He nearly ran over Eden as he came out the door, but he made sure he heard it click shut behind him before he spoke. "You saw."

"I saw enough."

There wasn't enough time to go through it. William would be texting him at any time, and there was still Lee to deal with. Still, he forced himself to slow down and look at her. "How's the eye?"

She didn't blink. "Hurts like a bitch."

At least that was honest. He didn't like the way she kept brushing off his concern. Eden might be more than capable of taking care of herself, but they were all in over their heads right now. He rubbed a hand over his face, feeling a thousand years old. "William will be starting the autopsy right about now. I should be there."

"I'll go."

It wasn't an option. She could observe, but he had to send someone else with her or risk getting called on the fact that he was allowing Martha Collins's daughter into the investigation officially. He cursed. "I sent Henry home, but let me see if I can find Chase to go with you."

"I don't need a babysitter. Just tell William that I'm there to observe, but not in affiliation with the department." She sounded like she'd done this before.

It was more than that, though. The killer had already hurt her once. Zach didn't like to think of it happening again. He held her gaze. "Take someone with you."

She rolled her eyes. "You really are a mother hen."

"All the same."

"I will." She reached out, hesitated, and then touched his forearm. It was only the briefest of moments, but it centered him all the same. Eden smiled. "Give 'em hell, champ."

CHAPTER
TWENTY-FIVE

Give 'em hell, champ? What the hell was I thinking? Eden trudged out of the police station, feeling like an idiot. It was a welcome relief from feeling responsible for all the murders, but that didn't mean it was comfortable. *Give 'em hell.* She'd never been as good with words as her mother was, but she was better than *that.*

"Eden."

She froze, blinked, and then grinned. "Hey, Vic."

He must have come straight from the airport, because he had a duffel bag slung over one shoulder and wore his usual jeans, boots, and a buttoned-up shirt. All were designed to play down how large he was and make him less intimidating. From what she'd seen, it never worked. His smile didn't quite reach his gray eyes, but she didn't take it personally. That's just how Vic operated. "Heard you were in a bit of trouble."

"I'm not in trouble. I'm taking personal time and helping out a new friend with a case—unofficially, of course."

"Of course." He raised his eyebrows, and they'd worked together enough years for her to read between the lines. He didn't believe she was an innocent bystander any more than she did.

Eden sighed. "Are you up-to-date?" It was an unnecessary question. She knew how he worked, and he'd have pored over the case files on the plane ride over.

Sure enough, Vic nodded. "You headed somewhere?"

"Autopsy." She jerked her thumb at her car. "Want to act as official FBI consultant while I observe as a curious civilian?" *And not just because Zach doesn't want me going anywhere alone.* She needed another mind on this—one that wasn't connected in any way, shape, or form to Clear Springs. She was too close. Zach was too close. And there was no one else. Britton kept his own counsel unless it was an emergency—and what constituted an emergency in her mind differed *greatly* from what apparently did in his. He preferred to have his agents reason things out themselves because he claimed they all had better information being on the ground floor of an investigation than he did reading the reports. Eden thought that was bullshit, but she couldn't deny she was a better agent as a result of his trial-by-fire methods.

Vic nodded and followed her to the car. He didn't speak again until they were pulling out of the parking lot. "So much for taking personal time."

"I was." It tasted like a lie, and she didn't make a habit of lying to her partner, so she cursed and clarified. "It was mostly personal. I knew there was a murder, and I knew it was connected with my past—which meant there was no way in hell Britton would approve of my coming here as anything other than vacation. I didn't expect *this.*"

He leaned back, extending his tall frame as much as he could in the passenger seat. The top of his head brushed the roof of the car just like it did in pretty much every vehicle they'd ever been in together. "Walk me through it."

So she did. The girls. The tattoos. The little present she'd been left. The fact she was pretty sure someone had been in her room at least once since she'd been in town, possibly tampering with her phone.

He waited a beat. "And your mother."

Damn it, she didn't want to talk about Martha. But then, that was the point, wasn't it? She hadn't exactly been forthcoming about her past the entire time they'd worked together, other than vague statements here and there. Vic didn't push. He had a past, too, and understood that some things were better left alone. Word in their unit was that he'd been married back before Eden joined the BAU, and he'd had a partner who'd apparently burned out pretty spectacularly right around the time his marriage failed. But Eden didn't ask, because she respected him enough not to ask about the bones rattling around inside her closet.

Except now he was.

"You read the report. You know."

He looked out the window, everything about his body language seemingly relaxed. She knew he was doing it on purpose, but that didn't stop it from calming her down just a little. "Some things don't come across in the reports. I know it's tough—"

"How the hell do you know? Those girls are being killed as some sick kind of bait to get me back to Clear Springs and keep me here until the unsub has accomplished whatever their purpose is—which evidence is piling up to be killing me." *How would he do it? Chase me down across the fields? Or bury me in the ground like they do their special little Persephone sacrifice?* Her chest tried to close at the thought, and she had to inhale slowly through her nose and out again several times before the screaming inside her head stopped. "You don't know what I'm going through. I can't even put it into words."

"I'd say you just did a damn good job of it."

She glared. "Stop profiling me. This entire situation is a fucking nightmare, and you know it. And, yes, I know that I'm not actually to blame for these girls' deaths, but that doesn't make the guilt magically disappear. Now there's another girl missing, and—" Her breath hitched and she forced steel into her tone. "Three is an important number for Elysians. Seven, too, but I doubt this unsub is going to stretch this out any longer than necessary. Even if he—or she—was willing, there just aren't that many teenagers that fit the profile without expanding their hunting grounds, and I get the feeling he doesn't want to do that."

The numbers were ones Martha had flat out stolen from other religions. Christianity valued seven as the ideal number or, rather, 777. Three showed up in everything from fairy tales to various world myths as a lucky number, a significant number. Eden had once asked her mother what those numbers meant to Persephone and Demeter, and she'd been forced to hold her wrist over that damn candle for seven minutes, and then for three more as punishment.

She refocused and kept speaking. "It's all about Elysia and that god-damn cult. Everything centers around that, including the location of the abductions and killings. He didn't use the same spot as a dumping ground, but that could be because he—and I'm aware that it could be a woman, because penetration doesn't always equal penis—ran Elouise into the ground. He's escalating, and escalating quickly. Either he already had Rachel before he dropped Neveah, or he took her directly after dumping the body. There's no cooldown period, and the methods are evolving all the same. Neveah was different."

"Why was she different?"

She almost snarled at him, her frustration choking her. "You tell me."

Vic shook his head. "You're right—I only know the facts as they're written on paper. You know this place and you know this cult. Your problem is that you're letting the guilt cloud your reasoning. So stop thinking like the daughter of Martha Collins, and start thinking like an agent."

"I *am* thinking like an agent." When he didn't say anything, she cursed some more. "I hate you a little bit right now."

"I'm strangely okay with that."

"You would be." Eden took a deep breath and tried to let go of all the shit clouding her head. "From all accounts, Neveah wasn't much like Elouise. The first victim flew under the radar. She might have turned Lee Whitby's head, but she was riding out the horror show of her life until she could get out of Clear Springs." Something Eden knew all about, though she'd never been as good at keeping her head down as Elouise had.

"Neveah Smith was . . . God, she was a hell-raiser. Her parents are church folk, but she liked to make waves. She had the boys following her around, and I get the feeling she really liked the attention. She was just in love with life and the high she got from defying small-town moral boundaries." If someone was taking notes, she had more in common with Neveah than Elouise, though it wasn't a perfect match by any means—Eden had been skittish about anything that could potentially tie her to Elysia or Clear Springs, and that included boys and sex. There were no foolproof types of birth control, and the thought of being a teen mom and having her mother potentially sweep in, of potentially repeating the history of raising a child on her own without the father around . . . She shuddered. Yeah, it hadn't been worth the risk.

Or maybe she just hadn't met a guy who'd turned her head enough to risk it.

Zach would have.

She pushed the thought away. "It's possible Neveah gave him more of a fight than he was expecting. Or maybe she ran in the wrong direction and he wanted her dumped in a specific spot. It could be anything." But she didn't think so. There was none of the frenzy that came when a serial killer started to flame out. This unsub had been a full three steps ahead of them the entire time, and she didn't see him making such a blatant mistake. "I think it was intentional, though I couldn't begin to tell you why he chose there and that time."

Vic nodded. "I agree. We haven't seen anything quite like this, but all signs point to this guy having a plan from the very beginning."

A plan they were all dancing to the tune of. She thought hard. "It could be that there are two of them—don't look at me like that, I know how rare serial-killing partners are. But if there *were* two of them, it could be that the body was dumped at that specific time to provide Lee with an alibi." Another option occurred, making her sick to her stomach. "Or it could be to create more tension in Clear Springs. It's a bomb waiting for the right spark to set the whole thing off. It's only a matter of time, probably sooner rather than later, especially with Rachel Carpenter missing."

A muscle twitched in Vic's jaw, the only sign of how pissed off that possibility made him. "If the goal was to draw you back here, the unsub accomplished his goal with the first girl. Maybe leaving her like that was about you, too—hard to say for sure—but I think it's possible he got a taste of fame and liked the experience."

She could see that. Zach had said Neveah was left in a similar situation and position as Elouise, but there could be a wealth of evidence they weren't seeing yet. The autopsy would say for certain.

"What about the girl who's missing?"

"She's not like either of them. Or, rather, she's right down the middle. Her dad died in Afghanistan after September eleventh, and it's just her and her mom now. They have a good relationship, from what I can tell, but Rachel's got ambition—her eye's on something better." She pressed her lips together, knowing all too well that she was too close to this. *Way* too close to this. "I liked her, Vic. She was a little prickly, and she's got angst to spare because she's got shit taste in friends, but she's a good kid. She doesn't deserve any of what that prick is going to do to her."

"None of them did."

"No, none of them did." Just like that, the guilt surged again, strong enough to choke her. "If—"

"I'm going to stop you right there, kid. You know as well as I do that letting the guilt ride you is guarantee of a fast burnout and a trip to a nice padded room. You can't shoulder the entire world."

That doesn't stop you from trying. She didn't say it. She never said it. Instead, she adjusted her grip on the steering wheel. "I'm only five years younger than you. I'm not a kid."

"You being a kid has nothing to do with age—or lack of respect— and you know it. Stop nitpicking."

Easier said than done. She wanted to nitpick until he snapped at her and she had a reason to lash out. It wasn't a fair response. Vic hadn't done a single thing other than show up here as backup that was sorely needed. She turned off the highway and followed the GPS instructions into Augusta.

It wasn't until she'd put the car in park that Vic said, "What happened to your face?"

She bit her lip. She really, really didn't want to tell him. She hadn't been being dramatic when she'd thought about Vic carrying around the responsibility of the world on his shoulders. He took the safety of Eden—of all his past partners—deadly serious. "I, uh, had a run-in." Despite his silence, she could actually *feel* his anger growing. "It's nothing."

"Don't try that shit with me, kid. I know what nothing looks like, and that isn't it. That knock you out?"

"Only for a little bit." Ten minutes was *not* a little bit, but she didn't like being treated like she was the kid he liked to call her. She wasn't. *Then don't act like an idiot.* "It's possible that I've got a concussion, but other than a wicked headache, I'm not having any other symptoms."

He snorted. "Not that you'd tell me if you were. You always have to play the hero."

"Pot, meet kettle."

She parked in the lot and they headed into the hospital. The morgue occupied the basement of the local hospital, and she was reasonably sure the temperature actually dropped as they descended in the elevator. The hallway didn't appear any different from the others in the hospital, but it *felt* different. Maybe it was the antiseptic smell, maybe it was just some preternatural sense that rose from being in the vicinity of death.

An older man wearing a pair of jeans and a long-sleeved T-shirt with a giant picture of Garth Brooks on it met them at the door. Eden did her best to melt into the background as the man eyed Vic, his glasses askew. "You must be the feds—and the civilian observer Zach mentioned." He turned and headed deeper into the morgue without another word, leaving them to follow. Eden appreciated that. She was really tired of the *Martha Collins's daughter?* comments. Augusta might be thirty minutes from Clear Springs, but Elysia's reach ran far.

"I took the liberty of getting the preliminary examination out of the way." The coroner—William, Zach had said his name was—moved to the body laid out on the gurney. Eden hadn't had problems with dead victims for years now, but there was something about seeing a girl with so many similarities to *her* on that table that spooked her. She started to rub her arms, realized what she was doing, and forced her hands to her sides.

William didn't seem to notice the lapse, but she caught Vic watching her out of the corner of his eye. *Damn.* There was nothing she could say to reassure him, and if she brought it up, she ran the risk that he'd realize exactly how off center she was.

The coroner started at Neveah's head, her dark hair now combed for evidence and out of her face. "There are a lot of similarities between this girl and the first. Both have bruises—though hers are newer, with no history of abuse that I can see—and both had sex in the last twenty-four hours before their death. There are marks on her feet that indicate she ran barefoot across some distance, and small slices along her shins and knees to back that up."

Well, shit. She hadn't really expected anything else, but she was hoping the unsub keeping the body and dumping it at a later time would have resulted in *some* sort of evidence.

But then William lifted the dead girl's hand, his brown eyes lighting up. "But there's something different. Our girl put up a fight, and a decent one from the amount of skin and dirt beneath her fingernails."

Eden exchanged a look with Vic. "That means—"

"Yes. We have the killer's DNA."

CHAPTER
TWENTY-SIX

Zach couldn't get any further with Joseph, so he refocused on Lee, all too aware of the time dwindling down to when he'd have to either arrest the man or release him. He ambled into the interrogation room and dropped into the chair. "You look tired."

"Yeah, well, it's been a long day—a long week." Lee's eyes were bloodshot, and he was shaking, just enough to be noticeable.

Zach nodded, doing his best to appear sympathetic. Good cop might not work on Joseph—or bad cop, for that matter—but Lee was cooperating, for the most part. "You want some coffee? Snack?"

"Sheriff, with all due respect, I want to go home."

"Just a few more questions." What he wanted was some concrete evidence that would put the person killing girls in Clear Springs behind bars, but Lee didn't seem to have that. No telling if that was the truth, though. Zach sat back, suddenly exhausted. He hadn't been this on edge for such a prolonged period of time since he'd been in the desert. He was out of practice—mostly because he didn't want to be *in* practice. He'd left war behind, and he never wanted to revisit it.

It didn't seem like he was going to have a choice, though this was a very different type of battle.

Working to keep as relaxed as possible, he stretched. "Did you know Joseph had sex with Neveah Smith?"

Lee frowned. "No. Christ, she's only seventeen years old."

"Was. She was found dead this morning, same as Elouise Perkins."

What was left of the light went out of Lee's eyes. "You think Joseph had something to do with this."

"Doesn't matter what I think. I want to know what you think." Maybe this would get the man talking. Zach studied the scratch on his hand that he hadn't even been aware he'd picked up. "Doesn't seem to me that Martha would take kindly to you and Joseph dipping into the local pool."

"That's not what it was with Elouise. It actually meant something." The words started out loud and ended almost in a whisper.

"Not saying it didn't—which is exactly what would have rubbed Martha the wrong way. She doesn't seem the type to share all that well."

Lee's mouth tightened. "It's not her. Not like that. She got her feelings hurt about Elouise, though that was never my intention. But she *knew* she'd won. Elouise chose to leave, and I chose to stay, and that was exactly what she wanted." He sounded bitter in the extreme, though Zach had a hard time being sympathetic. If he'd loved the girl as much as he claimed, he should have packed his bags and left with her, Elysia be damned. Maybe Elouise would still be alive if he had.

Or maybe they'd both be dead.

There was no telling.

He switched tactics. "What about Neveah Smith?"

"What about her?"

"Did Martha know about her and Joseph?"

Lee shook his head. "Martha knows everything. But she's not the one with the problem with Neveah. That was Abram. He didn't like the girl—he considered her disrespectful."

Zach could see that. Abram seemed to take everything to do with Elysia—and Martha, especially—seriously. He would have no patience for thrill-seeking teenagers who poked into the commune looking for a wild ride. He frowned. "You ever see him threaten her?"

"I don't know. No, I don't think so." Lee rubbed his hands over his face, his shoulders drooping. "I can't go back there. Or at least I can't stay. I don't know where it got all twisted up, but I can't stay with Martha or in Elysia."

Zach pushed to his feet. He didn't think he'd be getting any more out of Lee for the time being. "You can leave when this is all over. Until then, stick close to town."

Lee sighed. "I thought you might say something like that."

Zach walked out of the room, but he left the door open. While he couldn't knock Lee off the suspect list completely, he mentally placed the man toward the bottom. He heard raised voices in the main room of the police station and picked up his pace. He burst in, finding Chase facing off against Martha and Abram. "What in the hell is going on here?"

"I should be asking you the same thing! Where are my boys?" Martha took a step forward, and when Chase didn't immediately move, Abram did the same. Chase's shoulders tensed, his hands fisting at his sides.

If this went on much longer, someone was bound to resort to violence, and then he'd have a whole new mess on his hands. Zach crossed his arms over his chest. "Lee is free to go."

"And my Joseph? Where is he?" She looked around as if expecting him to pop out of the woodwork.

Zach didn't have the time or patience for this shit. "Cut the act, Martha. There's no one here to perform for." He moved forward before he finished speaking. "Chase, tell Joseph he's free to go."

Chase opened his mouth like he wanted to argue, shot a glance at Martha and Abram, and seemed to think better of it. But if the heaviness of his footsteps was anything to go by, he wasn't pleased with the new development. Well, fuck, that made two of them. But the truth was that Zach didn't have jack to hold anyone on. This case was high on the circumstantial evidence and low on *actual* evidence, and the circumstantial stuff seemed to point at both everyone and no one at Elysia. Since he couldn't bring in and question the entire community without starting a riot, he needed to let them go and regroup once he had a chance to sit down with Eden and her partner.

Martha leveled a look at him that sent a chill right down to his bones. "I don't like the way you're handling this case, Zachary Owens."

"Well, ma'am, that's really none of your business. I go where the evidence leads me. You wouldn't want the person who killed two teenage girls to get a chance to bring his kill count up to three, would you? You know he's kidnapped a third."

There was no shock on her face at the news, but he had no way of telling if that was because she was that good an actor or because she already knew about both the abduction and the second killing. The latter would be common knowledge around town by this hour, and he needed to find the killer before the Smiths gathered their wits enough to head out to Elysia for a witch hunt.

My life would be easier if I could just sit back and let it happen.

He shut that temptation down *real* fast. A mob was an unpredictable thing, and he still didn't know for a fact that someone at Elysia was behind this—not beyond a shadow of a doubt. Beyond that, there were kids out there and a few hundred people who likely *weren't* involved in this nightmare. Once a mob got rolling, it wouldn't discriminate. It would be chaos, and the innocent were more likely to get hurt than the guilty.

Martha wilted, and Abram immediately put an arm around her shoulders. She wiped at dry eyes. "It's just horrible about those girls. If you think of anything I can do, you tell me right away, you hear?"

"Funny, but your daughter *did* ask for help, and all she got for her trouble was a knock on the head and you giving her the runaround."

She pressed a hand to her chest. "Now, Sheriff, that's simply not true."

So now he was *Sheriff.* Go figure. He stepped back as Joseph and Lee walked into the room. Joseph went immediately to Martha, engulfing her in a hug that appeared to be genuine affection. Was there a damn person in that cult who actually acted and reacted honestly? He was starting to think the answer was no.

Lee, on the other hand, stalked directly to the door, not looking at anyone. He was gone by the time Joseph let Martha go. She looked around, a frown on her face. "What did you do to my Lee?"

"You can't lay the blame for this one on me." Lee was falling apart, but that had more to do with him realizing what Zach and Eden had known all along—that one of Martha's flock was likely responsible.

And that Lee having feelings for Elouise had likely drawn the killer's attention to her in the first place.

Zach stood back and watched Martha and Abram herd Joseph and a reluctant Lee to the SUV they'd parked by the street, unable to shake the feeling that he'd be seeing one—or all of them—again very soon. Frankly, he wished it weren't so. If Martha was involved in all this, it would hurt Eden. It didn't matter that she'd been estranged from her mother for ten years. A mother was a mother, which meant Martha was uniquely qualified to deal devastating emotional blows to her daughter. He didn't like it. He'd shield Eden from that if he could.

The problem was that he couldn't.

He had a feeling they'd all need a shield before this thing was over.

His phone rang, and he breathed a quiet sigh of relief when he saw that it was Eden. Even knowing she was with her partner didn't stop him from worrying about her. Rationally, he knew everyone in the city limits wasn't under his explicit care, but rationality had no place in their current situation. "You find anything?"

"She had DNA under her fingernails." She gave a breathless laugh. "She fought, Zach. She's going to be the key to unlocking this."

Elation hit him, quickly followed by the ever-present guilt. A girl had to die in order for them to get this break. It wasn't right and it wasn't fair, but neither was the world they were living in. He moved to the window and watched Abram hold open the door of a Suburban for Martha. Joseph prodded Lee into the back and then climbed in behind him. "They won't submit to DNA tests without a warrant."

"Martha wouldn't let them even if they were inclined. She's bred the distrust of the government too deep."

And he'd stake his badge on the fact that someone in the car pulling away from the curb was directly responsible for those girls' deaths. Zach put aside all his personal bullshit through sheer force of will. "I'll give the judge up in Augusta a call. It may take some convincing, but I'll get us a warrant by morning."

Judge Tanner used to hunt with Zach's old man back in the day. Now, the tough son of a bitch preferred golfing and gardening, though he often complained it was harder on his knees than sitting in a tree stand for hours had been. There was no telling what side of this thing he'd come down on with the warrants. He wasn't the type to do favors if he thought it went against the law.

A man's voice murmured in the background—Vic—and she said, "Why don't we meet you here? We can compare notes and get on the same page."

"Sounds good." He craved the sight of her, even in the midst of their current storm. Maybe *because* of their current storm. "I'll see you soon." And hopefully tomorrow they'd be one step closer to bringing Elouise and Neveah's killer to justice.

CHAPTER TWENTY-SEVEN

"That key is the, well, the key." Eden followed Zach into the court-house. She tapped her chest another time. "Martha didn't want to talk about it, and it's the one thing that sets the girls apart from your average cult member. And she dodged the subject every time I brought it up." She'd been given it after the Persephone ritual, but Eden had left Elysia before she'd been introduced to the so-called mysteries. She'd her doubts that she would have been even if she'd stayed, though. Beth and Jon hadn't known anything about the key, and if every girl who was buried alive got one, Beth herself would have one already.

"It's the one thing that sets *you* apart, too."

She didn't look back to where Vic brought up their merry band of law enforcement. "It's linked up with Persephone, though hell if I could tell you how." *Maybe it's the key to the underworld? But if that's the case, why would they glorify it with a tattoo? Martha preaches that the underworld is dirty and wrong and something to escape.* She shook her head. "We don't have enough information." For all her goals of sliding back into Elysian life and mining the people there for everything they knew, it hadn't worked out like that at all. Too much had changed. She wasn't one of them any more than she was a citizen of Clear Springs. She didn't have a place.

Zach led the way down a hallway to a door with the plaque declaring it Judge Tanner's office. He glanced over his shoulder. "Let me do the talking."

He hadn't said much since he'd shown up, but she could see how the stress was getting to him. She didn't blame him. It was making her tweaky, too. When they opened the door, the man behind the desk looked up. "Zach Owens."

"Judge."

The judge seemed more bear than man. She suspected when he stood, he'd be at Vic's height, nearly six and a half feet tall, but where her partner was on the leaner side, this man was wide enough that he might have to turn to walk through doors. Combine that with a full head of silver hair that blended in with a beard that hit the middle of his chest, and the flannel that would do any lumberjack proud, and he was a little overwhelming. He eyed them. "You brought me the feds as a present. And I thought we were friends."

"I'm here on business."

"I figured." He huffed out a breath and looked at his watch. "I'm off the clock in exactly thirty minutes, and I have an appointment with my butternut squash. Make it quick."

Eden blinked. She should know better by now than to take people on their surface looks, but the judge seemed more like a man who'd go out and take down a deer with his bare hands than someone who'd make appointments with butternut squash.

Zach didn't sit down. He braced his legs shoulder-width apart and laced his hands behind his back. She doubted he realized he'd just taken an at-ease position, but once a Marine, always a Marine. He cleared his throat. "I need a warrant for DNA samples from Martha Collins and her three lieutenants—Abram, Joseph Edwards, and Lee Whitby."

Judge Tanner didn't seem surprised, which made her wonder if he'd known they were coming. The gossip network in small towns was intricate enough to do the CIA proud. "You have legitimate evidence to point to that commune, I'm assuming, since poking that damn hornet's nest is going to make all our lives a damn nightmare. Martha's rage is legendary, and she holds a grudge like nobody's business. She might be too snooty to bring her business into Clear Springs, let alone Augusta, but she knows the law almost better than I do. You make her angry, you can be damn sure she'll be reporting every violation she can to make life harder for your people."

"I wouldn't ask if I didn't have sufficient belief that one or all of them are connected." He shifted his stance as if bracing for a blow. "There are marks on the bodies that could be done only by someone with intimate knowledge of the inner workings of Elysia, and both girls had romantic—or at least physical—relationships with two of the suspects." He took a deep breath. "And now there's a third girl missing who has those same connections. If we don't move on this, in roughly seven days she's going to be found the same way as the first two."

Judge Tanner looked at each of them in turn and then sat back in his chair. "Give me the file."

Eden found herself holding her breath as he read through the evidence they'd compiled. When all was said and done, it wasn't much. There was a lot in the way of circumstantial and not much that could conclusively point any fingers. The findings beneath Neveah's fingernails were their first break, but they wouldn't do a single thing if there wasn't something to match them to. Vic could run them against the ViCAP database, as was standard with this kind of investigation, but this wasn't some garden-variety serial killer—if there could even be said to be such a thing.

This was someone with an intimate knowledge of Elysia.

Someone like her mother.

Judge Tanner finally set the file down. "It's not much."

"It's what we have."

He turned eyes a startling shade of blue on her. "And you two. What do you have to say about this?" He squinted. "Wait a damn second. I know you. You're Martha Collins's daughter."

"I'm not here officially." She fought down her instinct to snap back. It wouldn't help anyone right now, least of all Rachel Carpenter. If she had the ability to convince the judge to give them this warrant, she was going to do what it took. "Consider me an expert civilian consultant, and I think we can both agree I'm uniquely qualified to say these murders were done by someone within Martha's flock—someone high up. The dead girls all share a tattoo that—"

"That you seem to have." He raised his eyebrows. "What a fortunate coincidence that you're back in town right as our girls start dropping dead, and they all bear a startling resemblance to you."

She knew that. Damn it, she knew that better than anyone. Eden gritted her teeth. "No one is more concerned with finding this killer than I am."

"I can't attest to that, and the fact that you're even in this room could potentially compromise the investigation." He eyed Vic. "You're one scary son of a bitch. Which branch of special forces were you part of?"

"SEALs. Team Six."

"Humph." Judge Tanner shook his head. "You damn frogs. I should have known. You have that dead look about your eyes."

Eden turned to stare at Vic. She'd known he was ex-military, but he'd never offered what branch, and she'd never asked—part of their policy. How the hell hadn't she known he was a goddamn Navy SEAL in another life? She made herself take a mental step back and look at him from the judge's point of view . . . and came up with nothing. She frowned harder. "How did you know?"

"Like recognizes like, little girl." He set the file aside and focused on Zach. "The most you're looking at is a warrant compelling them to give oral swabs. Even that may get thrown out in court, because any attorney worth his salt would argue that my being on good terms with your old man means I'm reaching with this warrant solely as a favor. And they'd be right." He shook his head. "I'll have it ready by morning. Now get out of my office."

They got out of his office.

Eden considering cornering Vic about the new information that meeting had revealed, but there was a time and place for such talks, and now was neither. She wasn't sure there *was* a good time and place to demand to know why he'd kept such an important piece of information from her—or how she'd missed it all along.

She'd met SEALs before—it went with the territory that sometimes they ran into the various military branches in various cases—and she just couldn't reconcile the differences. Those guys were scary sons of bitches. Usually when they looked at her, she got the feeling they were mentally compiling a list of ways they could kill her and dispose of her body without anyone being the wiser. It wasn't personal—it was just how their minds worked. She'd never once, not in five years, gotten that vibe from Vic. Sometimes he was too intense, and he was overprotective to a clinical degree, but a SEAL?

It just didn't compute.

"You're going to give yourself a headache—worse of a headache. Let it go."

She turned to face her partner. "How did he know? I'm trained in reading people, and I've worked with you for years and I had no idea."

Vic shrugged. "It's like he said—like recognizes like. He was a Ranger, if I don't miss my guess."

Zach came to stand next to them. "Back in Vietnam."

That, at least, she could see. Eden rubbed the bridge of her nose, all too aware of how much her face hurt. She was going to have to rest soon. No matter how wired she was right now, the day would catch up with her. "We need to get all our ducks in a row before the DNA test."

Vic shook his head. "I spent all day on the plane. I'm going to do some looking over the files again and walk around to see if I can get a feel for the town."

She started to say that wasn't a good idea, but stopped. Vic might not advertise it, but he was easily as deadly as Abram—and that went doubly if she took into account that he was a former SEAL. There wasn't much Clear Springs could offer that would be dangerous to him. *Not to mention the unsub is focused on* me. That was almost a relief. She could deal with a personal threat better than worrying that someone around her might be hurt.

Someone like Rachel.

She swallowed hard. "I'll update Britton."

"No need. I'll make the call." He turned gray eyes on her—wolfy eyes, she'd always thought. "You need to sit your ass down before you fall down."

Zach snorted. "You took the words right out of my mouth." He considered Vic. "If you want to drive her car back, I'll take her and grab some food and then make sure she doesn't get a wild hair."

"I am standing *right here*." She sounded petulant and hated it. "And if you talked to me like an adult, you'd know that I plan on going back to the B&B and getting some sleep." There wouldn't be much in the way of sleep tonight, no matter how brave a face she put on it, and she didn't trust the current situation enough to take the sleeping aid the doctor had prescribed months ago. Hell, she didn't take it most nights. With a job like hers, she could be pulled from sleep at any time and expected to operate on all cylinders without missing a beat. There wasn't the luxury of shaking off a pill-induced haze.

Or that's what she told herself.

The truth was that the pills made the nightmares worse—and impossible to escape.

She turned to them both. "There's a girl who's missing—a girl who's probably going through some seriously scary shit right now, and if we don't stop it, she's going to end up just like the other two. Even if we get the DNA swabs, that takes *weeks*. You can't put a rush order on it when there are dozens of other rush orders in the mix."

Zach pointed at his cruiser. "You want to yell at me because you're frustrated? Fine. Get in the damn car before you do. We have an audience."

Eden belatedly realized there was a handful of people in hearing range, all watching with avid expressions. *Damn. Damn, damn, damn.* She should have noticed them. More so, she shouldn't need to be reprimanded like she was still green. She tossed her keys to Vic and turned without another word to stalk to Zach's vehicle. *Stupid. So stupid. You're reacting instead of acting, and it's fucking with your head.*

It didn't matter if that was the truth. She couldn't afford to skip a beat, not with Rachel counting on her. *She's just a kid.* They were *all* just kids.

Whoever was doing this was known to her, no matter how tentative the relationship. They *had* to be in order to know about the garland. That fact alone meant they were in Elysia at the same time she was. The only problem with that was that every single one of their suspects had been, too. Even if the unsub hadn't actually seen her making the flower chain, they could have gleaned the information from someone who had. Even though there were more secrets in that cult than there were trees in the Rockies, it didn't stop members from getting together and talking—gossiping. But that wasn't the way to think about it, because if they went in that direction, they were back to anyone in Elysia being a suspect.

Eden rubbed her face and then winced when she came into contact with her bruise.

If she could just figure out the missing piece, she could put an end to all this.

CHAPTER
TWENTY-EIGHT

Eden kept up a running commentary as Zach drove them back to Clear Springs. She'd always worked better when reasoning through things aloud, and she wanted a head start before she bunkered down tonight and started making lists. "He's coming after me eventually. Maybe I can do something to take his attention away from Rachel and up his timeline." It would be tricky, though, because they ran the risk that the unsub would kill Rachel before the timeline indicated. She tapped a finger to her lip. "If it was the unsub who hit me earlier, he had a chance to take me and passed it up. This guy is controlled—freakishly controlled—and that indicates he has a plan with a timeline he's sticking to. Which we already knew, but it's still good information. At this point, *any* information is good information."

She looked up and realized they'd taken a turn off the highway while she was occupied with her thoughts. "Where are we going? I thought you were taking me back to the B&B." She'd already mentally geared up for a night spent poring over the case file yet again and making notes.

Katee Robert

"If I drop you off, you're going to get straight to work and forget to eat." He didn't look at her. Every muscle in his body was tense, like he was preparing for a fight. "Maybe you aren't concerned with taking care of yourself, but I am."

She blinked. *Uh, okay.* The last thing she needed right now was to deal with another person's feelings, and she hadn't forgotten the way he'd talked to Vic over her back at the courthouse. That macho bullshit might work with the women around here, but it wasn't Eden's cup of tea. She didn't find it sexy, and if he was going to make a habit of it . . . *What? You're leaving when this case is done. You always leave. There's no future here. There never was.*

He climbed out of the car and headed for his front door, leaving her staring after him. For a few seconds, Eden actually considered trying to hotwire his car. It'd been a very long time since she'd done it, but some skills didn't disappear with time. She reluctantly let go of the impulse. Grand theft auto wouldn't solve anything.

But it would be extremely satisfying.

She started after him, finding the front door open. They needed to get to the bottom of whatever had crawled up his ass so they could move on to more important things—mainly stopping the unsub.

Eden found him in the kitchen, pouring a healthy glass of whiskey into a tumbler. She frowned. "I didn't think you drank hard alcohol." He might have the easygoing small-town sheriff thing down pat, but she recognized the inner control freak he kept on a tight leash. She doubted he'd been drunk anytime in recent memory, and he'd only had that single beer the other night before he switched to water.

Today must have really gotten under his skin if he was breaking that habit.

"I'm making an exception." He downed it in a single shot without so much as flinching.

Impressive. She crossed her arms over her chest. "What's got you in a tizzy? Because throwing a tantrum without warning isn't a positive trait, no matter which way you swing it."

He poured another glass. "Have you always been so damn reckless?"

She straightened. "I don't know what you're talking about."

"Yes, you do." He raised the glass, stopped, and set it down. "I thought it was just that you were driven to find this killer, but that's not it, is it? Your partner wasn't surprised by the bruise on your face, which makes me think this kind of thing has happened before."

She'd never been taken down quite in the same way before, but she didn't think he was talking about that. She lifted her chin. "Being with the BAU comes with risks. Every type of law-enforcement job does."

But he was already shaking his head. "That's not what I'm talking about, and you know it."

"What the hell do you care?" Anger made her voice sharp, but she didn't try to temper it.

"Do you push everyone away, or am I just special?" He downed the second glass and set it on the counter with a clink. "Who am I kidding? There's a wall between you and the rest of the world. You even hold your partner at a distance."

"That's none of your business." Why was he forcing the issue? Especially now, when there were so many other things on the line. Who cared if she didn't have much in the way of close friends? It was just how she operated. She knew the hard way that there were no guarantees in life, and letting people within arm's reach was just asking for a knife in the ribs.

"I can't pretend that I know what you went through growing up, but living your life without roots isn't the answer."

The pressure in her chest got worse. He was putting into words things she barely allowed herself to think of. "I don't remember signing up for a therapy session, Zach. Back the fuck off."

Instead, he circled around the island and stalked toward her. "There are people who care about you. Your partner. Your boss." He stopped in front of her, too close, and slid his hands up her arms to cup her chin, forcing her to meet his gaze. "*Me.* I see you, Eden. And you matter, no matter what you seem to think. If something happens to you . . ." He growled, the sound so low she felt it more than heard it. "It won't. I won't let it." Then Zach kissed her.

Zach didn't know what he was doing. He meant to keep things simple between himself and Eden until the rest of the world became sane again. But anger seared through what was left of his self-control. He'd never had much when it came to her.

He needed her to understand that she was worth something, at least to him. In the back of his mind, he knew that was a thing she had to decide for herself—it couldn't come from the outside—but with her going soft in his arms and her mouth against his, he didn't give a damn. He laced his fingers through her hair, tilting her head back to give him better access. She tasted of cinnamon—a little bite, a little sweetness—and he craved more.

This time they weren't going to stop.

He pulled back enough that they shared breath. "Say yes, Eden."

"I . . ." She blinked those big dark eyes at him, looking vulnerable and all too human. "This is a mistake."

"Almost definitely."

She laughed softly. "I'm still very angry with you—and this conversation isn't over."

"We can fight later." He kissed her again, slipping his tongue into her mouth. She opened to him immediately, her hands clutching his shoulders. Pressed against her like this, it was almost astounding to realize how small she was. When they were talking or fighting, Eden seemed larger than life. In reality, she topped out at maybe five feet six inches, and while she had muscles, she was still petite. *Anything could happen to her. It doesn't matter how capable she is. She was laid out today and helpless. She could have died.*

That last thought spurred him on. He backed her up and lifted her onto the kitchen island. They were separated for precious seconds while he slid off her shirt and dropped it on the floor, but then she was in his arms again, kissing him with all her might. She yanked his shirt over his head and tossed it behind her, then ran her hands up his chest. "Damn, Zach."

He knew what she was seeing. The scars. They weren't anything like what some of his squad had come home with, but shrapnel left its mark all the same. He didn't talk about it with people in Clear Springs. What was there to say? He'd made it home alive, which was more than many could say. No one knew about it except his parents, and that was only because the military had called them when he was hospitalized. "It was a long time ago."

Her fingers stopped on the curved cut across his left pec. "Not long enough."

No, not long enough. Maybe in another ten years he'd have left the nightmares behind, but he didn't think so. Some things just stayed with a person.

He didn't want to think about that right now, though.

Zach jerked her to the edge of the counter and unbuttoned her jeans, needing to have her, needing as much of her bare skin pressed against his as possible. There was no telling if either of them would make it out of this unscathed, let alone alive. That was becoming readily clear the longer this case went on. "I need you."

"Good." She lifted herself up so he could pull her pants off to join their shirts on the floor. "Because I'm tired of talking."

It wasn't over. It might never be over. He didn't care right now. Zach ran his hand down from her neck, between her breasts and down her stomach. She had scars of her own, scars that he doubted had anything to do with the line of duty. *And she still came back here to face her demons.* "You are so fucking brave."

Eden shook her head. "Come here." She hooked the back of his neck and kissed him, the move pressing his hand between her legs. He nearly groaned at how warm and welcoming she was there. For him.

He had no right to the surge of possessiveness he felt at the thought, just like he had no right to yell at her for taking unnecessary risks. She wasn't his.

But maybe I want her to be.

"Promise me." He pushed a finger into her, cursing at how good she felt there, at how beautiful she was with her head back in abandon, pleasure written over her face.

"Promise you what?" She didn't open her eyes.

He opened his mouth, but what could he say? There were no guarantees, not in life and not in this. So Zach kissed her again, stroking her slowly, gauging her responses to see exactly what she liked. He needed her release, needed to feel in control of this little corner of their world, at least in this moment.

Eden pushed him away. He had a second to wonder if she was putting a stop to this—and if she wasn't the smarter of the two of them—and then she hopped off the counter. "You're wearing too many clothes." She went for his belt buckle, divesting him of his pants in record time. "Condom."

"Bedroom."

"Go get it."

He didn't ask why she didn't want to be in the bedroom, mostly because he could barely string two thoughts together with her standing in his kitchen, gloriously naked. Her tattoos snaked down to her elbows, melding together into a mural that only seemed to highlight her beauty, framing her breasts to perfection. He headed for the bedroom before he could throw caution to the wind and touch her again.

It took a grand total of thirty seconds to grab a handful of condoms and come back.

She raised her eyebrows. "Someone's optimistic."

"Once won't be enough, and you know it." He grabbed her hand with his free one and towed her into the living room. The dogs were safely locked outside, and there was no one around to see now, any more than there had been last time. He wanted to watch her where the late-afternoon light would turn her golden skin even more so and to kiss her the way he intended to.

She straddled him, wasting no time in grabbing his cock and sinking onto his length. They cursed in the shared breath between them. She was so damn tight around him that he tried to slow her down, but Eden was having none of it. She raised herself up and sank down again. "Zach."

"I've got you." Maybe if he said it enough times, she'd understand that he meant it in more than orgasms. He wanted her in every way that mattered—or at least wanted a chance to really explore it without the damned case hanging over their heads.

He gripped her hips, guiding her strokes, watching her face as she lost herself in pleasure. She was softer like this, more woman and less federal agent. The woman he was hopelessly attracted to.

The woman who wouldn't hesitate to put herself in the line of fire if it meant she could bring this killer down.

Zach gripped her chin. "Promise me, Eden. Promise me you won't take any stupid risks."

She held on to his shoulders, meeting his gaze as she took him deeper yet, sealing them as close as two people could be. Her nails pricked his skin, the light pain only making his pleasure sharper.

But she didn't promise.

In the back of his mind, he'd known she wouldn't. She kissed him, the soft gesture completely at odds with the harsh contact of his body into hers. "I'm not a liar, Zach."

He reached between them and stroked her clit, needing to have at least *this*. He transferred his grip to the back of her neck, holding them sealed together as he drove her crazy with the little circles his thumb made.

"Yes, yes, *yes*." She threw her head back, her body milking his as she came.

He couldn't hold on. Zach flipped them, pounding into her, chasing his pleasure the same way he'd chased hers. He came, her name on his exhale, and collapsed to the side. But he didn't release her. All too soon, she'd be off again, beyond his limited circle of protection.

He had to hold her close while he could.

CHAPTER
TWENTY-NINE

Eden woke to the sound of her phone ringing. She stretched, smiling a little at how deliciously sore she was. Last night might have created more complications than it had solved, but it had been good. So damn good. She rolled over and dug through the pile of clothes Zach had dropped next to the bed for her still-ringing phone. She frowned at the unknown number, but gave a mental shrug and answered. "Eden Collins."

"Eden?"

She shot straight upright. She knew that voice. "Rachel? Rachel, where are you?"

"Eden, I'm scared." Rachel sobbed. "He's hurt me . . . so much. He said it's your fault."

The buzzing in her ears got worse, but she managed to keep her voice even. "Rachel, tell me everything you can about your surroundings and who hurt you."

"It's so dark . . ."

"Rachel, focus."

A pause, and then a click. For a second, she thought the call had ended, but then Rachel's voice sounded again. "Eden?"

"I'm here." She was clutching the phone so tightly, it was a wonder it didn't break apart in her hands. She could sense Zach awake behind her, but she couldn't move, couldn't do anything but cling to the voice on the other end of the phone. "Honey, you need to focus."

"Eden, I'm scared." She sobbed. "He's hurt me . . . so much. He said it's your fault."

She almost dropped the phone. *Not Rachel at all—a recording.* "I know it's not her. You can stop now."

But it just kept playing on loop until Zach extracted the phone from her hands and ended the call. He pulled her into his arms, and she actually let him, sinking into the feel of his skin on hers. The comfort was a lie, but she took it all the same. "She could already be dead."

"He kept the other two alive for almost a week."

But things had changed between Elouise and Neveah. The unsub was learning, evolving. Elouise had been his first—she'd stake her badge on it. Maybe not his first killing, but his first ritualized killing. With Neveah, he'd perfected his technique, added elements that hadn't been there with Elouise. *Why?*

That was the question. Or, rather, it was one question to add to the growing list currently threatening to drown her.

"We can't take anything for granted." She slipped out of his arms and stood. The sun no longer felt like a welcoming friend. Now it was a glaring reminder of a time slipping through her fingers. If Rachel was still alive, she was on borrowed time. And there wasn't a damn thing Eden could do about it.

Nothing except find the piece of shit who was doing this.

He. "Rachel said 'he' in the recording."

"We always thought it was a man." Zach hadn't moved from his spot on the bed, watching her get dressed with an unreadable expression on his face. "The evidence of sexual activity indicates it."

"That can be faked." At least to some extent.

He narrowed his eyes. "You think there's a woman involved. Why?"

"I don't know." There was something there, something she couldn't quite put her finger on. "It's just a gut feeling. The entirety of the Elysian faith centers around this powerful woman and her daughter—who is equally powerful if one were to look at it like that."

"What do you mean?"

She pulled her shirt over her head and met his gaze. "What no one seems to remember is that Persephone wasn't only Demeter's daughter or Hades' wife. She was the queen of the underworld in her own right."

He studied her, almost as if seeing her for the first time. "Martha considers you her Persephone."

"Yes." She sat on the bed to pull on her socks. "And so does the unsub."

His sigh was so quiet, she half wondered if she'd imagined it. She knew what he wanted—for her to promise to be safe and to actually follow through on that promise, but she couldn't do either. If putting herself into the path of danger meant Rachel would survive this, she'd do that without a thought. That was her job. She'd signed up for it when she took the badge. Rachel was just a kid.

Once upon a time, Eden had been just a kid caught up in the dangerous world of Elysia. No one had come to save her back then, but Rachel had a whole team working to ensure she got out of this alive.

She pushed to her feet. "We need to get moving. Hopefully forcing them to give DNA samples will spook the unsub into action."

"You mean action like making an attempt on you."

That was exactly what she meant. She turned to face him, squaring her shoulders. "We don't have time for this."

"Make time." He stood, and she got temporarily distracted by the sheer sight that was Zach Owens in the nude.

She forced herself to look away. "You don't understand."

"I understand all too well." The sympathy in his blue eyes almost did her in. "You can't change what happened to you. It wasn't your fault, and it was beyond your control. You've made something of your life that would make anyone proud. Getting yourself killed isn't going to do anything but guarantee that they win."

She glared. "I know that. I have no intention of getting killed."

"That's not the same as saying you'll be careful."

"For fuck's sake, Zach, enough. You're not my mother." Her mother, who might be involved in this deeper than she wanted to think about. "You're not my brother. You're not my goddamn boyfriend. You don't get a say."

She hadn't realized he was allowing her to see the anger on his face until he shut it down. "Fine."

She blinked. "What?"

"Fine. You want to shut me out? Shut me out. That's not going to make me stop caring if you're okay, and it's not going to make it any easier to keep out of my bed."

She actually took a step back. "I'm out of your bed. Right now, in fact."

He gave her a look like she was a few crayons short of a full box. "Eden, I could have you right now, and you'd be screaming on my cock inside of five minutes."

She opened her mouth to tell him he was wrong, but her body was already tingling, her nipples pebbling, and things low in her stomach clenching, making the words a lie. "You're a jackass."

"No. I just call it like I see it. You need to retreat after last night—fine. But don't go rushing headlong into some harebrained scheme because you're afraid I'm going to put you in a cage."

"You couldn't put me in a cage if you tried."

He nodded like she'd said something else. "I'll get dressed and give you a ride into town. I have a few things to take care of before we do the DNA tests, the main of which is organizing another search party for Rachel." He saw her look and shook his head. "I know, but it will keep folks busy, and that's important right now."

He was right. She knew that.

Zach continued. "I'm assuming you want to be there when I bring Martha and her men in."

"I do." She rocked back on her heels, not sure how to handle the change in his demeanor. "I thought we were fighting about this."

Zach sat on the bed long enough to pull on a pair of jeans. "Fighting isn't going to accomplish anything. I care about you, Eden. But you're right—I'm not your mother, your brother, or your boyfriend. If you don't want to take my concerns into account, you don't have to."

That's what she wanted . . . so why did it make her chest hurt to hear him say it? She was an emotional mess right now, and going toe to toe over the fact that Zach *wasn't* fighting with her would just waste their time. She finally nodded. "Okay." Really, there was nothing else to say.

And they didn't.

Silence reigned during the entire drive back to the B&B. Zach parked out front, and she opened the door and hesitated. "I care about you, too."

"I know."

The surety in his voice made her want to smack him. "I just can't let that get in the way of bringing this unsub down. There's a girl's life at stake."

"Eden, there's more than that, and you know it."

She shut the door without answering. She did know it. There was *her* life, sure, but there was also the fate of every person living in Elysia. She'd fought very hard not to think about the implications of there being a killer loose in Martha's inner circle. Her mother would try to spin it, and she'd try to spin it hard, but there was only so much she could do once the courts became involved.

And if Martha is behind these deaths . . .

Eden headed inside, ducking into the stairwell before Dolores could look up from the magazine she was poring over and start questioning where she'd been all night. It really was too easy. Anyone could come and go from this building if they had the slightest bit of stealth. She didn't breathe easy again until she had the door closed and locked between her and the rest of Clear Springs, and even then she couldn't relax until she'd searched every inch of her room. Nothing *seemed* disturbed, but there was once again the faintest prickling at the nape of her neck suggesting that someone had been here, going through her things.

She closed the curtains and stripped, needing a shower to clear her head so she could face the challenges the day was no doubt going to bring. With the water beating a rhythm against her bare skin, her fears once again reared up and kicked her in the face.

If her mother was responsible, she'd lose any property to her name. It would most likely pass to Eden.

I don't want it. What the hell would I do with a hundred acres in Montana? With all the people who live off the land there? The thought of letting them continue to worship Demeter and do their yearly burial of Persephone filled her with revulsion, but to the individual, they had given Martha every single thing of worth they owned. If they were forced back into the real world, they would be starting from nothing— from less than nothing. And that wasn't even considering people like Beth and Jon who'd grown up in the cult.

Or how brutal deconditioning cult beliefs could be.

Eden closed her eyes and ducked her head under the spray, wishing she could wash away her fears as easily as she washed off the scent of Zach and sex.

There were no easy answers.

It was almost enough to have her hoping Martha had no connection to the killer, but she couldn't even afford to wish for that, because it could color her investigation. *I shouldn't be here. I never should have come back.*

A creak sounded from somewhere close, and she jerked out of the spray, blinking the water from her eyes. Seconds ticked by, the water cooling to a temperature slightly less than scalding, and she started shivering, the belief she wasn't alone only growing with each careful breath she exhaled. *Where is my gun?* She almost cursed aloud when she realized she'd left it in the nightstand. *How did Eden Collins die? Oh, that idiot? She was shot with her own service weapon.*

She held the metal rings of the shower curtain to keep them from clinking and then carefully stepped out of the shower. The cadence of the water changed without her there, but it wasn't something a person would notice unless they were listening for it. She padded across the bathroom floor and angled to peer out the doorway and into the rest of the room. One second, two, three, and nothing moved. Her gun lay where she'd left it, damn near taunting her with its nearness. She could dive forward, roll across the bed, and come up with gun raised before anyone in the room could react.

If they haven't already tampered with the gun by removing the bullets.

She was just a little ray of sunshine today.

When the seconds ticked into minutes, she couldn't wait any longer. She leaped out of the bathroom, clearing the space to the bed with a single move, rolling across the mattress and scooping up her gun when she did, and ending up crouched behind the bed with her back to the wall. Her hands shook where they held the raised gun, but she clicked off the safety all the same. It took her a few moments to process what she was seeing.

Nothing. No one. Her room was empty.

Eden rose and walked to the closest, poking through the handful of clothes hanging there and finding nothing. She turned to double-check that the door was locked and froze. Not only was the lock not engaged but there was a gift basket sitting on the desk that had most definitely *not* been there when she'd gotten in the shower. Fear rose, cloying and thick. She'd been naked and as helpless as a person could be, and there had been someone in her room, maybe even in the bathroom, a few feet away, and she hadn't known.

You did know. You heard something.

But not soon enough.

She checked to make sure her gun was, in fact, loaded, and then moved to lock the door. *I can't sleep here. The unsub—if that's who it is, and who else would it be—can get in whenever he wants to. I can't keep him out.* She was fine with the idea of playing bait, but there was a world of difference between going into a situation with guns blazing, so to speak, and lying in that bed and waiting to hear the lock turn as someone broke into her room. She shuddered. *I can't do it. Not that.*

Realizing she was stalling, she turned to the basket. It looked like any other gift basket that went out around the various holidays—woven plastic and that crinkly plastic wrap that partially obscured the contents. She moved forward, feeling like she was in a haze, and undid the jaunty ribbon at the top, using the barrel of her gun to ease the plastic wrap down. Eden bit back a scream at what was revealed.

A dismembered bat in a bed of daises.

She took one step back and then another, her stomach lurching into her throat. It was only the fact she hadn't eaten anything yet this morning that kept her from needing to rush to the toilet. She reached blindly for her phone, dialing while watching the dead bat, half-afraid it would twitch or something. She'd lose it on the spot if it did.

"I'm kind of busy, Eden."

"Zach." Was that her voice? She sounded weak and terrified. Eden cleared her throat. "Zach, I—"

Instantly, his tone changed, all anger disappearing. "What happened? Are you okay?"

"Someone broke into my room while I was in the shower."

"Shit." On the other end of the phone, tires screeched, and there was a massive amount of background noise like he'd just gone off-road. "I'm coming. Go into the bathroom and lock the door."

That got her moving again. "I already searched the room. There's no one here but me." *Now.*

"That's the first step. This is the second time someone's been in there—that we know of—so he can get in again." A thump, and the background noise died down, as he must have hit pavement again. "You have your gun?"

"Yes."

"Good. The second reason you need to go into the bathroom is so you don't shoot me on accident when I come through the door."

Eden backed away from the door in question. "I would never shoot you on accident."

"No, but after our conversation this morning, it might be a little more on purpose than that."

She knew what he was doing—pushing her to get her back on solid ground—but she still snarled. "Give me a little credit here. One fight doesn't mean I want to shoot you." *Much.*

"I'm ten minutes out. The bathroom, Eden." His voice dropped. "Please."

"Okay." She hung up and started for the bathroom before she realized she was still naked and the shower was still running. She cursed and grabbed the first thing she found—a pair of jeans and a white T-shirt—and walked into the bathroom. Her hands shook as she locked the door and then turned off the shower, but there wasn't a single thing she could do about it. The longer she waited, the worse the shakes got, until she had to set her gun aside because she was afraid she might actually shoot herself by accident. *Guess Zach wasn't too far off on that one.*

She didn't hear sirens, but exactly ten minutes later there were pounding footsteps down the hallway, and the main door to her room was thrown open. "Eden, it's me."

She bit back a borderline hysterical sob and shoved to her feet. "In here."

He came through the door slowly, as if aware of how close she was to losing it. She let him see her, let him see she was okay—and then she threw herself into his arms. Her body shook despite her mental command for it to remain still. He held her closely, his hand stroking her hair and his voice soothing. "I'm here. You're safe. I'll keep you safe."

She buried her face in his neck, letting his words roll over her. In that moment of weakness, Eden almost believed him. That she was safe, that he would keep her safe.

That she had someone she could truly lean on.

CHAPTER THIRTY

Zach drove to the station, Eden in the passenger seat next to him, his vision painfully clear. He knew it was adrenaline, knew that the letdown would kick him in the ass, but he couldn't keep it locked down. It was one thing to know Eden was potentially the ultimate victim of this serial killer, but it was something else altogether to know that bastard had been in her room. The gift basket with the dead bat was in the truck, carefully packaged up to preserve what little evidence there might be. He wasn't optimistic. The only evidence they had to date was beneath Neveah Smith's fingernails, and they were looking at more than a week's turnaround time, even with a rush order.

Plenty of time for the killer to finish what he started with Rachel and move on to Eden.

There wasn't any doubt in Zach's mind that she was his next target. Everything was escalating to that event, and he could actually feel the seconds slipping through his fingers. Not enough time. There hadn't been enough fucking time since they'd found Elouise's body.

Eden tilted her head back against the headrest and closed her eyes. "I'm a little surprised that the unsub killed the bat. It's a punishable offense in Martha's world." She didn't give him a chance to respond before she cursed. "But then, killing Persephone would be pretty damn frowned upon. With no Persephone, Demeter would ravage the earth with eternal winter. Crops would never grow. Spring would never come. Who the hell would want that?"

"I don't know." He'd said it so many times since the start of this case that it felt like a mantra.

"It doesn't make sense. So much of this doesn't make sense." She pulled a hair tie out of the pocket of her leather jacket and yanked her hair up. "Well, this DNA test will shake something loose one way or another."

He climbed out of the cruiser and waited for Eden to join him. "I need to get the basket."

"I know." She took a breath, and when she spoke again, some of the sharpness had bled out of her voice. "I'm okay. It scared the shit out of me when I saw it, but I'm okay now. You don't have to tiptoe around my feelings—just get it."

It was less about tiptoeing and more about the fact that she was a little too wide around the eyes, and her hands shook when she thought he wasn't looking. It was understandable that this situation was getting to her, but if she wouldn't just admit that fact, he didn't know what he was supposed to do.

Maybe her partner would know.

"Vic going to be here for the DNA testing?"

"Yeah." She yanked out her ponytail and redid it. "He's bringing my rental here as we speak."

Maybe having her partner here would help settle her. He tried not to resent that. She'd called *him* when she was in trouble and panicking. That was more than he would have expected given how their last encounter had ended. It was hard to be patient with her, but his current stress had more to do with the murders than with Eden. He would be patient, damn it. "I'm going to take Chase and go round them up."

"We'll follow you up." When he hesitated, she rolled her eyes. "The warrant says they need to submit to the swabbing, not that they have to do it in the police station. You're more likely to avoid a fight if you take it to them and ambush them in Elysia. And I happen to have an open invitation to be there, so no reason I can't tag along."

As much as he wanted to argue just for the sake of keeping her away from that place, she had a point. Zach caught sight of her rental coming down the street. "Bring your partner up-to-date. I'll get the swabs and the warrant."

He left her standing in the parking lot, looking so damn alone it made his heart ache.

It took ten minutes to get everything sorted out. He was loading the swabs into a small case when Chase strode into the station. He looked like shit, but he was wearing a different shirt than he'd had on yesterday, and he'd taken the time to shave this morning. So, really, he was holding up as well as any of them were. Chase narrowed his eyes at the case in Zach's hand. "DNA?"

"Yeah. About to head out to the compound right now."

Chase nodded. "We need to put this monster away for good."

"Yeah. Sooner the better." *I hope. I seriously fucking hope.* The details were there, laid out by Eden time and time again. It had to be a cult member, and it was unlikely it was anyone too low on the totem pole, because they wouldn't know a damn thing about the key tattoo all the girls had on their sternum.

It was just a matter of figuring out which member of Martha's inner circle was responsible.

Could be any of them. All of them.

The thought made him sick to his stomach. Bad enough that one person had hurt those girls—if it had been a group, that just seemed so much worse. But cults had gone bad in the past, and killing two teenagers was nothing compared with what Manson's people had done back in 1969, or the suicide pacts that had cropped up over the years. It wasn't beyond the realm of possibility, by any means.

"I'll keep you updated."

◆ ◆ ◆

"We're tipping our hand in a big way. Lots of risk." Eden didn't take her eyes from the cruiser in front of them as they followed Zach toward Elysia. In the distance, the gates rose, larger than life, as ominous as tombstones. Or maybe she was just being dramatic.

She didn't feel dramatic, though. Her gut churned, and every muscle tensed like her body was ready to flee, whether her mind was willing or not. She rubbed a hand over her eyes. "This is a mistake."

"You're letting your emotions get the best of you."

She'd never wanted to hit her partner more than she did in that second, which just served to prove he was right. "We're going to spook him."

"It's possible."

Damn it, why was Vic being so closemouthed *now*, when she needed the fight? She had the answer almost before the question formed. *Because a fight is going to divert our energy, and he knows I'm being stupid.* She shifted in her seat. "I don't want anything to happen to that girl."

"No one does."

She turned off the main road, squinting against the dust Zach's car kicked up. "There are some people I need to talk to here."

"Uh-huh." Vic huffed out a laugh. "Is that your way of trying to get me to volunteer to get a ride back with the sheriff?"

"Maybe." She drummed her fingers on the steering wheel. "There's a girl here I grew up with. We used to be friends." As close as she'd had to friends in this place. "I'm missing something, and I'm hoping if I can get her alone—no Martha and no husband around—she'll spill whatever information she's hoarding. She knows something. I'm sure of it."

"All the more reason for me to be your backup."

That was logical. And yet . . . She shook her head. "You don't know these people, Vic. They barely allow me back in, and I'm Martha's daughter. They'll take one look at you and close up. Which means I'd have to come out here again, and that's going to waste everyone's time. If I can get a chance to talk to Beth alone, I want you to go back to Clear Springs with Zach."

"I don't like it."

"I know." Zach wouldn't be crazy about it, either, especially after what had happened yesterday. She touched her face. Had that really been only yesterday? It felt like weeks ago. Her head hadn't stopped aching, but it had dulled to the point where she could mostly ignore it.

She'd gotten really good at ignoring pain. Practically an expert, after her childhood.

Put it away. Lock it down. Being on the verge of a meltdown isn't going to help anyone.

Easier said than done. She parked the car next to Zach's cruiser and climbed out. He met her between them, the sight of him bringing his earlier words back to the forefront of her mind. *I'll keep you safe.* She couldn't allow herself to lean on him, not when she most needed to be strong.

Even now, hours later, her hands shook just the slightest bit. She kept seeing that bat, kept hearing the faintest creak of a person putting their weight on a floorboard in her bedroom. Those things on their own were plenty creepy, but it was the *other* that was bringing her down. The one thing she'd been doing her damnedest not to think about.

Neveah Smith had been buried alive.

The coroner couldn't say for certain that it had happened like that—only that she had a film of dirt over her skin and dirt beneath her fingernails along with the DNA. There was no telling how those things had come about.

Except Eden knew.

She'd been there, after all. She'd lain in the grave that wasn't called a grave and watched the faces of the people she knew as the dirt rained down, covering her from her feet to her chest, a weight she'd never really escaped, the suffocating feeling sometimes visiting her in her nightmares and making her wake up in a cold sweat.

"Eden."

She latched on to Zach's voice like a life vest, letting it ground her. "I'm fine."

"No, you're not. And that's all right."

"I'm better than this, Zach. I've faced worse." She didn't reach for him, but she wanted to. God, she wanted to. "This shouldn't be messing me up so bad."

"Our personal demons always get under our skin." He didn't touch her, didn't offer false comfort. There were eyes on them even now, and any show of weakness would be noted and used against them in the coming confrontation. "It's going to get worse before it gets better—*if* it gets better. Some cases break you if you don't learn how to bend."

She didn't have a backup plan. The BAU fulfilled her in a way nothing else had managed to for her entire life. She wasn't going to let that go—not for anything. She unclenched her hands, forcing herself to meet his direct blue gaze. "I won't take any unnecessary risks."

"I thought you weren't going to lie to me about that." One corner of his mouth quirked up, but the expression died there. "Just . . . watch your back, okay? If something happened to you . . ." He shook his head and walked away without finishing the sentence.

It was just as well. She didn't know what she was supposed to say to that. She looked around the courtyard, shivering as a brittle wind kicked up. Winter was coming, and coming fast. She tried not to see that as an omen.

She tried really damn hard.

CHAPTER
THIRTY-ONE

Zach saw exactly how things would play out the second Martha got a look at the warrant. She drew herself up to her full height, somehow seeming to tower over him despite the fact she was a good four inches shorter. "Zach Owens, I expected better of you."

Guilt surged, but he fought it down. He didn't have a damn thing to be guilty for—the response was the same as if his mother gave him *that* look and spoke to him in *that* tone of voice—though in that case he most likely *had* done something wrong. He kept his body relaxed, though he watched Abram out of the corner of his eye. "Ma'am, I'm sorry you feel that way, but this is a court order. You, Abram, Joseph, and Lee are all required to submit to an oral swab. If you try to resist, you will be brought in to the station, and you will still be required to take the test."

She studied him, and he could almost see the wheels turning in her head, debating which course of action would benefit her the most. Zach had always known Martha was a force of nature, but it was only after spending time with Eden that he realized exactly how much of her responses were cherry-picked to get the outcome she wanted.

Finally she jerked her chin at Abram. "Get the boys and bring them to my office." Martha turned to look at Eden, where she stood at the edge of the group. "I suppose you had something to do with this. You always did think the worst of me."

Zach started to step between them, but Eden just shook her head. "If you didn't have a murderer running loose in Elysia, this wouldn't be necessary. That's on you—not me. And if I thought for a second I could subpoena your video footage, I'd do it. Hell, I'd have already done it."

"If there wasn't a murderer running loose, as you say, you wouldn't have come back." Martha gave a tight smile. "And we both know you have only circumstantial evidence, and no judge without a personal connection to our dear sheriff would violate my rights."

Alarms blasted through Zach's head at the comment. Some part of him hadn't been able to believe that Martha actually had anything to do with this. She might be controlling and had something of a god complex, but murdering teenagers? It had been too crazy to contemplate.

But now, with her looking at Eden with that bittersweet expression on her face, she seemed almost *thankful* her daughter was back, no matter how horrific the event was that had brought her home.

Martha wasn't a small woman. She could have easily overpowered both Elouise and Neveah. And, as Eden pointed out, the recent sexual intercourse didn't necessarily mean the killer was a man. His stomach lurched, but he managed to keep it off his face. He hoped.

"Shall we, ma'am?"

She shook her head at him. "You say *ma'am* and yet manage to sound so disrespectful at the same time. It's a disgrace." Martha turned and led the way into the main building, leaving him to follow her. He glanced at Eden, but she shook her head again. Zach hesitated. He didn't like leaving her out here alone any more than he liked the fact she was here in the first place. If he had his way, he'd have put her on the first plane back to Virginia, even if it meant never seeing her again.

At least that way he'd know she was safe.

But there was no real safety in this world, something he knew all too well, so he turned and followed Martha into the building. The sooner they got the swabs, the sooner all of them could get out of Elysia for good.

◆ ◆ ◆

Eden waited until the door closed behind the group to exchange a look with Vic. "I'm going to find Beth."

He hesitated, then nodded. "Be quick. I have a feeling your mother won't like you poking around while she's occupied."

No, she wouldn't. Especially if she knew that Eden had the password to get into her computer room and go through the feed. Since that could potentially take hours she didn't have, she'd focus on Beth first and then see where things shook out. *One step at a time.* First, Beth. Then she'd see what she could find.

The compound was eerily quiet as she skirted around the buildings toward Beth and Jon's house. It was Thursday, so if she wasn't mistaken, everyone should be taking their midday rest right around now. That explained why Martha was lurking around the courtyard. She was probably taking the downtime to get her own agenda done. She rarely rested, even when she required it of everyone under her command.

Eden knocked on the door as quietly as she could and held her breath until the door cracked open, revealing Beth's white-blonde hair and big blue eyes. "Eden? What are you doing here? It's our resting time."

"I know." She hated the stress that appeared around her friend's eyes. "I'm sorry. I just was hoping we could talk a little more."

Beth cracked the door open a bit wider. "Does Martha know you're here? I don't want you to get into trouble."

"I won't." She pressed closer to the door. "And I won't let you get into trouble, either. Just a few questions, I promise."

"Okay." Beth stepped back, allowing her into the house.

Eden took a quick look around, but everything was the same as it had been the last time she was here. She wasn't sure what she expected. The place just seemed so *normal*, considering it was built on cult property and two long-standing members lived here. There was comfort in that, though. Maybe life for Beth and Jon wasn't all that bad. It had been bad for *her*, but maybe that didn't mean it was bad in general.

And maybe you're just trying to assuage the guilt you feel for leaving them behind. For leaving all of them behind.

She'd been little more than a kid when she'd left. She couldn't have saved anyone else. She'd barely managed to save herself. Not to mention, no one else in Elysia actually *wanted* to be saved.

Still feels like I'm rationalizing.

She couldn't help that. Hell, nothing seemed to help that. It was Eden's burden to bear, no matter how irrational it was.

"Jon's out spending time at Montana State." Beth moved into the kitchen, her hands fluttering a little as she picked up a coffee mug and set it back down again. "Can I get you anything? Coffee? Tea?"

"No, thank you." She took in the other woman's nervousness, her gut twisting. "Jon wasn't here when I visited that first time, either."

"His calling requires a lot of time spent outside the commune."

Eden narrowed her eyes. "Calling?" She'd thought Lee was in charge of the recruiting. That wasn't to say there wasn't a whole legion of Elysians who worked to bring more people into the fold, but from her understanding, they generally spent most of their time in the larger cities and college towns in the Pacific Northwest and came here only for retreats, which were designed solely to bring in new followers. They cycled in and out of the commune, because Martha couldn't afford to have anyone outside her grasp for too long for fear that the conditioning would wear off.

But Eden didn't think any of those recruiters were people who'd grown up in Elysia. It just didn't make sense. Lifers usually kept inside the walls, working the fields or weaving or watching the children of other members.

Jon was young and attractive, but he'd spent his entire life behind the walls. She doubted he had the social skills necessary to slide into a group, pick out the people most susceptible to Martha's influence, and manipulate them into thinking about joining up. It just didn't fit with what she knew of him.

Maybe you don't know him anymore.

Beth kept twisting her mug, the scrape of porcelain on the counter setting Eden's teeth on edge. "He's become very intense in the last few years. He spends more and more time outside the commune. He's . . . searching for something." She looked up, her blue eyes shining with unshed tears. "I don't understand. Why isn't Martha enough for him? Why aren't *I* enough?"

Eden didn't have an answer to that. What she did have was a growing fear that she could now put a name to the unsub. "Beth, do you know if he was gone the night of September seventeenth or September twenty-second?"

"I don't . . . He was." Beth's lower lip quivered. "He's gone more often than he's here."

Oh, God. Not Jon.

But it fit. Jon had grown up alongside Eden. He could have very easily seen her making the garlands out in the fields when she was a child. And if he was disillusioned, maybe he'd thought trying to bring Persephone—to bring *her*—back would help. It made her sick to her stomach to think about. "Beth, I'm going to need you to come with me."

"Come with you? Where? Why?" She clutched her mug to her chest like a shield. "I can't leave, Eden. It's time for resting. I'm leading small groups tonight. I have to be here."

"I know that." She carefully took the mug out of her friend's hands. "And I'm sorry. But we need to go get Jon." *We need to bring him in.* "You need to call him and tell him to meet you . . ." She thought fast. "Meet you at the Gas 'N Go. Tell him it's about Martha, and you don't feel safe here." The Gas 'N Go was close enough to the outskirts of Clear Springs that the chances of anyone being caught in the cross fire were minimal.

Beth looked doubtful. "I don't know, Eden. I'm worried about him, but this seems like it's too much."

She stomped down on her impatience. The only person whose call he'd answer if he was off the rails was Beth. Even then, there was a chance he'd ignore her. *Rachel.* She cleared her throat. "Does Jon have anywhere in Elysia that he goes to be alone? Somewhere he wants to be undisturbed?" It was a long shot, but if they could get to Rachel before Jon knew they were onto him, it would ease everyone's mind.

Beth frowned, but then her expression cleared. "He built a little cabin out by the forest line. We share the chores out in that quadrant with the Jones family, and we, uh, go out there . . ."

"To be alone."

Beth blushed, her fair skin going pink. "I love living so close to the center, but there isn't much privacy with the houses so close. We haven't been out there this summer, but we used to go a lot after we were first married."

Eden understood, to an extent. They'd known each other the same way she and Jon had known each other—somewhat at a distance. To go from that to the single most intimate relationship a person could enter was jarring, to say the least. It made sense that they'd wanted to carve out a little spot for themselves and get to know each other.

Except apparently no one had known Jon as well as they'd thought.

She debated, weighing the need to track Jon down immediately against every instinct she had screaming that the cabin was the key and that was where Rachel was being kept. *The priority has to be Rachel. If we can secure her safely, then we can focus on bringing Jon to justice.* She took Beth's hands, looking into her eyes. "Beth, can you take me there? We'll call Jon afterward, but it's important that you take me there right now."

"I can take you there." The words were little more than a whisper. Beth's lower lip quivered. "Is this about those girls who were hurt?"

"It might be." She wasn't willing to say one way or another until they had Jon in custody and Rachel safe. Beth was a good girl, but she'd had ten years to get used to putting Jon first—and her entire life submitting to Martha. Eden couldn't trust her to be left alone for a minute or she'd tell *someone*, and that was all they needed for vital information to escape. "Come with me, okay?"

"Okay."

Movement at the edge of her vision had the small hairs at the back of Eden's neck rising. She turned, reaching for her gun, but something hit her head, and the last thing she saw before blackness claimed her was Beth's horrified face.

Then there was nothing at all.

CHAPTER
THIRTY-TWO

Zach took the last swab, closed the bag, and sealed it. He looked from one face to the next, taking in the set jaws and the flinty eyes. They might be a house divided right now, but they were unified against the enemy—him. Even Lee looked furious. Zach stored the bags in the bag he'd brought and straightened. "If you're innocent, you have nothing to worry about."

Martha lifted her chin. "If it's all the same to you, Sheriff, please get the hell off my property. Unless you're planning on arresting one of us?"

He kind of wanted to arrest *all* of them on principle, but that wouldn't do a damn thing but make him feel better for a few seconds. Zach nodded at each of them in turn. "Ma'am. Gentlemen. I sincerely hope I won't be back to arrest one of you for the deaths of both Neveah Smith and Elouise Perkins. If one of you was involved, it'd be best to come forward now."

No one so much as blinked.

He nodded again. "Thought as much. I'll just collect my people and be out of your hair." He was so focused on getting the hell out of there that it took him several long seconds to process Vic laid out on the ground next to the police cruiser.

Everything snapped into place at the bright red on the ground next to the man. Zach rushed forward, scanning the surrounding area as he went to his knees and checked for a pulse, finding one. "Martha, this had better not be your doing." He breathed a little sigh of relief that died the second it reached his lips. *Where the fuck is Eden?* The blood was from a cut on the back of Vic's head, and it was bleeding pretty good, but nothing crazy enough to worry about.

Not when Eden was missing.

He looked up to find Martha standing over him, her men at her back. She frowned at the scene they created. "What's going on?"

"That's the question, isn't it? Did one of your people do this?" *What if it was the killer? Fuck, fuck, fuck. I had these four closeted up, and some-one was attacking Vic not twenty feet away.*

"I don't know what you're talking about."

Vic groaned, his eyes flicking open. "Took her." He groaned and put a hand over his eyes. "Didn't see who. Eden was in the trunk, and I went to figure out what the fuck was going on. Someone hit me."

There seemed to be a whole hell of a lot of ambushes lately. He used a hand on the other man's shoulder to keep him on the ground. "Which car? What did it look like? Did you get a plate?"

"The rental."

Damn it, he should have noticed it was missing. He dug out his phone and called the station, but when the phone rang and clicked over to the answering service, he cursed and immediately dialed the Augusta station. It was a long shot, but the faster he got in the BOLO, the better chance there was of someone catching the car before they took her . . . wherever the killer had been holding his victims. He passed over the information to the operator and hung up.

All the while, Martha had stood by with a dawning expression of horror on her face. "The person who hurt those girls has Eden?"

There was something there, a lingering knowledge behind her words. She knew something. He wanted to cross the distance between them and shake the life out of her. Her daughter was directly in the line of danger, and she was still playing games. "You know damn well that's what's going on. It's one of your people, Martha. Don't waste our time with protests of innocence. If you're not going to help me, you'd better get the fuck out of my way, because that psychopath has been working his way up to hurting Eden, and now he's got her." Panic welled, and there was no fighting it.

So he used it.

Zach snapped his fingers at Lee. "Get something to stop the bleeding. Now." He waited until he knew the man would obey to look down at Vic. "You'll live, I think. What can you tell me about what happened?" Any little detail that could help them find Eden faster was worth its weight in gold.

But the FBI agent made a frustrated sound. "I didn't see a damn thing. That asshole got the jump on me." He shook his head and winced. "I knew my instincts were a little rusty, but that's unforgivable."

Zach thought so, too, but he might be more forgiving if Eden's life wasn't on the line.

Lee ran up with a dishrag, and Zach pressed it against Vic's head. Already, the bleeding had slowed. He put Vic's hand over the rag. "Don't move. I'm going to call in backup, and even if it looks like you're going to be okay, head injuries are tricky."

"Find her."

"I will." He wished he felt as sure as he sounded. Zach shoved to his feet and turned on Martha. "Which one of your people did this?"

"I don't know." She threw up her hands. "I might be a leader, but I'm not a god."

He had his doubts about her beliefs regarding that. He ran his hands through his hair, thinking hard. Something was there . . . something dancing on the edges of his memory. He paced a quick circle. Vic hadn't seen . . . "That's it." He spun around. "The cameras. Eden said you have them set up all over Elysia. One of them must have seen *something*."

Martha went pale; then her mouth firmed. "I don't know what you're talking about."

She definitely knows something. He stepped forward, getting right up in her face. "Your daughter is going to die—and die horribly. Do you want to know what that sick fuck did to Elouise Perkins and Neveah Smith—and probably Rachel Carpenter, too? He tattooed them, kept them locked up for over a week, and—"

"Stop." Her entire frame shook, her skin so pale she looked half a second from passing out. Well, too fucking bad. He didn't have time to handle her with kid gloves, and she didn't deserve the preferential treatment after how she'd stonewalled the entire investigation—was *still* stonewalling it.

Abram stepped in, his expression unforgiving, but Zach was having none of it. He pushed the other man back and lowered his voice. "He raped them, Martha. Do you know what kind of terror living like that for a week had to have caused? Elouise was choked repeatedly to the point of unconsciousness, and Neveah was buried alive and then dug back up again. If he did that while working his way up to Eden, what do you think he's going to do to her?"

Still, she didn't move, didn't say anything. Zach cursed. "Do you really love your daughter, Martha? Or was that all a lie, too?"

Something cleared in her eyes. She seemed to reclaim herself, pulling her shoulders back and her chin up and resuming her commanding air. "This way."

"Martha—" Abram stopped short when she pinned him with a look.

"That's my daughter. They're doing this because I claimed her as my Persephone, and you know it. What is this worth"—she motioned around her—"if she dies?"

"You'll regret it in the morning."

Zach clenched his fists but managed to keep his mouth shut. Time was of the essence, so going a few rounds with Abram wasn't going to solve anything—even if it would make him feel a little better, at least temporarily.

Then he processed what Martha had said. *"They."*

But she was already moving, striding across the square to the house situated in the center. Zach rushed after her. "You know who's doing this. Damn it, Martha, you could have put a stop to it before the first death."

"You're wrong. I knew something was going on, but I had no way of knowing it went any deeper than sex. My people need to let steam off sometimes, and I'm inclined to allow it."

He was on her heels as she climbed the stairs. "You should have told me."

"You're lucky I'm telling you now."

He knew that. He also knew there was a decent chance she'd deny anything said or done during this little trip. Zach glanced behind him at the glowering Abram and wondered if this was all some elaborate trap to ensure the DNA samples never made it to the lab. *Don't think about it. Get Eden back and worry about the rest later.* He tried to take in the bedroom Martha led him into, but she didn't stop there, marching into what appeared to be a closet until she plugged a code into a little pad on the wall and a doorway appeared with a click.

Inside, it was like walking into the twilight zone. Monitors lined the walls of a room almost as large as the bedroom itself, each seeming to record a part of the Elysian community. On the video, everyone went about their business, likely having no idea they were being recorded.

No wonder her people think she's a prophet. She knows all their secrets. He pointed to the one showing the police cruiser and a now-sitting Vic. "This will be the one."

Abram was the one who moved past them to the control system, typing a few commands into the system. The screen went black for a few seconds and then cleared to show a blonde girl who looked about sixteen hauling Eden's unconscious body—*please let her be unconscious*—into the trunk. Zach winced when her head made contact with the trunk as the woman dumped her into the space. The blonde disappeared, headed off in the direction she'd come. Less than a minute later, Vic rushed up to the vehicle, and there was a flash of movement behind him, the impression of the blonde wielding a baseball bat, and then he was down. The woman tossed the bat into the backseat, climbed into the driver's seat, and drove away.

He pointed at the screen. *Only one. Maybe Martha is wrong? But that doesn't make sense . . .* "Who the fuck is that?"

"Beth. She's been with us since she was a small child. Her grandmother was one of my first followers, though she left unexpectedly seven years ago." Martha smoothed back her hair, and it was only because he watched her so closely that he noticed her hands shaking just a bit.

Zach shot a look at Abram. Did "left unexpectedly" mean she left of her own will? Or was she kicked out? Or . . . ? He filed away that piece of information to investigate later. Right now there were more pressing things to deal with. "Where is she taking Eden?"

Martha's breath hitched. "I . . . I don't know."

Eden thought she'd felt pain in her life. She'd been wrong. So goddamn wrong. Her head pulsed with each heartbeat like a giant exposed nerve, feeling huge and too big for her body. She had to open her eyes—it was imperative that she figure out where she was—but she couldn't quite manage to make the command reach the body part in question. *Oh, God, oh, God, oh, God.*

Stop.

Breathe.

Inhale. Keep it steady. Exhale.

There. Just like that.

Keep going.

Each breath brought a little more steadiness to her, though the initial panic hovered at the edge of her mind, just waiting for her to miss a step so it could pull her under. It was so hard to *think*.

What happened?

That, at least, was easy enough to answer. She'd gone to see Beth, and then she'd realized that Jon might be the one who was doing this. Had he come home unexpectedly? Had he hurt Beth after he knocked Eden out? *That* got her moving. She opened her eyes, blinking into the shadows. It wasn't pure darkness, but the light made her wonder how much time had passed while she'd been out. *Losing time like that is bad. So fucking bad.* She tried to see as much of the room as she could without moving her head. She'd have to evaluate her injuries, but not right this second. Getting the lay of the land, so to speak, was first.

That's right. One step at a time. Keep the panic at bay.

Judging from the rugged exposed wood and lack of drywall or anything that would mean a finished house, she was in the cabin Beth had mentioned. The cabin that only a handful of people in Elysia knew about, and no one had reason to connect her with. She had to close her eyes and concentrate on getting her breathing back to normal. *Okay, so no one is going to swoop in like a knight in shining armor. I have to get out of this myself.* It sounded simple enough . . . as long as she didn't think about the fact that this unsub had killed two girls to date.

Rachel.

She opened her eyes again, forcing herself to twist a little to see the rest of the room. There wasn't much to see. A simple table of the same unfinished look was set against the single window—no glass, to speak of—and there was the bed she currently stretched out on. *Do* not *think about the bed.*

Eden tried to move farther, but her wrists were tied over her head. She twisted a bit more, ignoring the pain that almost made her black out to see what restrained her. *Rope. I can work with rope.* Or she could if she could reach anything remotely sharp. The comforting weight of her gun was gone, and her boots were, too, which meant they had her backup weapon. *This is bad, but I've been in worse . . .* Except she couldn't think of a worse situation. Footsteps sounded, and she had a half a second to debate whether she wanted to pretend to be unconscious still. She chose to meet her attacker with eyes open instead.

The door, which was just a cloth hung over a door-size opening in the wall, fluttered open, and a man walked through. Eden had prepared herself for facing off with one of her childhood friends. Or she'd thought she had.

That was why it took her several long seconds to process the fact that the man now looking down at her was *not* Jon. She blinked, blinked again, but he didn't change. Eden swallowed past her suddenly dry throat. "I don't . . . I don't understand."

Chase smiled. "You never did." He reached down and ran a finger down the side of her face, laughing when she jerked away as much as she could. "Stubborn to the very end. Just like she said."

Do not panic. Do not *panic.* If she hadn't realized Chase was even a suspect, it was unlikely Zach would, either. There was such a disconnect that she didn't even know how to begin processing it. Eden looked around, but the cabin didn't change. "This is Jon and Beth's cabin." *Beth.* "What did you do with Beth?"

"Nothing, silly." The feminine voice made her stomach lurch. The nausea only got worse when the woman in question walked through the doorway and slipped under Chase's arm. That kind of body language and comfort meant they'd been lovers—and probably for some time.

Didn't see that coming. Didn't see any of it coming.

"How did you even meet? Where is Rachel?" She didn't know if she really wanted the answer to the second question, but if she could get them talking, maybe she could figure out a way free. *Long shot.*

Shut up.

"It was a gift from Persephone." Beth went on her tiptoes and kissed Chase. Her eyes shone, and she looked like it was Christmas morning and she'd just discovered her entire list beneath the tree. "Things started so promising with Jon, but it's been so incredibly hard the last few years. I met Chase while I was chasing down one of our wandering alpacas."

"The rest is history." Chase's grin made the bottom of Eden's stomach drop out. If there was fanatical brightness in Beth's eyes, there was only cold calculation in his. *He's not a true believer.* She didn't know if it was better or worse that he'd hurt those girls for his own purposes rather than because he was a secret religious zealot.

Beth smiled. "It's time. Are you ready?"

"What?"

But it was Chase she spoke to. He cupped her face, managing to not look too eager about what was to come. "I've never been more ready, baby. It's time to take what's ours."

She had to say something, do something, to snap Beth out of it. "Beth, we've been friends for years. You don't want to hurt me."

The woman went to her knees next to the bed and pulled out a little knife. She cut down the middle of Eden's shirt, frowning at the tattoos spanning her chest. "You covered it."

Not completely. She could see the faint outline of the key beneath the other tattoo, if she looked hard enough. A constant reminder that she could never truly escape her past. "I never wanted it to begin with."

Beth shook her head. "You left your legacy behind, just like you left me behind." She traced the faint outline of the skeleton key with a reverent finger. "Oh, Chase, I wish we could see the original how it was intended." She frowned. "I didn't get the others quite right."

"It's just a stupid key." *Keep them talking; keep them talking.* She pulled on the ropes around her wrists, but there wasn't a damn bit of give. "It's not real. Nothing Martha says is real."

Beth slanted her a look. "You would say that. You were always the chosen one." She tapped the tattoo with her finger. "You don't know what it was like for the rest of us growing up under Demeter's reign."

Eden bit back a hysterical laugh. "I think I know better than anyone."

"I thought so. But then you left, and it all became clear." She tapped the tattoo again, harder this time. "You left just like Persephone left, and Demeter's gone mad with grief. She won't release her power, won't even share a shred of it, so it's left up to us to take it. If you're not going to take your rightful place, someone else will. You were always the key."

"I was just a kid." She'd felt guilty for leaving people behind, but that was the truth. "I was barely able to save myself, let alone you, too."

"You had to go alone. It was foreseen. But then you never came back, and we've been floundering ever since." She looked up at Chase. "It's time. You need to start prepping her."

Since Eden had a pretty good idea what they meant by *prepping*, she had no interest in it starting. *If he's going to rape me, getting that close might give me the chance to get free.* She yanked on the ropes binding her wrists again, making the bed frame shake. *Then again, maybe not. Fuck.* She looked around again, but no magical way to escape presented itself. *Need more time.* "How did Chase get involved?"

"That first day, I saw Beth and knew we had something special between us. I stopped to see if I could convince her to give me the time of day." The smile he shared with Beth made her stomach churn. "She ended up converting me on the spot."

"I'll just bet she did. And whose idea was it to throw a bit of rape into the bargain?"

Beth rolled her eyes. "Oh, please, don't be naive. You know as well as I do that Hades raping Persephone is part of her journey to power. A necessary, if unfortunate, step."

Except Martha never taught the story that way. Eden knew the scholars typically agreed with Beth's version of events—that Persephone's abduction was really a rape—but no one in Elysia shared that belief.

She didn't share that belief.

She couldn't reason with Beth, so she turned her glare on Chase. "Did you have your eye on those girls for a long time? Watching them grow from children into teenagers must have been a trip. I bet it was your idea to go after Clear Springs teenagers instead of the ones in Elysia."

"Come now, Eden, you know the rule. You don't shit where you eat." Beth made a face. "I've never liked the language in that saying."

Eden ignored Beth, focusing on Chase—the weak link.

His face went red, and he took a step toward the bed. "You don't know a damn thing about it."

Oh, she'd bet she knew more than most. He didn't lean toward the younger set—that much was clear—but it might as well be a giant red button for her to push. Getting him to lose control would probably be a one-way trip to the morgue, but a man going berserk was less likely to take the time to rape her before he killed her.

It's really bad that I'm thinking like this.

She lifted her chin. "I think I know more than most. I'm Persephone, remember? I'm more than Demeter's daughter. I'm Hades' bride, which makes me the queen of the underworld." It felt weird to say the words aloud, especially to people who might actually believe them, but she'd do whatever it took. "You'll regret this."

Chase leaned down, his brown eyes cold. "No, I don't think I will."

"You might be Persephone now, but you won't be once you're gone—just like the others." Beth stood. "Then it will be my turn."

Oh, shit. "It doesn't work like that."

"Yes, it does. Martha's said as much every time spring comes. Do you know how many times they've put me into the ground?" Beth looked away, her breath catching. "You left. *I've* been here. It's my turn to take the reins, whether that old bitch wants to hand them over or not."

Did she realize how roundabout her logic was? First Eden was Persephone, and now she was a Persephone that could be replaced. But then, they had to have some rationale for killing her. She jerked harder on the ropes, but there wasn't any more give than there had been before. "Where's Rachel?"

Beth shook her head, her expression sad. "She wasn't any more worthy than the others."

No. "It's too soon to have killed her. It's only been three days. You wait eight."

"Don't worry about her." Chase turned to Beth and cupped her face. "You're going to want to leave, honey. You don't like this next part."

Eden forced herself to keep her breathing even. If she hyperventilated, she'd be helpless to fight him—she was *already* helpless to fight him. *No, I'm not. I just need to think. There has to be a way.* She shifted her feet, testing the strength of the foot of the bed. It didn't wobble, but if she kicked, she might be able to . . . *I have to try.*

She forced herself to watch as they kissed, because she'd only get one chance at this. Beth left the cabin, her gaze lingering on first Eden and then Chase, and then she was gone. "How the hell did you get her to agree to you raping the girls?" She put a little more emphasis on *rape*, because it had been a trigger before.

But apparently no longer. He stripped off his shirt, revealing the tattoos all the cult members had—a torch on his wrist and a sheaf of wheat on his hip. She'd bet if he turned around, there would be a bat on his shoulder blade, too. Chase's hands went to the button of his jeans. "Martha might have cleaned up the myth, but the original is far more brutal. I happen to like brutal."

CHAPTER
THIRTY-THREE

Zach had never wanted to strike a woman as much as he did in that moment. "You're a smart woman, Martha. Where the hell would they take her? It's on Elysian property. It has to be."

"You don't know that."

Abram stepped forward, touching Martha's elbow. "The cabin."

Zach didn't wait for her to give permission. He focused on the other man. "What cabin?"

"Jon built it years ago. He and Beth thought no one knew." Abram's mouth twisted. "We allowed them the illusion."

Because it served Martha's purpose. In a way, Zach understood. If a person was held too closely with no freedom, they were more likely to revolt. He looked at her. *So goddamn manipulative from beginning to end.* "Where is it?"

"The north side of the property, just inside the tree line. It's twenty minutes from here." Her voice was barely above a whisper.

Abram rattled off a series of coordinates that Zach instantly memorized. He needed to call in backup and call them in now, but they wouldn't do a damn bit of good if they didn't know where they were headed.

For the first time since he'd met her, Martha looked at a loss. She crossed her arms over her chest. "If they follow the rituals to bring back Persephone . . ." She turned and clutched Abram's arm. "Go get her. Bring my baby home."

Now she understood the danger Eden was in.

Zach wanted to shake her, but there was no time. There was no time for a single damn thing, not the least to demand to know what the hell she'd taught her followers—or just how closely Beth was replicating these teachings with the murders. He would, though, when this was all over.

He stepped back to allow Abram to precede him down the stairs, but he followed on the other man's heels. The last thing he saw before he was out of sight of Martha was Joseph putting his arms around her. Anger burned his stomach. She didn't deserve the comfort. If she'd been up front about what she'd known from the beginning, they could have put a stop to this so much earlier.

Maybe we could have saved Neveah.

He hit the door at nearly a run and found Abram climbing into the driver's seat of his battered old truck. He rolled down the window. "Follow me if you want, but I'm not slowing down for you."

"Fine by me." This might be the only time in his life that he and the other man were on the same side, but he wasn't about to look the gift horse in the mouth. Martha had commanded that her daughter be brought home safe, and Abram would die making that happen if he had to. Zach paused to help Vic into the passenger seat. The Elysians might not be enemies at this point, but there was no way he was going to leave the fed helpless in their clutches. Too many "accidents" could happen.

He tore out of the main living quarters on Abram's truck's tail and grabbed the radio. "Chase? Henry?"

"Henry here, Sheriff. Chase took off a little bit ago to grab some grub."

It would just figure that the deputy chose *now* to listen to what Zach had badgered him about through the entire case. He cursed. "Get every cop Augusta can muster, and send them to these coordinates." He passed on the location Abram had given him. "The killers are a couple from the compound by the names of Beth and Jon, and they have Eden. Henry, get them there as fast as they can."

"Will do." He clicked off.

Zach did some quick math in his head, but no matter which way he looked at it, it'd be almost an hour before any of his backup arrived. *Guess it's just me, the fed, and Abram.*

Fuck.

"Drive faster."

He didn't glance at Vic. "How's your head?"

"Don't worry about me. Worry about Eden." Vic leaned back and closed his eyes, his skin an unhealthy color. "They're reenacting the most traumatic parts of her childhood. If we don't get there in time . . . there's more than her life on the line."

He pushed the pedal farther to the floor, the cruiser bucking and dipping as it fought its way across the dirt road that could barely call itself a road. *Twenty minutes, and that's in addition to the time we wasted dancing around the truth with Martha, and however long Vic lay on the ground, bleeding. Fuck, fuck, fuck.* Too long, no matter which way he split it.

She's capable. You've been thinking that from the beginning.

Yeah, he had. But he'd been thinking of Eden, fully healthy and able to kick ass as needed—not suffering from her second head wound in twenty-four hours and unconscious in a trunk. Zach held his breath and drove faster.

◆　◆　◆

Fear clogged Eden's throat as Chase came toward her, his hands on his belt buckle. She couldn't wait any longer. If he got his pants off . . . *No.* Being naked might slow him down, but it would be one less barrier between them if he got her pinned. *I'll die first.*

It's now or never.

She kicked with everything she had, years of merciless physical training making it possible to swing her legs up and over her head, and then pushed with her arms to complete the flip and come to a crouching position on the other side of the head of the bed.

Chase blinked at her. "Well, I'll be damned."

Eden didn't waste any time, kicking with everything she was worth at the joint where the leg of the bed met the rest of the frame. It cracked but didn't bust open, so she kicked it again.

Chase shook himself. "That's fine, Persephone. I can take you like this. I actually prefer it."

No.

She kicked again, using her grip on the rope to bear down and leverage her weight into something more. The bed cracked even more, creating a gap large enough for her to slip the rope through.

Which was the exact moment Chase got his hands on her. He shoved her over the headboard, bending her in half. Eden's breath left her in a whoosh, black spots dancing across her vision. She wouldn't pass out. She fucking *refused* to. While he fumbled at her clothes, she twisted her arms beneath her, aiming to slide the rope through the gap she'd created. It hurt. It hurt so damn bad.

The rope popped free of the frame with a lurch that had her blinking and wondering if she'd imagined it. But when she brought her arms back beneath her, there was no tension. *Free. Just need to get this monster off me.*

She forced herself to go supple, to stop fighting him, and was rewarded with a grunt of what might be approval. Acid rose in her throat, but she fought that down just like she'd fought down every instinct demanding that she fight and claw and scream. There would be one chance to make this work.

"That's a good girl." His grip on her softened just a bit, and that was all the opportunity she needed.

Eden brought her elbow back into his stomach as hard as she could, twisting as much as possible to give the blow extra momentum. She didn't give Chase a chance to recover; she slammed her heel into his instep and slid around to hit him on the side of the head with both fists. It flipped him onto his back, his expression dazed.

Finish it.

She knew exactly how to do it. She could loop the slack rope around his neck and pull, putting all her weight into it until he passed out. Until he could never hurt anyone else the way he hurt those girls. The way he'd wanted to hurt *her*.

She could put an end to it, once and for all.

Eden had never felt more like Martha Collins's daughter than she did in that moment, coldly considering putting this semiconscious man down like a dog.

"That's not who I am," she whispered. "I am Eden Collins, BAU agent. Federal agent. I am *not* a murderer." But she was also human, so she kicked him while he was down and then bent over to retrieve his service weapon. She patted him down as best she could with her hands tied, finding a knife in a sheath at his hip but nothing else. She needed to tie him down, but the cabin was empty except for the bed, and she didn't have time. Beth would be back at any moment, and though she was reasonably sure she could take the other woman, if Chase recovered by then . . . Eden couldn't take them both. She'd more than proven that.

She kicked him again for good measure, part of her taking a sick satisfaction in the way he groaned.

Rachel. Focus on Rachel. And getting the hell out of here.

Eden eyed the doorway but ultimately moved toward the gap in the wall that seemed to function as another door into a different room.

Jon did a piss-poor job building this—and thank God for that. She ducked into the room, the gun held loosely in her hand. There was a second bed in here, shoved up against the far wall. Her breath caught in her throat as she saw the slumped body next to it. She took a step before she registered that it was a man, and another before she recognized *Jon*, his skin waxy and ashen, his eyes vacant.

Not Jon, too. Goddamn it.

"They killed him," Eden whispered.

It was only then that she noticed the huddled form curled up in the corner of the bed. "Rachel?"

She padded the rest of the way into the room, every instinct demanding she get out of this closed space where she could be trapped. Chase wouldn't be down forever, and she wanted to be gone from here when he was. *Probably need my hands untied, too.* The rope was too tight for her to be able to wedge the knife in there without cutting herself, but she might have to try it anyway if Rachel couldn't walk on her own.

Please be okay. Please.

She crouched down next to the bed, keeping a careful distance away from Jon's body, half-sure she could feel his judgment despite his being dead. *Should have been smarter. Should have known something was wrong with Beth, with Chase.* "Rachel?" There was a single sheet over the girl, and she had the horrified thought that Rachel was dead and they just hadn't gotten around to dumping her body yet. Steeling herself, she yanked the sheet down.

Rachel shoved her hands over her eyes. "No more. Please no more. Just kill me."

"Rachel, it's me. Eden. I'm here to get you out." She shot a look at the doorway, but Chase didn't appear. "But we have to move now."

"Eden?" The girl opened her eyes, blinking as if she'd been in the dark for some time. "You're really here?"

"I'm really here." How many times had Rachel imagined someone coming through that door to save her, only to discover it was Beth or

Chase, ready and willing to hurt her again. *It's only been a couple of days, and she's alive. That's more than the others can say.* Cold comfort if there ever was one.

They weren't out of this yet.

She started to finish pulling off the sheet but stopped when she realized the girl was naked. "Can you walk?"

"I don't think so. My ankle." Rachel sat up, swaying, and stuck her leg out from beneath the sheet. It was ugly and swollen, a myriad of blue and purple and black. *Definitely sprained if not broken.* She hiccuped, obviously fighting to keep control and not break down. "I tried to run. They made it so I couldn't."

"Brave girl." But they wouldn't be making a grand escape fleeing for their lives. She checked the door again. "I have a knife, and I need you to cut me free. Can you do that, honey?"

"I think so." She took the knife with shaking hands, and Eden had to brace herself against the mental image of the girl accidentally slitting her wrists. *Stop it.* She held as still as she could while Rachel sawed through the thick rope, the binding finally releasing with a pop.

Eden rubbed her wrists, wincing at how raw they were. *How am I going to get us both out of here?* She couldn't carry Rachel and reliably aim the gun, but leaving the teenager behind wasn't an option. Neither was giving her the handgun. "We're going with a fireman's carry, okay?" She was reasonably sure she could run with the girl draped over her shoulders. It wouldn't be fast, and it wouldn't be pretty, but it was the only option.

Rachel nodded, her entire body shaking. "Okay."

"Good girl." After a second of consideration, she shoved the gun into the waistband of her jeans. Like everything else about this shitty day, it was the best of a bad situation. Without her holster, she'd have to make do. She hauled Rachel onto her shoulders, pausing long enough to adjust her hold, and then headed for the door.

Her heart stopped at the sight of the empty cabin.

Chase was gone.

No, no, no.

I should have killed that monster.

"What's that smell?"

Eden inhaled deeply, swaying. "Gasoline." The word came through numb lips as the truth hit her with the strength of a freight train. *They're going to burn the cabin.*

She looked around, but no alternate escape route presented itself. With enough time and a good ax, she could chop herself a new door, but she had neither. Not to mention that if Chase and Beth were waiting to ambush them the second they walked through the door, it would be child's play for one of them to block any hole she made to crawl through. There was only one option, and it might as well be a death sentence—the front door.

Well, they could choose to burn alive, but she wasn't all that keen on leaving this world while wreathed in flames and smoke.

"I smell smoke."

"Me, too." There was no more time for stalling. They had to take their chances. She headed for the doorway. "If I go down, you get up and you run. I don't care if that fucking ankle is broken, you run. Do you hear me?"

"Yes." A whisper, nothing more.

Even if Eden didn't get out of this alive, she'd do her best to make sure Rachel did. "They're going to be focused on me." That, at least, she could do for Rachel. If she kept them occupied long enough, the girl might have a chance.

Except there were miles between the cabin and Clear Springs, miles where Chase could hunt her down just like he'd hunted down Elouise and Neveah.

Don't think about that.

"But—"

"Get ready." She rushed through the doorway and into the afternoon light. Her eyes didn't have time to adjust, which was probably the only reason she heard the heavy footsteps to her right. Eden threw herself left, sending Rachel flying, and she actually felt the air move as whatever Chase tried to hit her with flew over her head. "Rachel, *run*."

She was so dizzy, it took her two tries to get to her feet, but she managed, pulling out the gun as she did. Chase held up his hands. "Now don't do anything crazy." His eyes shifted slightly over her right shoulder, and that was the only warning she got before something came down hard on her collarbone. Sharp pain sent her to her knees, but she managed to keep hold of the gun through sheer force of will.

Another blow knocked her to her stomach. She cursed and rolled, bringing the gun up even as Beth raised a crowbar. "Do *not* move." *Can't see Chase. Damn, damn, damn. This is so bad.*

Beth eyed her, as if considering whether she'd really pull the trigger. "Put down the gun, Eden. This will be over shortly."

"Funny, but I don't think I'll do that." Her hands shook so bad; she knew it was only a matter of time before she dropped the gun or shot Beth by accident. *I know which one I'd prefer.* No, that wasn't right. If she shot the other woman, she'd do it on purpose. "Put the crowbar down."

"I don't think I'll do that, either." Beth looked over her shoulder, and Eden followed her gaze to where Rachel was limping away from them at a speed barely above walking.

Good girl. Keep going.

Beth shook her head. "Pathetic. She doesn't deserve to be Persephone, even symbolically." Her face twisted. "Neither of you do."

She was *not* going another round with this level of crazy again. Eden tried to see Chase without taking her eyes off Beth, but it was impossible. It was only a matter of time before he got the drop on her. *Shit.* A shadow fell over her, and she raised her gun as Chase bore down on her, a knife in his hands.

A gunshot cracked through the near silence of the afternoon, and for a second, Eden thought she'd pulled the trigger. A dark stain blossomed in the middle of Chase's shirt, spreading outward like some kind of warped flower. He hit his knees next to her, his eyes full of too much knowledge. "Beth." Then he was on the ground, the life bleeding out of his eyes.

"Eden!" Zach's voice, somewhere in the distance.

Eden switched her aim to Beth once again, but the woman wasn't looking at her. She shook her head, blonde hair swinging wildly. "No, no, no, you're *ruining everything*." She advanced on Eden. "*You* ruined everything. Why can't you just die like you're supposed to and *stay in the ground where you belong?*"

She pulled the trigger, knocking the woman back a step. Beth sank to the ground next to Chase, still shaking her head. "This isn't how it ends."

"*Wrong.*" She finally let the gun sink to her side. She let loose a hysterical laugh. "You stupid bitch. No one beats Persephone indefinitely. Not Demeter, not mankind, and sure as hell not Hades."

"I should have been"—Beth slumped against Chase—"Persephone."

"You don't deserve the name."

"Eden!" Strong arms came around her, pulling her to her feet as Zach seemed to touch every part of her. He glanced at the couple at their feet and then focused on her. "Are you okay?"

"I'm fine. Rachel—"

"Vic has her."

Sure enough, her partner crouched next to the girl about a hundred yards away, not touching her but obviously comforting her all the same. She'd always been in awe of how he managed to do that, to turn off the hard-edged fed and turn on the human being full of empathy. Eden had never mastered that trick.

Zach touched her face gently. "Are you . . . did he . . . ?"

"I'm *fine.*" She hesitated. It felt too much like a lie to let stand between them. "I'm not fine. I might not be fine for a long time. But I'm alive and Rachel is alive and we got the people responsible. That's about as positive an outcome as anyone can reasonably expect."

His mouth thinned. "I could have done without you being in danger. I didn't know if I hit him at first. I thought for sure it was too late."

Zach had been the one to shoot Chase. She should have known. Eden hugged him, surrendering to the need to both give and receive comfort. "I'm sorry. You shouldn't have had to be the one to do that."

"I would do it again if it means you walk away from that fight." He held her so tightly she could barely draw a breath. "Fuck, Eden, I'd set the world aflame for you."

CHAPTER THIRTY-FOUR

The next few hours passed in a whirlwind of activity. The coroner showed up to deal with the bodies, the paramedics showed up to deal with Rachel and Eden and Vic, and it seemed like every cop east of the mountains showed up in response to Zach's call. For her part, Eden wasn't too keen on being fussed over, but it saved her from having to answer questions because everyone assumed she was in shock.

The truth was she didn't want to face her mother.

Abram had come with Zach, and Martha hadn't been far behind him. Eden wasn't sure how Zach had figured out where she was so quickly, and she didn't have the energy to ask, but she *knew* who was responsible for Beth's death.

Her.

Martha sank down next to her with a sigh. "Are you okay, baby?"

"I was kidnapped by a pair of serial killers and almost murdered. What do you think?"

Martha twined Eden's hair around a finger, a small smile on her lips. "I think you're more torn up about the fact that you shot that girl before you bothered to notice she had a gun on her."

Eden turned so fast she almost fell off the tailgate. "What did you say?"

"A mother always knows."

That was bullshit, and they both knew it. She turned her glare at Abram where he stood just out of earshot. It was the closest he'd managed to come to subtle in all the time she'd known him. "She was going to kill me."

"But you didn't know that when you pulled the trigger." Martha patted her hand, still not looking at her. "Your secret is safe with me."

Eden jerked her hand away and instantly regretted the motion. She'd as good as verbally confirmed her mother's belief. *Well, she is right.* She pulled the blanket the paramedics had given her more tightly around her shoulders. "I'm not back. There's not a damn thing you can say or do to bring me back."

"I'd settle for coffee once or twice a year."

She almost said yes, almost gave in to this weird moment where it seemed like her mother might actually *be* a mother, instead of the devil incarnate. And then she remembered everything. "I didn't expect it to be her. Not Beth."

Martha was silent for a beat. "Did you know she had quite the following among my people?"

She looked at her mother, that single sentence making things click into place. Hadn't she just recently considered how little Martha liked to share power? She wouldn't have done it for her own daughter, let alone an upstart she'd half raised. Eden turned to watch the coroner take pictures of the bodies. "She was always well liked when we were kids."

"That didn't change as she grew into an adult."

No, it wouldn't have. And if Beth had decided to break from Elysia, she might have taken a considerable number of people with her. If she stayed, she might have even been able to wrest away Martha's power for herself, given enough time. "You knew."

"Knew what, baby?"

Knew what Beth and Chase were doing. Knew where those girls were being held. Knew *everything*.

She didn't have to say it. The glint in her mother's eyes told her enough. Martha might not have put the idea to kill those girls into Beth's head, but she'd let the woman walk down that path without stepping in.

Anything to remove the competition without getting her hands dirty.

Eden pushed off the edge of the tailgate, hating that she wobbled a little on her feet, but refusing to sit in this woman's presence another moment. "We're not having coffee. And if you contact me again without my permission, I will do whatever it takes to get a restraining order in place."

She made it a single step before her mother's voice stopped her. "You're more like me than you care to admit. You wouldn't fight against this if it wasn't true."

Enough. Eden spun and stalked back to Martha, getting close enough that she got a face full of her mother's hyacinth perfume. "There are two girls *dead* because you gave Beth enough rope to hang herself with instead of removing her from Elysia like you should have. There would have been another murder if things hadn't worked out the way they did. Don't think for a goddamn second that I don't know the truth—*nothing* happens in Elysia without your knowledge. With that camera network, you knew that she was up to something, and you didn't say a fucking thing. Those girls' blood—*Jon's* blood—is on your hands as much as hers."

Martha's smile disappeared, leaving her dark eyes cold. "There isn't a court in this country that would convict me, so don't you go wasting your time and energy on it. As far as I was concerned, Beth was sneaking around on her husband."

Bullshit. But . . . that didn't make it any less true—or easier to swallow. She wasn't going to roll over and play dead, though. Eden stared her mother straight in the eyes. "You step out of line once and your ass is mine."

There was nothing left to say. She strode away from the truck with as much dignity as she could muster, her mother's words ringing in her ears. *You're more like me than you care to admit.* Maybe, or maybe she was more like Abram. He was the one who wouldn't hesitate to pull a trigger to remove a threat. Too much had flashed through Eden's mind in that millisecond. She didn't have the ability to put it into words.

So she went in search of Zach.

He was in a group of cops, their heads down as they spoke in low voices, but he managed a tired smile when she limped over. "Hey."

"Hey."

The cops took one look at her and drifted away. There wasn't much left to see. The scene had been worked, the bodies removed, Rachel and Vic taken to the hospital. There was a team of forensic folk just showing up to work the cabin, but most of the people currently on the scene weren't vital to the investigation.

Really, at this point, it was just a matter of tying everything up all pretty, complete with a bow.

Zach pulled her into his arms, and she hugged him tight, his warmth driving away some of the ice caused by the conversation she'd just left. *Take me home.* She started to hold the words back, but the sheer enormity of the day crushed what was left of her resistance. Eden buried her face in his neck. "I don't know how much more of this I can stand."

His grip tightened on her. "I have to finish up here, but I can get Henry to give you a lift back to the B&B if you want."

"I'll wait." She didn't want to be alone. She hesitated, then changed the subject. "You solved the case and got the bad guy. What are you going to do next?"

"Get back to normal, and hope no one on the national media circuit gets wind of this." He didn't want the glory any more than she did. The fact that the media hadn't sniffed out this story up until this point was a miracle from on high—and it wouldn't last. If she had her way, she'd be long gone by then.

Except . . .

For the first time in her life, the thought of leaving someone in the rearview filled her with a loss she didn't know how to deal with. It should be too soon to feel something like that for this man, but logic had no place here.

Zach didn't speak until she'd leaned against the side of his cruiser, her blanket still wrapped firmly around her. "Do you want to talk about it?"

She opened her mouth to tell him no, but that wasn't what came out. "I shot her, Zach. Maybe I didn't think that the world would be a better place without her in it, or consider the fact that if she lived, she'd probably get a lighter sentence because she didn't look like she could hurt a fly, let alone orchestrate something like this . . . but I shot her before I saw that she had a gun." It wasn't what a white knight would do, and maybe it had saved her life, but she couldn't get her mother's words out of her head. "I'm *not* like her. I don't care what Martha says. I'm not an apple that didn't fall far from the tree."

He took her hand, the warmth of his skin settling her like a final piece of a puzzle sliding into place. "You lived, Eden. You got the bad guys, and you saved the victim who could be saved, and you lived. That's as close to a win as you get."

"But—"

"Don't think for a damn minute that I'm going to ask you to apologize for surviving." He squeezed her hand harder. "God, Eden. I was so fucking sure that I'd show up and you'd be gone. I thought I was rushing to the scene of your murder."

"I can't stay." She clung to him, her eyes on the cops working the scene behind him. "Being so close to her . . . I can't do it. Not even for you. But I don't . . . I . . ." She didn't even know how to put it into words. "If there was a person in this world who'd make me want to stay in one place long enough to figure out if this was something worth pursuing, it would be you."

His thumb traced a pattern on the back of her hand. "I'm not done with you, Eden. Not by a long shot."

"How will this even work?" She found herself holding her breath, waiting for him to say something to magically solve all their problems.

"I don't know."

Zach spent the rest of the week tying up loose ends. Martha was no more cooperative than she had been from the beginning, but there was no denying the evidence found in the cabin Beth and her husband, Jon, had built—the cabin Jon had met his end in. So much goddamn evidence. It made him sick to think about what those girls went through before they died.

What Rachel was going to have to live with.

She, at least, was looking at a full recovery. Her mother hadn't left her bedside, and Rachel had managed to give a surprisingly detailed account of how Chase had come to her house, claiming that Zach had a few more questions for her, and then proceeded to kidnap her. Her story lined up with what Eden had witnessed, that apparently Chase and Beth had formed some kind of relationship, which then evolved into them killing local girls in some twisted following of the practices Martha taught.

Martha, who claimed not to know a damn thing about what had been going on right under her nose.

He looked up as Vic walked into the room. The big man had barely stayed in the hospital an hour to get his head bandaged before he was up and moving again, going over the evidence alongside Eden and Zach. Wrapping everything up like it was fucking Christmas morning.

And then Eden was there, looking tired but happy to see him, and hell if he didn't feel exactly the same way. He knew he hadn't given her the answers she wanted when she asked how this thing between them would work, but there *weren't* easy answers.

She couldn't stay here. Not with Martha so damn close and willing to meddle. Not with her job that she obviously loved. He understood that.

He didn't want to let her go.

She smiled at him and dropped into the chair across the desk from him. "DNA evidence just got back to us. As expected, it's negative across the board for the original four. It *does* match Chase, though."

Part of him had almost hoped to find out that Martha or one of her men was more directly involved. It would remove her from the equation and . . . but that was his selfishness talking.

Vic took one look at them and hightailed it back out of the station, leaving Zach and Eden in relative privacy. He leaned forward, bracing his elbows on his desk. "Lee's gone."

"I saw him heading for the bus stop." She pulled her hair out of its ponytail and shook it out. "I give him a year."

Zach didn't disagree. The man moved like he had one foot in the grave. It was only a matter of time before he took that final step. But it wasn't Lee who was his top concern right now. He took her in, just drinking in the sight of her. She'd spent every single night in his bed since the kidnapping, just content to let him hold her. There had been nightmares, but he was always there to pull her back into wakefulness. "Eden . . ."

She pushed to her feet, the very picture of nervous energy. "Since this vacation time didn't end up being all that relaxing, Britton has informed me that I'm to take a *real* vacation. Immediately."

"I see."

She gave him a strangely tentative smile. "I don't suppose you have some time saved up? I hear Jamaica is nice this time of year. Or Hawaii. Or, hell, Oregon. I'm not picky, as long as it's anywhere but here—and you're there."

Zach stood and circled around the desk. "You want me to go on vacation with you."

"I want a week or two to spend getting to know you without a case or life getting in the way. After that . . ." She shrugged, her dark eyes large and vulnerable. "After that, we'll figure something out. People do long-distance relationships all the time. It's not the end of the world."

"It's really not." He pulled her into his arms, slowly drawing her closer until she was pressed against him. "Yes. Let's go to Jamaica or Hawaii or Oregon. I don't care where we are, as long as I'm with you."

ACKNOWLEDGMENTS

The art of creating stories is a strange one. You file away information across a wide spectrum of subjects, and suddenly two completely separate ideas will fuse together and you'll have a story with legs that demands to be told. And sometimes that story will launch you into a genre that you've never set foot in before. That's exactly what happened with *The Devil's Daughter*.

So thank you to God for giving me such a twisty, strange mind that allows these kinds of characters and villains and plotlines to percolate and merge into something complete and whole.

Huge thanks to Laura Bradford for taking my delving into the dark side in stride and for reading the proposal and going, "This one. This is the one." Your support has been such a vital part of this journey. Thank you!

Thank you to Krista Stroever for helping me whip this book into shape and really getting what I was trying to accomplish. Eden and Zach's story wouldn't be the same without you!

Thank you to Chris Werner and the rest of the team at Montlake. You have been so incredibly welcoming and supportive, and I am beyond geeked that you're as excited about the world of Clear Springs and Elysia as I am.

Big thanks to John Nave for your endless patience with the many texted questions regarding everything from murder to traffic violations. See! It *is* just for research and not because I'm burying bodies in my yard. Promise!

No path is ever straight, and sometimes the journey starts many, many years before you even realize you're heading in a particular direction. Thank you to my grandmother Gayle Reid for introducing me to fairy tales as a child and for teaching me that some stories don't end happy. Thank you to my grandfather Thomas Reid for telling me stories that prove that the best ones *do* have a happily ever after. And thank you to my uncle Gary Reid for never losing patience with a small niece following you around and asking endless questions about history. I wouldn't be half the storyteller I am now without your influence and support.

Thank you and big hugs to my readers! Thank you for taking a chance on something a bit different, a bit darker, and sticking with me after many years and many more books. I couldn't have done it without you, and I am forever humbled by your support. You are beyond amazing.

Special shout out to the Rabble! You all were the first ones to see the opening page of this book, and your excitement was contagious. I hope you enjoyed reading about Clear Springs as much as I enjoyed writing it. You rock!

Last, but certainly not least, thanks to my family. Being married to a writer—or being the child of one—is sometimes fraught with conversations that trail off into silence, vacant eyes as a plot point slams into place, and more pizza than one family should probably eat. I love you all.

ABOUT THE AUTHOR

New York Times and *USA Today* bestselling author Katee Robert learned to tell her stories at her grandpa's knee. She found romance novels at age twelve, and they changed her life. When not writing sexy contemporary and romantic suspense, she spends her time playing imaginary games with her children, driving her husband batty with what-if questions, and planning for the inevitable zombie apocalypse. Visit her at www.kateerobert.com.